Golden Apple

Golden Apple

Angela Kaufman

Copyright © 2021 Angela Kaufman

The moral right of the author has been asserted.

All rights reserved.
No part of this publication may be reproduced, stored in a retrieval system, or transmitted, in any form or by any means, without the prior permission in writing of the publisher, nor be otherwise circulated in any form of binding or cover other than that in which it is published and without a similar condition including this condition being imposed on the subsequent purchaser.

Published by Trash Panda Press

ISBN 978-1-7362544-4-8

Typesetting services by BOOKOW.COM

Foreword

Golden Apple is a work of fiction. The first draft of this work was completed in December of 2020. Any resemblance to current events are the byproducts of keeping a pulse on current sociopolitical tensions and imagination. For authenticity purposes, I have used the names of specific cities, towns and landmarks in the Saratoga NY area. Yet the events described herein are not based on actual people or events in these areas.

You may recognize landmarks like Stewart's shops, and a place that sounds a lot like Lee's Park. These places are real, but the activities described as taking place in this story are completely fictitious and unrelated to the operation of such locations. And yes, there is a mobile home park nestled between the Stewart's and the Fire Department. But this is not a book about any events that took place in that park, nor is it about anyone residing in that park. Any similarities are coincidental.

To my knowledge, as of the time of this writing, the group Golden Apple does not exist.

Golden Apple deals with themes that are real and as such are deeply troubling. Some of the subject matter may be triggering to some readers. Again, for the purposes of authenticity, phrases and words used herein to describe bigoted, racist, misogynistic, ableist, anti-Semitic mentality as well as other expressions of oppression serve only to reflect the climate of hatred and bigotry as it exists at this time in the United States, and as it has existed since the establishment of the U.S. government.

Though it is not my intention to further harm members of marginalized communities, words and phrases used to describe oppressive ideology are part of the story as it is a story that deals with a fictional white supremacist hate group.

For authenticity, names and references to actual people and historic events are referenced. While it is grammatically correct to capitalize the first letter of a proper name of a person or group, I have intentionally kept the first letter of the name of the 45th president lowercase. I've given the same treatment to names of actual historic and modern hate groups. The chapters are numbered, and you'll notice they go from 44 to 46. This too was intentional.

Acknowledgments

This book began as a writing prompt based on a line from the song MacArthur's Park, by Richard Harris. The cake reference was deleted in earlier drafts, but the completed work would not have been possible were it not for the ongoing guidance and inspiration of many people.

Specifically, Linda Lowen and the Boxers as well as Alice Barden and the Promptly Writer's Group. Also, thank you to Debbie Horan for your feedback on earlier drafts.

The formatting for this book was provided by Bookow.com and the cover was created by James at Go On Write (goonwrite.com).

I should probably also acknowledge all of the people who provided excellent character research, even though none will ever read these words and most have blocked me over the past year. Know that your social media posts provided valuable insight into the world of various cults and mass delusions.

Finally, a debt I can never repay is owed to Michael Dahlquist, who painstakingly edited several drafts of this work.

"All of us assign blame in our own best interest, right? Well, if we assign blame in our own best interest then that means that blame is relative. And if blame is relative then one of the important functions in society becomes 'who controls
the blame pattern?'"
Utah Phillips

Preface

Chorus:
    And here She is
    The wretched one
    Her presence void of charm and grace
    You'll recognize Her by Her name
    In your fellow man, you'll see Her face.

She's made her mark upon your world
    In every Golden Apple spoiled
    Your suffering is Her delight
    And as you waste the hours in toil,
    That you may have what others lack
    You'll not escape their suffering
    For in a mansion or a shack,
    The gift of strife this Goddess brings
    And who would want Her at the feast?
    Yet for this rejection, you'll feel Her pain
    Destruction of human and beast
    To Discordia, it's all the same
    -Book of Discordia

New Dwarf Planet Named for Goddess of Discord; Pluto Demoted

Southern Adirondack Tribune
September 15, 2006

Sky-gazers have something new to celebrate- or not. It seems the discovery of the largest Dwarf Planet, originally named 2003 UB313, has led to discord within the astronomical community about the definition of a planet.

At the time of Eris's discovery, astronomers believed this new Dwarf Planet was actually larger than Pluto. However just recently, as a result of an ensuing debate about what constitutes a planet, the International Astronomical Union has revised the requirements of planetary status, demoting Pluto along with other celestial bodies as Dwarf Planets.

It is fitting, then, that the recently discovered orb that started all the fuss has been renamed Eris, after the Greek Goddess of disharmony and chaos, called Discordia in Roman mythos.

Eris was first discovered by M.E. Brown and D. Rabinowitz at the Palomar Observatory in California.

Part I Park Reaganomics

Chapter 1

Marie

August 2020

The road along the lake winds into what looks like a campground for carnies. RVs and trailers line the path on either side. Worn down. I imagine the owners still getting a kick out of their Billy Bass fish. I expect to see Pink Flamingo lawn ornaments any minute now.

Or Tiki Torches.

But what I don't see is the number I'm looking for. Nor do I see any For Sale signs as I drive slowly through the park. I pull over to the side of the road, not wanting the locals to think I'm dropping by for a visit. Careful to avoid blocking the tiny parking spaces. But I can't escape their notice. A man in an undershirt, shorts, and suspenders, eyes me suspiciously from his lawn chair. I park a few feet away under the awning of his bright green trailer.

Don't worry, I think to myself, I'm not coming for your gun or your trump flag.

I look down at my notes, scrawled on a paper on the passenger seat. *Trailer park. Off Route 9R, right after the State Boat Launch by Saratoga Lake.*

I've already driven back and forth on Route 9R, from Stewart's Shop to shining Stewart's Shop. Nothing.

I turn back to the main road, pull into Stewart's parking lot. I don't want to go in, but it's getting late. The woman standing at the counter is wearing a Thin Blue Line mask. I don't want to talk to her.

"Excuse me," I begin, "I'm looking for the mobile home park." I hold up the real estate listing.

"You mean the trailer park," she says, squinting one eye as if she is now suspicious of me.

"Yes."

"Yeah, you go down a few feet, turn left."

"Is there a sign?"

"Nope, it's a private road. If you get to the Fire House you passed it."

"Thanks."

I pull out of the lot and back onto the road. It doesn't take long for me to see the drive she indicated. Concealed from unsuspecting travelers by overgrowth of trees, lawn and shrubs. The entrance is set back from the road. There's something to be said about living in a place that's hard to find. I see the first trailer on the left. Not bad. Then on the right. Spoke too soon.

It's not where I want to end up. But I suppose that's what everyone tells themselves when they move here. The park doesn't need a sign. It doesn't need a name. Rows of trailers doing their best to hold up patchworks of sinking roofs. Small yards of sunburned grass stocked with inventory. The landscape tells the story of downward spirals and failed safety nets. The clutter of furniture and toys, not good enough to be housed indoors but too valuable to throw out, is all the signage needed.

Welcome to Park Reaganomics. I think to myself.

And then, I think I've spotted one that isn't too bad. A trailer on the left with newer siding. But the relief is washed away almost as soon as it appeared. A fleeting moment of hope replaced by heaviness in the pit of my stomach as I drive closer to the house.

An assortment of trump, thin blue line, and other flags hang from posts on the far corner of the yard. American flags in abundant supply as if the trailer's owner has dementia and needs to remind himself of which country he resides.

Some of the homes don't have curtains. Or windows. Insulated instead by flags that read "Don't tread on me."

I drive past slowly. Following the numbers, surveying the rubble. Tires, rusted cars, and old appliances line the road like tombstones. Monuments to life snuffed out by credit card debt, medical bills, divorce, and loss.

Shit rolls downhill and we are in the valley.

I see it, finally. Not the worst. Not the best. My welcome mat to the middle lower class. Fenced in from the world, a perfect place to wait out the end of civilization.

I pull into the tiny patch of dry grass beside a shiny car, clearly a newer model than mine, which I assume belongs to the realtor. Mask in place, I step out of the car. A colony of feral cats lay out in the sun, staring up at me from the lawn beside the trailer. At least someone is happy to be here.

A hefty orange cat lounges lazily on the caving trailer rooftop next door. I think of the Cheshire Cat. What did he say?

We're all a little mad?

Indeed.

Sounds of screaming and laughter erupt behind me. I backtrack toward the main road and see a cluster of children, all mask-less. The kids roll in the dirt and dart in and out of the road. Oblivious to the risk.

Why shouldn't they be?

I take out my phone and text the realtor.

"Here, sorry I'm late."

And wait, trying to scan the trailer to assess what I can of its condition. Like I know what I'm even looking for. A roof, walls, a place to start over.

Another of the cat brigade saunters around the edge of the front steps and drops a present at my feet.

A dead mouse.

He grins up at me, the Cheshire Cat look on his face not proud but daring.

"Hello! Mario?"

The realtor's voice calls my attention back from the rabbit hole. She's wearing a mask. Must not be from around here.

"Yes, sorry I'm late, I couldn't find it."

"No worries. I'm Rita."

I follow her through the door, grateful she didn't try to shake my hand. The trailer is small enough to take in the main area, open kitchenette, and living room. Bedroom and bathroom the size of a closet. Surprisingly, it looks the same in person as in the photos.

"And you said the washer and dryer work?"

"Yes, all appliances included and working." She continues to review the amenities and specifications.

I linger for a moment, touring the same two rooms. What is there to decide? I've run out of options. It's simpler compared to when I bought my house more than a decade ago. The one I sold last year. Before the shit hit the fan. There had been inspections and applications and bargaining back then. It was nice to have bargaining power.

But that's gone now.

"Did you say you were prepared to pay cash?" Rita asks.

"Yes."

"Well, how fortunate. There was another interested party, but I'm stalling because you contacted me first."

Fortunate? Maybe. But all things considered, I'd give up the cash to have my grandmother back. To be back in my house. A real house. In a neighborhood with sidewalks. And no trump signs.

But I don't bore Rita with these details. She looks like she wants to get out of here as much as I do.

Only one of us gets to leave.

Fortunate.

"Yes. Cash."

I hand it over. She slides a paper across the table. One paper. I sign it. And like a cheap Vegas wedding, the deal is done. 'Til death do us part.

"So that's it?" I ask.

"Yes, keys are on the counter. Congratulations. It's all yours."

CHAPTER 2

Dottie

"We're going to have a visitor, Hathor." I tell her of my premonition, but she's not listening. Obsessed instead with the food dish in my hands. So much for good conversation.

I set the dish down and step aside. All these cats, I swear to the Goddess, if I ever up and died on this trailer floor, they'd come running in and feast on my body. Eat me right down to the bone! Not that there's much left.

I step over the plump fur-babies who purr loudly as they gobble their breakfast.

"Slow down, Isadora! Don't be so greedy!" I chastise my Torti girl, who has pushed her way past her brother to eat his food, having wolfed down her own. A visitor is coming. I saw it in my dreams. Someone who will need my help. And it's time to prepare for what's coming next.

A sharp knock at the door interrupts my thoughts.

"Well, Goddess, you're not wasting any time now, are you?" I ask Her, chuckling to myself. But it isn't the visitor She foretold, nope. It's Dave from across the street.

"Dorothea, I got a notice from the post office. My package was delivered here yesterday," he says. Only one in this park who calls me that name. Hell, no one called me that name since the nuns in high school. Hated it just as much then, too.

"I don't know what you're talking about. I haven't gotten any packages, but I'll keep an eye out if I see one…"

"You stole my package. Now, why would you steal my package, Dorothea? We're all civil and neighborly here, and you're the only one who has to stir up trouble. Why?"

Now I'm pissed. I may be less than five feet tall to his six five, but I step down off my porch, finger jabbing him in the sternum for emphasis.

"I didn't steal your package, fool. What is it with you men? You think everyone wants your package?"

He backs up but only a few steps before crossing his arms over his chest. Hmph, as if he could scare me. Goddess already showed me when it's my time to go and it ain't today, so whatever he thinks he's going to do to intimidate Crazy Dottie, he's got another thing coming! He puffs himself up and rants.

"You really don't want to cross me, Dorothea. I already called the Post Office. Inspector is coming today. I told them your address. You can deal with them."

"You can bite me!" I tell him. I know damn well no postal inspector's coming out to look for his stupid package.

"You got a mouth on you!" he tries to chastise me.

"Blow it out your ass!" I tell him. And maybe I shoulda stopped there. But I'm older than him and that means I've been putting up with shit long enough to have run out of fucks back when Moses wore short pants. So, I keep going.

"And that's one thing men like you hate. Women who use our voices. I feel sorry for your daughter."

Now the neighbors are peeking out their doors, and windows, and I don't care. They think I'm crazy. I'll show them crazy.

"I suppose you think she's better off living with someone like you?"

"I could teach her a thing or two, that's for sure. I've seen men like you my whole life. You have a pecking order, because you think with your cock. You're at the top now, but you'll cave as soon as an even bigger cock comes along."

"What's this about a cock, Dottie?" a calm voice interrupts from the distance and I turn to see the Caretaker approaching, holding a cooking dish.

"Oh, hey there darlin' don't you get jealous. I was just talking with Dave here about his package."

"Is that so?" The Caretaker saunters over and nods to Dave, smiling. Dave's face is turning red, and I am here for it.

"Well, Dottie, I was just stopping by to drop off some banana bread I baked last night, but if you're busy, I can come back later." He hands me the plastic container, reused from some past trip to a restaurant. I can see the banana bread inside.

"Oh, it looks divine, thank you. Good to know some men around here know how to act."

Dave grunts under his breath and leaves. Muttering about how I better keep out of his mail.

"Everything okay?" The Caretaker asks when Dave's out of earshot.

"Oh, yeah, I can take care of myself. I'm a tough old bitch, don't you worry about Crazy Dottie."

He smiles. "I was worried about Dave."

"I see we have a new neighbor," I change the subject.

"Yeah, haven't met her yet. I think it's just the one lady. Looks like she's not from around here."

"Citiot?"

"It's possible. Time will tell. Hope it isn't too big a culture shock for her though."

"Well, I have to get back inside. Something big is coming. I've got to get ready. Thanks for the bread."

* * *

The heavy curtains block out the light completely. I can meditate, go real deep, even in the midday, with no problem. And I'm almost there, too, except the crash brings me out of it.

Scares Isadora too, poor thing curled up on my lap nearly claws my leg off as she jumps to run from me.

"Jumped up Jesus, what now?" I snuff the candles out and step out of the trailer and back into the blinding daylight. My ceramic fountain, the big one with the fairies on it, is now in shambles, pieces strewn all about the lawn. Fat tire tracks trace the path over my lawn and back out to the road, toward 9R. I look back again and see they came from Dave's driveway.

Just a big prancing cock, I think to myself as I clean up the mess. Strutting around until the next biggest cock in the pecking order comes along. And Karma is a bitch.

Chapter 3

Marie

Max Romeo's voice carries from the speakers, asking rhetorically if it is really over.

No need to ask. I already know it's the end of the line.

I sit on the back deck, forcing myself into the sunshine. Next summer may not come. I bargain with myself. You can have some needed vitamin D if you continue to work.

I stare into the blank screen as the electronic abyss stares back at me.

The disembodied voice again croons the question. *Is it really over?*

The end of the line. When it becomes clear that your partner of ten years has found president trump a more attractive prospect than another minute with you.

Some people love the illusion of a successful businessman.

No need to wonder who's stepping into my shoes.

And it wasn't just that. "Business is business, you just have to understand." That's what my editor had said.

Who's stepping in my shoes?

I found out. When I made the mistake of perusing the recent catalog for Saffron Publishers. The same hacks and their trite but easily digestible titles. The bodice rippers, the long line of memoirs. The recycled plots, predictable characters, and tidy endings.

Nothing left to do but face the music.

"Marie, we know you're a good writer, but we can't take a chance on you gain. Not given how Soldier of Fortune underperformed our expected sales goals." Sylvia had said when we last spoke months ago. What she added next was intended to be helpful. "You're missing your market. If you want to write political fiction, you've got to make it YA for the woke crowd. Adults just don't read this genre. And besides, after this year, trump will be out of office and everything will go back to normal."

You really want to make this mistake again? I wanted to ask her, but it was useless.

Tears roll down my face.

Of all the times I wanted one more chance to do better, to learn from past mistakes, to try harder.

The door is closed.

I look around the yard, there's a pond in the far-left corner. A glorified puddle, really. A brothel for mosquitoes who are then the buffet for the family of frogs, each of whom I've taken to calling Bubbles.

This is nice. I tell myself, trying to find the silver lining. Once I pay off the trailer, lot rent is manageable. I can hide away here until I die, writing bullshit that no one reads. No questions asked. No strings attached.

But I always thought there would be one more time.

Hadn't I just wanted some quiet time at home, during the past two years almost nonstop tour promoting *Soldier of Fortune*? After passing through St. Louis, Tacoma, Portland, Albuquerque, Houston, Dallas, Nashville, Denver, Even fucking Ohio, for the second, then third times.

Watching landmarks through dirty bus windows. The arch, the Mississippi, the museums, theaters, even the Quaker Oats building. And I would think to myself, next time I'll plan a longer stay. Walk around more. Do some sightseeing. Maybe find an armadillo meandering down the road.

Never once imagining next time would never come, and not just because of the pandemic. Because long before COVID closed the door, Saffron Publishing had made it clear there would be no second chances.

I sigh and squint through tears and afternoon sunlight. How many times did I plan for next time, taking for granted there would be one more?

One more book signing. One more conference. One more Greyhound bus, one more plane trip, one more visit with my grandmother, who was in good spirits on her birthday in February. The last time I saw her. When she had eaten half a piece of chocolate cake and smiled, reminding the nursing home staff who walked by that it was her birthday. That her granddaughter had come to visit.

"You'll come and visit me again, real soon, right Marie?" she had asked when I kissed her goodbye.

"Yes, real soon."

But COVID was already making the rounds. There would be no return trip. No chance to say goodbye before the doors closed, for good.

Chapter 4

Marie

The earbud pops out of my ear as I laugh at Andre's jokes.

"Hang on," I tell them as I use my ungloved hand to reinsert it. In my other hand, concealed by a too large rubber glove, I squeeze the fouled water out of a rag that I've been using to scrub the floors and walls. The bucket I dip it into has a concoction of peppermint oil, bleach, and floor cleaner.

I begin to cough and wheeze.

"Damn, sis, time to tickle your brain with a Q-Tip," Andre teases.

"No," I gag, trying to catch my breath. The windows are open but in the July heat the air is heavy and unhelpful. "It's not COVID. In fact, according to the president...*cough*... this should cure me of it... *cough*."

"Oh? You're drinking bleach now?"

"Pretty close to it. Trying to get rid of the mice."

"That's why you call Orkin, fam," they tell me. Although they're on the phone in my back pocket, I can see their face. I imagine their eyes twinkling, one corner of their mouth upturned in a sly smirk. I miss them.

"You know I don't want an exterminator. That's genocide. It's not their fault."

"Watch it, sis, they have disease and it's 2020. You're gonna end up with buboes on your neck."

I can't help laughing. "I know, but then again, I'm more likely to catch something from the infestation of Karens here than from mice. I just don't want to be their roommate."

"I don't understand why you had to move to Dogpatch. You could have come back to the city." Andre turns serious now.

"I couldn't afford the city, not long term. I expect to be underemployed for a few years, even when this blows over. I had to go where I could afford to buy or rent."

"Why buy or rent when you can do both?" Andre quips back, a reference to the typical combined mortgage on the trailer and monthly lot rent.

"True, true," I admit. "But it's paid. Grandma would roll in her grave if she knew what I spent her money on. But I can deal with whatever comes next. Plus, it's got a yard. I need a yard so I can rescue dogs."

"You with the dogs again. I been hearing you talk about dogs for years. Now you're seriously going to get one?"

"Got an appointment with the shelter tomorrow to meet a German Shepherd mix named Jackie. If they approve me, she'll be here later this week."

"Good for you," Andre says, "But I hope you understand I won't be bringing my fine ass up to Green Acres to celebrate when you throw her a birthday party, even after the pandemic. No offense. Even if I wasn't trans, no way I'm going to be within gunshot range of your white neighbors out in Dogpatch."

"None taken," I tell them. "I wouldn't want to put you in that kind of danger. When the time comes, Doggie and I will come to visit you."

"You better," they tell me. "I miss you."

"I miss you too."

Chapter 5

Marie

I walk along the unpaved road, away from the lake where weekenders gather, mask-less, believing themselves immune or the virus a hoax. At my feet, Jackie pulls at her leash and tries to run circles around me. She's filling out now, her ribs no longer show like they did when I first brought her home from the shelter. Her light tan and white coat filling in as well.

Are you happy with your new home?

I wish I could ask her.

"C'mon," I urge her, untangling her leash from my legs. Trying to keep her on the far side of the path where she won't be tempted to stray toward the neighbors.

One, who introduced himself as Vinny, stands at the helm of his grill. It's one of those ridiculous models. The Hummer of barbecue. He's entertaining. An older woman sits tethered to an oxygen machine, kids spray each other with squirt guns and squeal, running around the grill. All unmasked. He gags and coughs and I tell myself it's just the smoke he's breathing. But I'm not completely convinced.

One of the kids approaches the older woman. Stretching his arms wide, he calls "Grandma!" He climbs up on her lap. His shirt is stained with ketchup or barbecue sauce, smattered over its one design, an Italian flag.

"Uncle Vinny, more hotdogs!" He then yells out to the man at the grill.

I prompt Jackie to move forward; the scene makes me think of my grandmother, and her parents. The generation that came to this country. I walk on. Thinking of their trek to NY from Calabria.

On their first trip, one of their children was sick. Based on a medical evaluation, he was denied entry and sent him back, over the ocean. What kind of person sends a child over the rolling waves alone and infirm?

A poor person, perhaps. Someone who is desperate to start over. Someone who can't afford to give up their one big chance. He was reunited with them, Eventually.

I imagine him. Small and chubby as the kid outside of Vinny's house. Except he would likely not have had an Italian flag on his shirt as he sailed to his new home with his family. Too on the nose. I imagine him sitting in some ship, alone and sick. And how was the rest of the family not sick if they had traveled with him?

These questions didn't occur to me when my grandmother first told me the story. But we weren't in the midst of a pandemic then. And now there is no one alive who can answer.

Was it worth it?

Contagion. Quarantine. Relocation. The themes circle through my mind. Judging by the crowds who mill around the main road, it seems I'm alone in being concerned about these things.

I survey the intersection, trying to decide whether to risk walking Jackie to the lake. Still too many tourists. We take another road. The early autumn leaves are changing, but it's still hot. My mask itches, but I try to not scratch my nose. I look at Jackie and think of the chance I could have had to start over somewhere else when thing first turned.

But first there was no money. Then there was some money, but not enough to move. By the time it was possible to find some place new to land, it was too late.

No Americans need apply.

The list of countries that have now banned U.S. residents is dizzying to comprehend. I missed my chance. Moved here instead. One last chance. A final refuge.

I should have gone. Where they have healthcare and sanity...

Jackie tugs at the leash and I indulge her nose as she sticks her face eagerly in a bush, pursuing whatever exciting scent has got her attention. I think of Italy, where people are now resuming a cautious baseline. Where crisis was an opportunity to learn and change, not to bury your head in the sand, or in the bush, as Jackie now proceeds to do as if emphasizing the point.

Why had they finally come here?

I never got a clear answer. The government was corrupt; the people living in poverty. They must have thought they were making a sacrifice for their future. For me.

Was it really that bad?

Not then. But it would be. By the time Mussolini was in power, they were already settled into upper working-class life. They dodged a bullet. But migrating country to country to stay a step ahead of fascism is busy work. Expensive. Impractical.

As Jackie resumes her walk, I'm lost in thought again. Great Uncle What's-His-Name, shivering, on a boat. Great Grandfather possessing all the clothes on his back and fifteen dollars. Did they ever imagine that in a few generations their destination would be worse than the country they fled?

I look at the debris lining the road. Bags. Beer cans. Discarded masks. Litter is disrespectful. Perhaps it's also rebellion. A vomiting of refuse, a slap in the face to the pearl-clutching class who must be reminded of the people they have discarded. As if to say, "we're still here! You won't look at us, so look at what we've left behind!"

When the next generation fares worse than the one before, who do we blame? Those who passed the torch, or those who received it?

I think again of my great grandparents, and then the child with the Italian flag shirt. Italy was hit hard by the pandemic. Stories spread of people dying in hospital hallways. And when trump's disciples took note, what did they say?

"See what communist medicine does?"

Just wait. I had replied, taking no pleasure in knowing that they could eat their words in only a matter of weeks.

They could have. If logic mattered to them.

Do they have rationality in Italy? Do they have facts? We've run out of both in the U.S.

I wonder if Vinny realizes that in the present day it would disgust Italians to know how little we give value human life in America. Would he then denounce his ancestry? Call them communists? Did he scoff at the images of people dying in hospital corridors, believing his fate would be better here?

I knew early on the pandemic was a big deal. How could it not be? A new virus doesn't just emerge out of nowhere, shut down entire countries, and then somehow miraculously miss the U.S.

"It will blow over in about a month," one friend after another tried to reassure me. Back in March, when "locking down" in NY was given as a temporary solution. Breadcrumbs, one week, then another, instead of just ripping off the band-aid and telling the cold hard truth.

"It's my intuition, this is short term, it will clear up by the summer." The Greek Chorus of wishful thinkers had recited, one after another.

"It's only going to get worse. And it's going to take years to get through this," I had responded.

Needless to say; friends stopped calling after a while.

People don't want to hear what they can't imagine. Too many people lack imagination.

Jackie lunges for a squirrel. I hold her back. She wags her tail and pushes her snout forward. As if her willpower will make the leash disappear. I can empathize. "This way, baby," I tell her and distract her by pretending to run in the opposite direction. She takes the bait and runs with me. "Okay, slow down." I tell her, setting a slower pace now.

The sun is setting. I squint to keep it out of my eyes. Jackie and I head back home.

I don't know how much time has gone by. Vinny's party is over. Just plates left out on picnic tables. A glance reveals a wedge of cake on the lawn by the road, frosting smeared across the grass. Besides the confection and remnants of the party, the lawn is littered with children's toys. Lots of them.

Because everyone wants what's best for their kids, nephews, nieces, grandkids, regardless of the sacrifice it requires. I think again to my great grandparents. Their sacrifice. Their journey.

How long did it take them to save? Or was it an impulsive decision?

My grandmother can't answer anymore.

I look at Jackie and think again, it's too late to start over.

Who did they leave behind? I wonder. Friends? Neighbors? A stray cat in the yard who would beg for scraps of food?

Was it worth it?

Chapter 6

Joni

Do you want to join with video? The app asks me. Heck no isn't an option, so I gracefully opt out of that Zoom feature. Madame Lynnaeus won't mind, others have come to the weekly Manifestation Circles on Zoom and kept their photos up. Fine by me.

No, no, no, I correct myself. Think gratitude. Think positive.

Deep breath.

Ahhh.

It's not that I'm embarrassed to be sleeping on a cot in my sister's addition in a trailer park, it's that I'm working on manifesting my ideal home. And I can't do that if I see the reflection of this shabby room during the seminar. I mean, it will interfere with my concentration and lower my vibes. So best to focus on what I do want rather than looking at the screen and seeing this reflected back.

As I say this, I gaze around what would have been an enclosed porch in other summers. I did my part to tidy it up, If I do say so myself, I've made many improvements. I painted it. Cleaned up all that trash and old boxes that were back here. Added some of my style. On a bargain in fact.

A few throw pillows, some blankets, soft lighting, aromatherapy diffusers, some paintings from my Paint Your Inner Child retreat, and voila, it looks.... Still like I want to keep my camera off. But, better.

I turn back to my tablet. People are signing into this seminar from around the world. It's kept me sane throughout this crazy lockdown. Our collective energies are going to bring about the awakening that Madame Lynnaeus always talks about.

She's so spiritual.

I plug in my earbuds to drown out the noise. Sitting on my meditation cushion with my silk meditation shawl wrapped around my shoulders- it increases the positive energy and I found it on sale for only eighty dollars- I close my eyes.

I follow her breathing in, two, three, four, and out, two, three…

A roaring sound breaks my concentration. I feel my body tense. My mind starts to go to negative thoughts about how much I wish Dave would not turn on the weed whacker during my morning Power Hour, since he's known since March this is something I do every week at the same time…

But no, no, no, I remind myself.

Love and light and gratitude for Dave for letting me stay here. Temporarily.

It's just temporary.

Now I feel my vibration rising again.

I can let go… I can relax…. I can manifest….

I see my home. My ideal future home. And it turns, it fades, and then I'm walking through my past home. The one I signed over to the group. Before I knew what was really going on. Before the crazy talk about dieting and the sleep deprivation, and the branding…

No, no, no, that's a bad thought.

I breathe again, trying to recenter myself.

I don't want to think about that place and the dreams I had for it. I have new dreams now.

I hear Madame Lynnaeus's voice, but more distant now, harder to follow.

Focus on the positive, I tell myself. But it feels like a chore.

Why is it easier for everyone else? I squint just enough to see calm and serene faces filling the screen, Brady Bunch style.

I breathe deep and let out a sigh again.

Let go of the past, just let it go, no attachment. I repeat the instructions in my mind.

The pain comes up. The sadness. The parties I won't have there, the boyfriend who never moved in, who said I chose a cult over him, the kids who wouldn't play in the yard, the way the sun would come in the front windows on a summer's day, lighting the spacious front room.

All gone.

No, no, no.

Poof! It's gone. In the past.

It's just an illusion.

It doesn't exist.

But my heart is racing faster now. I'm fighting with myself.

Why is it easier for everyone else?

Breathe and sigh and focus and….

A crash startles me and my body jumps.

So much for serenity. With the boys running around the house. Kids will be kids. I can't wait to get out of here. The Zoom session is ending now. Everyone chants the sound of "Ommmm" in unison, but I don't. I don't want to sound silly. Maybe that's why I'm not manifesting things now, I wonder. So, I try it.

"Ommmmmm," even as I hear the kids snickering on the other side of the paper-thin walls.

Little brats.

No, no, no, how lucky I am.

I tell myself.

How lucky I am to spend time with family during a time when so many are far apart. I sign out of the seminar and think "better luck next time."

Chapter 7

Marie

Jackie nudges me with her snout. I reach down to pet her. Might as well. I've been staring at the screen for hours and so far, my contributions to the novel are...

Chapter One...

Every line I write seems wrong. Delete. Delete. Delete. Rainy nights like this usually help. Not tonight.

I click the screen for Google and change songs on YouTube. Maybe a different soundtrack will stir something. In the background, I hear thunder.

Word and I continue our staring contest. So far, Word is winning.

Jackie sighs and I pat my lap. I couldn't afford to hire movers to transport the couch, so now I sit on the floor. She circles around, eclipsing the laptop and then plops comfortably on my lap.

She licks my shirt diligently. I scratch behind her ear. Lightning flashes and she pushes her head on me. I hug her and coo in her ear.

A few lines, then a paragraph.

But I'm not fully invested.

YouTube cues up another song. I recognize the opening piano. It doesn't matter that you didn't write the song. I liked the way you played it better. But I can't find a library of the past on YouTube.

Grandma used to say in the old days people chopped up pianos because they couldn't afford to move them. I couldn't move the piano when you left. I sold it. When the movers' fee was accounted for, fifty dollars created an empty space where you used to play. Better than Tim Moore. Definitely Better than the Art Garfunkel cover.

Seventies Valium music, you called it.

I hear Tim Moore's voice as he sings about how we can no longer make it, he's found a new place to live his life.

Indeed.

The screen blurs. This isn't helping.

He laments about not shaving in her looking glass anymore. Tough life, I think to myself.

Are you still feeding the birds? Or has Fox taken that from you as well? I wonder.

I don't want to hear about *Second Avenue* anymore and flip screens to click on the next song on the list. Thunder reverberates overhead. I hear a crash in the distance. No sense getting up to look.

Jackie leans up, licking tears off my face. I have a dog now. That is something you never wanted. Not even when we found a stray outside the grocery store on a crisp October night.

"You don't know what diseases it has," you had said.

I should have left you there and brought the dog home. I would have if I had known what you would do a few weeks later.

Chapter 8

Vinny

"Watch your arm, Ma," I tell her before shutting the passenger door.

"Hey, Vinny!" I hear Dave's voice and try not to make a face.

Not now, I'm busy, I say inside my head. But to him, I just smile and wave.

"Hey, yeah, what's up?" No avoiding it. He's walking across the lawn in my direction. Smiling. He only talks to me when he wants something, even if he's smiling. I known him enough to know he don't consider me a friend.

"Hey, you know that storm we had the other night?"

I do. It was a bad one. Took down a branch in the yard. Didn't hit the roof. Thank God for small favors.

"Yeah. That was something, huh?"

"Something, it's a pain in my balls. Limb came down on the roof." He stops to look around my shoulder and sees Ma in the car. "Oh, I'm sorry, didn't realize you were busy. Hey maybe after you come back from taking your mom home you could come over and give me a hand fixing up the roof? I got the kit just need someone to hold the ladder."

I been here long enough to know his tone. The look in his face. A look that says, "You're not going to say 'no' to me." I also know that when he says hold the ladder, he means I'll be on the ladder and he'll be sitting back watching, drinking a beer maybe. I shouldn't be doing that kinda work, doctor says. Not with my emphysema, and definitely not with my bad back. I feel my lungs tighten up just thinking about hauling myself up and down from a roof. But It's not a good idea to make trouble with Dave.

"You think the Caretaker could help you out?" I test the waters, asking him this.

"I don't ask that fag for help. Guy's funny. I ask you because I can count on you."

He pauses.

"I can count on you, can't I?" His voice takes on a more sinister tone.

"Yeah, of course. Just that I'm taking Ma back to the home and didn't want to keep you waiting if it was an emergency is all."

"No hurry. We'll just do it when you get back."

"Sure."

"Hey, you see the new neighbor yet?" he changes the subject.

"No, saw the U-Haul van, but that's about all."

"Lady. Maybe a nice piece of ass around here for a change, eh?" He grins and raises an eyebrow.

"How's your wife doing?" I ask him.

"She's a pain in my ass. What else is new, right?"

"How long is her sister staying with you?"

"Too long already. She's a kook. I'll be glad when she gets her own place and I can have my sunroom back. But Shari gets pissed every time I bring it up. So here I am, a prisoner in my own house. Can you believe it? Women. Well, I'll let you get back to taking your mom home."

He waves to Ma. She waves back and smiles. I watch him as he walks back to his place. Cursing myself because once again I let myself get roped in. And it's never a small fix. Not with Dave. It's always a little of this, a little of that. I sit heavily in the car seat and let my breath out in a huff. Slamming the door.

"What's the matter, Vin?" Ma asks.

"It ain't nothing, Ma." I tell her.

Chapter 9

Marie

"If you could promise not to chew the wires, it wouldn't have to come to this," I tell the mouse. He looks terrified. I hold the DIY soda bottle trap high over Jackie's head.

"And if you could refrain from peeing in tracks everywhere you walk," I add.

"But that's not realistic of me to expect from you, is it? And I know it's not fair, but I will make it worth your while. Promise." The mouse stares back, blinks, doesn't look convinced. I don't blame them. I wouldn't trust someone holding a bottle after trapping me in it, either.

I look at Jackie, who is eager to play with our latest catch. I imagine her bouncing all over the car, trying to get at him and scaring the poor mouse to death. As this defeats the purpose of a catch and release trap, I give her the bad news.

"Stay here, baby. You watch the house for me. Good girl." She groans and lays down on a pile of blankets on the floor.

"I'll be right back," I remind her. She looks at me from the other side of the door and stomps a paw in protest as I close the door, leaving her behind. She whines twice, but by the time I get to my car, I no longer hear her protests and assume she's settled in.

Sliding into the car, I wedge the bottle, mouse and all, onto the passenger side seat. To ensure it won't slide, I place my copy of *A Handmaid's Tale* in front of it like a doorstop.

"A little light reading. You'll enjoy it," I tell the mouse.

We head to our destination. At least four miles away, the website instructed. Otherwise, they can find their way back. So persistent. I don't know if I would walk four miles to end up back here.

Our destination is a Price Chopper plaza on the other side of Saratoga Springs. It's early and even those designated to do shopping before the usual crowds come in, a COVID precaution instituted over the spring, are not here yet. The lot is mostly empty.

"Wait 'til you see this feast," I tell the mouse.

I pull the car around to the back of the store. Careful, I don't want to be too obvious. I park out of the way and walk along the edge to get to the dumpster. Leaning down to open the trap. The mouse sniffs the air for a few moments, then makes a beeline for the dumpster. Mission accomplished. I turn to go back to my car. I want to leave before anyone stops to wonder why I'm hanging around the dumpster at five in the morning. But before I can take another step toward the car, I see motion in the distance. A vehicle, black, white, and menacing. The words Saratoga County Sheriff lining the side. I see another. Then another silently making their way to the far corner of the lot.

They remind me of hornets.

Still holding the trap, upright to not look too suspicious, I walk along the greenery at the edge of the lot, approaching the caravan of police cars.

The officers have vacated the cars, they've gone farther into the back of the lot. As I approach, I see why they've come.

In the back of the lot, there is a clearing. A small patch of dirt amidst the trees and shrubs, overgrown for the most part.

Far from view of the public, who in this town would definitely not approve.

And that's why the cops are here, isn't it?

Someone saw this place. They discovered the secret Saratoga tries so hard to hide. That lurks behind the hotels, condos, galas. Lingers amidst the backdrop of museums. Fades into shadows out of sight of the trendy bistros and yoga studios.

Golden Apple

The other Saratoga.

Scratch the surface of this city's gilded veneer and you'll find the working class. You'll find the disaffected. You'll find the unhoused.

Someone found them living here.

Someone who didn't approve.

They saw the encampment, about five tents, some the real deal, some makeshift and weathered. They saw the collection of all the worldly goods left in possession of the small group who live here. An assortment that could easily fit in the back of a small car with room to spare.

And from the warmth of their sprawling loft or mansion home, they had called the police.

One cop takes a utility knife out of his pocket and without pausing for thought runs it down the walls of a tent.

I should stop them...

Another officer kicks a smaller tent flat on the ground, oblivious to whether anyone had been sleeping inside it. Luckily, no one was.

They seem angry, as if the small camp had offended them somehow.

I see myself intervening, yelling for them to stop. But in reality, I stand in the shadows, watching.

Another officer opens his fly and pisses on the remains of what had been a third tent. The other two tear the remaining gear, sleeping bags and clothes, to shreds.

I reach for my phone and start taking video, but the lighting is too dim, and nothing registers. They leave now. Not concerned about the mess they've left behind. Only satisfied in knowing what was once a last resort is now uninhabitable.

Mission accomplished.

CHAPTER 10

Marie

Driving back from the dumpster, I wanted a distraction to rid my mind of the scene of police stomping out some family's last hope, but this wasn't what I had intended as I flipped stations.

Dave Mason's voice fills the car. Singing about how long he's been away, how he hasn't seen you in a while.

"One, that's redundant and two, fuck you," I say out loud.

It was probably about this time of year. Do you remember? I heard he was coming to Albany and surprised you with tickets. You got his autograph. It was back before…

"Fuck You!" I yell louder, slamming my hands on the wheel for good measure. I wonder if the people in other cars can see. Is it strange for them to see a woman driving around and crying this early in the morning? It's 2020, and why not?

We just disagree…

I miss the days when we could just disagree. When it only meant a difference of opinion and not…

The road ahead of me fades and I see you in the kitchen making dinner. "I voted!" I announced, setting down my bags.

"So did I."

I thought you were kidding. Did you know that? It had been so long since you had left the house. I was sure you didn't mean it.

"You voted? For whom?" I had asked.

"I voted for… Not Hillary."

"You voted for Bernie?" I asked, in a moment of excitement. What you said next shattered everything.

Or rather, what you tried not to say. What you didn't want to admit, at first.

We just disagree. I tried to tell people. It's okay. That's what makes a democracy, isn't it?

But by the time you left, we no longer just disagreed. By the time nazis killed a woman in Charlottesville, I was done regretting losing you. So why the fuck am I crying now?

I slam off the radio. Home now. Or something like it. A little hole in the wall, Really no place at all.

Fuck You.

Chapter 11

Marie

I hold the razor and carefully consider what I am about to do.

Fuck it.

I plug it in. The noise bothers Jackie, and she chases her tail. I thumb the off switch and kneel beside her. Her face level with my neck.

"It's okay, baby," I tell her softly as she nuzzles deep into my hair. "It's okay."

Her anxieties mirror my own. But she doesn't mind going out to face the world while I would stay hidden inside if it wasn't for her. I reach into my pocket and grab a treat to reassure her. She sniffs it once, twice, and a wet tongue swipes it from my hand.

"Good girl," I tell her.

Distracting her with her favorite toy, a stuffed replica of Lamb Chop but with a squeaker in the center. She settles at my feet, licking and chewing at the toy, her paws wrapped around it. Occasionally, her brown eyes look up at me, searching for approval.

"Good girl. Chew your dolly," I tell her.

I look back up at the mirror. My dark brown, curly hair is now chopped to tiny tufts. I look like the poster child for mania. But if I am off balance, shaving my head to adapt to a now broken shower is not a marker of insanity. It's probably one of the most rational ideas I have had in a while.

I run the razor across my head, mowing a stripe of visible scalp amidst uneven stalks of what my mother would certainly say looks like a rat's nest if she were here to see it. Thank god she isn't.

It's cheaper than a plumber. I keep telling myself. *And who the fuck is going to see me any time for the rest of this century, anyway?*

Row upon row, brown tufts of hair take flight and cascade to their doom, cut short in the prime of life by an electric razor. A tuft lands on Jackie's nose and she sneezes, shaking her entire body. I laugh. The sound of the razor no longer bothers her. It's amazing what a treat will do.

Calm a nervous dog, convince a person to work one more hour, then another, then a year, then a decade, then a lifetime, to have nothing to show for it.

But we were given treats, and so we sat, shook, rolled over, found toys and distracted ourselves.

I clear off the razor now and wipe the tiny specs of hair, now making my neck and head itch. Surprisingly, it's not too terrible. My round moon face no longer concealed behind what I always thought was my best physical attribute. Once the mess is cleared away, I think I can get used to this.

Good, I tell myself, *because you'll be taking sponge baths for a long time* …

Chapter 12

Derrick

"Come with me, Derrick Torrey."

She's distracting me again. I look up from my laptop. "What did I say, Dee? I have to finish this project."

"It's not school."

"I know. It's something I want to do, though. Do you understand that?" I snap. I lost my temper. Again.

"I'm sorry, Dee," I tell her. Her face remains stoic.

"Dee," I get her attention again and take out my phone, "look, I'm setting a timer, for fifteen minutes. You can play with your toys, and when you hear the alarm, that means it's time to play."

"Yes, Derrick Torrey," she answers.

"Okay," I turn back to my laptop. She continues to stare at me. I try to ignore it and just concentrate on my coding. A slow fifteen minutes under her surveillance paces and my alarm sounds.

I turn and find her standing in the same position she's been in. I'll never understand how she can be so restless but also stand like one of the Queen's Guardsmen when it suits her. She gets obsessive when she wants something.

"What are we going to play?" I ask her.

"Fiver needs his walk." she responds.

Her rabbit, named for the main character in her favorite movie, *Watership Down*. She watched it constantly for months. That Mom finally broke down and got her a rabbit was inevitable. Though Mom thinks it's gross and makes her leave it outside. She sneaked out of the house to sleep outside its cage at first.

But several times each day, we walk Fiver. I swear, that rabbit goes for more walks than most dogs.

I grab my shoes and keys and take her by the hand, but she pulls away, insisting on putting her hand on the outside of mine. Like always.

Walking out to the hutch, I reach in to grab Fiver and load him into the red wagon covered with a frame and chicken wire. I made the wagon myself a while back. Modeled it off a pattern I found online. Built it from scraps left out around the park when she first had the idea to walk Fiver.

The air around Fiver's hutch is becoming pungent with the smell of ammonia.

"Dee," I tell her. Her eyes are glued to Fiver who busies himself grooming his paws. I continue as if she is listening. "Fiver's house needs to be cleaned. Do you smell how stinky it's getting?"

"Yes, Derrick Torrey." I know I'll have to walk her through cleaning the hutch which basically means I will clean it. Like always. I don't mind. She loves Fiver.

She hugs Fiver and holds the handle on the wagon and she even feeds him. She always remembers to feed him. She pets him and holds him and tries to sneak him into the house whenever she can. She cleans the cage once in a while but usually I have to stay on top of it.

She grabs the wagon handle and turns toward the road. Up ahead, the other kids are playing. They're always out. Anytime it's nice out and sometimes when it isn't.

We approach with Fiver in tow. One of them, the youngest, Scott, stops dead in his tracks and stares at Dee.

Don't be a douche, don't be a douche, don't be a douche, I chant in my head.

He doesn't say a word, but contorts his face, mouth open and twisted, eyes crossed. Dee has no idea, but I know he's making fun of her.

I glare at him. His older brother, who is about eleven, ups the ante.

"Why do you have a rabbit in a wagon?" he asks.

"Because she doesn't have real friends!" Scott says.

Don, the older brother, throws rocks. One hits Dee on her forehead.

"Cut it out!" I yell to them. I wish I could punch them, but Mom says they are too young, and I would be wrong. She doesn't see what they do. They're monsters.

"Cut it out!" Don taunts me, changing his voice to a falsetto and shaking his hips side to side. They laugh and I steer Dee and in turn, Fiver, to avoid them. There is only one road, so no chance of a detour. I can veer to the left where the path is wider. I try to get her to follow the dirt trail to the garden, at the far edge of the park by the main road. The kids and losers in the park don't go to the garden. It involves work and they don't like work. So, it's a safe place to stay away from the creeps.

Dee is becoming upset. She might have a meltdown. I don't want her to do this.

"Dee," I try to redirect her quickly, "Dee, look at Fiver, see how happy he is to go for a walk?" It works this time. It's hard enough for her to make friends as it is, even when we were both going to school. Before the lockdown. But the kids here in the park have never been nice to her. Maybe that's why she likes the animals better.

We walk to the garden where I name the different vegetables. She grabs some fistfuls of lettuce and starts feeding them to Fiver.

"Dee, that isn't ours, you shouldn't do that," I tell her, trying not to sound angry. A voice cuts in.

"It's fine. This food is for everyone. This year, there's plenty."

I look up.

It's the Caretaker. He's kinda weird. I usually try to avoid him. He does all the shoveling and odd jobs for the park owner because the park owner lives far away. Mom says he's got a checkered past. That he's an ex-con. They say he's the Caretaker because he's really poor. Like, even more poor than we are. The only way he can afford to live here is to do work on the park, like gardening and lawn work and repairs and stuff.

Anytime I get a bad grade, Mom says, "Do you want to end up like the Caretaker?"

"Thank you," I tell him, "but I don't want her to get into trouble with the neighbors," I try to explain.

"Well, if anyone gives you trouble about this, you tell me, okay?"

This is creepy. I wonder if he's what my friend John at school calls a Kiddie-phile. Why else is he being so nice to us kids all the time? He's so weird. He doesn't have any friends. Maybe because he's an Ex-con. I don't want to make him angry, so I just agree.

"And here," he says, and he grabs an entire head of lettuce right out of the raised beds nearby. He hands it to Dee.

"What's your Rabbit's name?" he asks her.

"Fiver Torrey."

She doesn't know not to keep her private life private. Mom says, "what goes on in this house stays in this house." But you can't expect Dee to understand that. It's not that she's chatty, but she doesn't have a filter. She's as likely to say what's on her mind as she is to just keep to herself.

Then she asks him, "What is your name?"

"Max," he replies.

She continues to stare. He doesn't know the routine.

"She has a thing for names," I explain. "She wants to know your whole name."

"Ahhh, well, names have power. You can call me Max Atrillion." He winks at me when he says this. I know it's not his real name. Who lies to kids about a name? A kiddie-phile weirdo who's an Ex-Con, no doubt. I feel chills go up my arms and neck.

"Thank you for the lettuce," I tell him.

Dee is busy feeding handfuls of the lettuce to Fiver. Neither seems to be fazed by the creepy Caretaker. Fiver chomps noisily. The next ragged piece of lettuce goes into Dee's mouth. She looks Fiver in the eyes and chews in time with him. She never eats salads when it's part of a meal. But she likes to mimic Fiver. I urge her along and we leave the garden and head for home.

As we walk into the yard, I see the Caretaker again. How did he get here ahead of us? Then I realize it's not him. It's the lady who moved in next door. To the trailer that had been a drug spot. Thank God those people are gone.

I'm not so sure about this one either. She had long brown hair when she moved in, but now she's shaved her head completely. It doesn't look bad. Maybe she's coming out. I had a friend who came out. It was cool. I don't care if people are gay. As long as they don't try to convince me to be gay. Mom's sister, Aunt Jenn doesn't feel the same but she's old school about certain things.

As far as I can tell, she lives by herself. She has a new dog, the dog is with her now. I take extra care putting Fiver back in his hutch. Some dogs eat rabbits. Coyotes can eat rabbits too, so we have to be careful to close everything up.

I look to Dee, who is fixated on the new lady's dog. The dog is big, fluffy, white and yellowish. Not a lab. From a distance, it looks like a white wolf or coyote.

Dee has her obsession look on again. Then she does something I almost never see. She waves at the dog, and then at the lady.

The lady waves back. She's wearing a mask, so I can't tell by her face if she's friendly or not. For some reason, Dee seems to like her.

Chapter 13

Dee

"Can he come in the house for dinner?"

"No, he's just eaten a ton of lettuce, that is his dinner." Derrick Torrey didn't tell us the lettuce counted as dinner. We were walking and eating. Not at a table. I sit on the ground and pet Fiver. Derrick sweeps hay and mess out of the cage.

Fiver wants to hug. We hug. He twitches his nose. I twitch my nose. I give him more lettuce. He eats it. He's still hungry. He knows that snack doesn't count as dinner. I eat some lettuce.

"Fiver doesn't want to live in a cage." I tell Derrick Torrey.

"Well, it's this or nothing. This is his home."

He doesn't want to go. Derrick Torrey said ten more minutes. I make a fence with my legs and Fiver hops over them and off my lap. I crawl along with him. He eats the heads off dandelions and I do it too.

"Dee! That's gross! Cats pee on that!" Derrick Torrey says.

Dandelions and cat pee taste better than lettuce. We hop and eat some more. Derrick Torrey picks up Fiver.

"No!" I rise to my feet and reach out my hands. Fiver reaches back. He wants me.

"It's time for him to go home for your dinner."

"I ate dandelions already."

"That doesn't count."

Derrick Torrey has strange rules.

"Say good night."

I walk to the hutch and look inside. Fiver eats hay. I tried it once. Dandelions taste better. And lettuce. Derrick Torrey turns the latch on the cage. Fiver is now in lock down.

I'm in a cage, too.

Chapter 14

The Caretaker

The car revs up again. It sounds like an old man with pneumonia, rasping once, twice, three times, trying to cough up something lodged deep. But it doesn't start.

"Damn." I pound the dashboard. Three hours lost to this. I can't get other work done today and I'm behind in the mowing. I hoist myself out of the seat and wipe my hands on a rag.

That's when I catch sight of what looks like trouble in the making.

The Swansen kids are out. Always hanging around. That's nothing new. But it looks like they're tussling. And I hear someone yelling the word "fag."

I clean myself off and head over to keep an eye on things. Still keeping a distance- kids need to learn to sort out their own affairs- I hang back by the tree at the edge of my lot.

Just like I thought. It's the older boy, Don. If I didn't know better, I would think he was named after the president. He's shoving Scotty around and calling him names. The neighbor boy is also in on it. I watch.

"You're a wimpy faggot!" Don taunts. His round face is ruddy in the heat and he looks like every bully from every cheap after school special since the dawning of the television age.

"Am not! You're a fucking Libtart!"

"You mean *Libtard*. Like that girl you want to be your *wife*!" the neighbor kid- Dalton or something like that- retorts.

I wonder whether I should inform him that technically, if he is going to accuse someone of being a faggot, he can't also accuse them of being married to a girl. I watch to see what happens next.

"No, I'm not! You want to marry her! You want to marry her and fuck her like they do on TV!" with this Scott emulates sex.

The shoving and name calling continues. I'm about to intervene, try to distract them, when another voice breaks in. It catches me by surprise; I was focusing only on the kids and hadn't noticed the new lady walking down the road with her dog.

She holds the dog's leash in a death grip, as if she's afraid someone's going to snatch it from her. She's got an entire bag overflowing with dog treats and toys. This woman packs to walk her dog the way some parents pack to take their toddler on a day trip. I wonder if she's also giving it Klonopin. One of them probably needs it.

"Hey, you kids are bigger than him. It's not right to push your little brother like that. You could hurt him," she says.

True, not fair. Best they get used to it early. But I was going to intervene before anyone got hurt.

This is going to get interesting. The semi-goth girl, big sister Jess, gets up from her reclining chair on the porch and wanders over to see what the fuss is about. She eyes the new lady with a look that reminds me of someone who doesn't know whether to laugh or be angry, so settles on a smirk instead.

That kid is a smartass, but knowing her parents, who can blame her. That family needs a smartass. At least that would be some kind of smart.

The new lady still holds her dog far from the kids as if they have the plague. Her dog doesn't seem interested in pursuing them. It seems she's a bit of a helicopter dog-mom.

"You can't tell me what to do! This is America!" Don yells, pointing a grubby finger at her. Only he pronounces it *'Murica*. I wish I had popped some popcorn.

"Well, if your free speech means you can call your brother mean names, then it also means I can tell you to stop calling him mean names."

"Hey, why are you wearing a mask?" Scott now asks, appearing to have forgotten he was just being bullied.

She pauses for a moment then says, "because there is a very contagious and dangerous virus going around."

"My dad says that's a hoax," Don is quick to reply.

Of course he does.

"Well," the new lady begins, "if it is a hoax, then what? I've taken a few extra minutes a day to put on a mask. But if I'm right, then what does that mean?"

Her question hangs in the air as she gives her dog a gentle tug and starts to walk away.

"Hey lady," Jess calls after her. I contemplate stepping in. Jess can have a mouth on her. But I wait.

"Yes?" she turns back to the girl.

"You're in for it now, you know. They're gonna rat to our parents."

The new lady turns back away and continues to walk toward the road.

The kids seem to have forgotten their mission to torment Scotty and are now taking turns impersonating liberals. No doubt parroting things they've heard from their parents.

"I'm a snowflake!" says Don in a falsetto. "Lock her up!" chants the other neighbor kid, Dalton or Aiden or whatever his name is.

I shake my head and return to the car.

Chapter 15

Dee

I look out the window. Fiver is asleep in his hutch. I can see his front paws sticking out from his wooden house. That's all.

"Dee, did you brush your teeth? Time for bed." Derrick Torrey says.

"I want to wait up for Mom."

"Mom's working late again."

I touch Fiver through the window.

Good night, Fiver. Sleep tight.

Mom works late. Again. I see someone moving around. It's the new lady. She moved into the place where people used to scream. And say 'bitch.' A bitch is a dog. Derrick Torrey told me. The man next door also used to yell 'cunt' and Derrick Torrey wouldn't tell me what that means. The old neighbors used to scream, and the lady used to cry.

The new lady cries there too, even though there is no one screaming. She doesn't call the cops all the time. Just her. And her dog. A dog is also a bitch.

She's out there now. In her car. Moving around.

Good night, Fiver.

I leave the window and go to bed.

* * *

Golden Apple

I can't sleep. Again. Mom is working late. I miss Fiver.

I also miss Taylor Bishop. Fiver is in a cage. I'm in a cage. Taylor Bishop is in a giant house. With stairs. They need it because she has a Mom and a Dad and two older sisters. A house with a pool. I went there once. For a birthday party. I didn't have a bathing suit. Taylor Bishop let me wear her old one. We threw water balloons at each other. And had a cake. And a clown showed up.

So many people were there. They asked me my name. I got scared.

"Will you come to my party again this year?" Taylor Bishop asked me at school, a year later.

Mom said I couldn't go.

"We don't have money for a present." Mom said.

But in school we made presents. We made crafts out of popsicle sticks and noodles, and beads.

I tried to make a present. Like we did at school. From elbow macaroni in the pantry. I ate one popsicle and put the other three in the sink to empty the box. I had found the glue in a drawer and made a present with the noodles and the sticks.

"Now can I go?" I asked Mom.

She yelled at me for wasting food. Derrick Torrey had come in and told her to go have a break outside.

"You can't go to the party, Dee. It's not just the present. Mom has to work late. No one can take you."

I had to tell Taylor Bishop. At the party I didn't go to, she became best friends with Kristen Jones. I didn't get invited to any more parties. I still used to see her at school. But now, I can't go to school. Because Mom has to work all the time. Because of lock down.

Like Fiver.

In a cage.

Chapter 16

Marie

The worst thing about living alone isn't lack of sex or even lack of company. It's losing things and not having anyone to ask, "have you seen my copy of *A Handmaid's Tale?*"

Fuck it, I ask Jackie anyway. Of course, she doesn't answer. I search the same spots inside for the fifth time before remembering I took it with me when I drove to the park recently with Jackie. I run out to my car but it's not on the passenger seat.

My car door is unlocked.

Chapter 17

Shari

It's bad enough my sister tries to tell me how to raise my own children, I won't have a stranger, especially *that* kind of stranger interfering in my kids' lives. I grab the filthy book and head out the door before Dave gets home. He'll have a fit. I know how to be a diplomat, at least. I can keep a level head. Dave can't do that. You know how a man is about his family.

I walk over to the dead end with purpose, head held high.

Will she flip out, like those people are inclined to do? Maybe I should just let the cops handle it. They all know us. But when Dave gets home, when he sees what our daughter *did* to herself! There's going to be hell to pay anyway. At least he won't have to know about this trash.

I walk up the front steps to her trailer and hear her dog barking inside. I've seen the beast. It's huge. If that animal ever gets out and comes after my kids, I'll call the police. I'll take her to court and I'll sue. I've already talked to Dave about it.

I bang on the door, three sharp raps. The mutt barks even louder. I hear it knock something over inside.

"Just a minute!" she yells. Probably in there fornicating or doing Lord only knows what.

The door swings back, and she pushes herself out before the beast can escape. She's wearing one of those ridiculous masks. A face diaper, we like to call them. She wears it to open the door! Does she wear it all day in the house? No wonder she can't think straight; with all the carbon monoxide going straight to her head.

Thank the Lord I'm not brainwashed. I refuse to live my life in fear!

"I can't control you being a bad influence on my daughter with your lesbian hairstyle," I begin firmly, "but you've crossed a line."

She furrows her brow.

"What? Who are you? What are you talking about?" she asks, muffled through her mask.

"My daughter, I'm Shari Swansen. My family and I live down the way," I motion down the road to my trailer, proudly displaying American Flags, back the blue, and not one but three trump 2020 flags.

"You gave my daughter this trash to read." I shove the book, *Handmaid's Tale*, back at her. She takes it by the corners as if I've spit on it. "Don't you ever give my kids anything, let alone this liberal trash, again. I don't think you understand the kind of people we are here in this park," I tell her, standing tall and looking her right in the eyes.

She gives me a nasty look, turns her eyes in the direction of my home and then returns her nasty face to me, saying "Oh I know exactly the *kind of people* who live here." Her emphasis on *kind of people* is supposed to be an insult. Then she says, "I didn't give this to anyone. I've been looking for it. It went missing."

"Are you saying my daughter stole it?"

"I have no idea. But I didn't give it to her. I don't even know your daughter."

"Well, she knows you. She came out the bathroom today with a bald head. Just like you. And I found this in her room. You're disgusting. Trying to turn an impressionable child gay. Do I need to remind you that seducing a minor is illegal?"

"Um, I'm not gay. I don't know your daughter and thank you for returning the book that mysteriously went missing from my car. Now is there anything else you want to say before I go and disinfect myself?"

Can you believe the gall?

I just say, "stay away from my daughter, we are on to you!" and with that I left.

I think I made my point clear. I hurry back home before Dave returns. Thank the good Lord I can stand up for myself. I am what they like to call an empowered woman. No one is going to mess with my kids. Especially not her kind.

Chapter 18

Lin

To avoid saying something I may regret, I say nothing.

It's easy to do. The clients, mostly white women who only work as a hobby, barely notice. They don't care what I think. They don't know that I think. They think I exist to wash their feet. To them, I exist to enable their illusion that their toenails are always prim and painted. To help them live the fantasy that they never sprout talons or develop blisters.

Well, if they develop blisters, it isn't from hard work.

I hear them say it. They assume I don't speak English and they air all their dirty laundry. I could tell the priest a few things they've left out of confession.

I keep my head down, avoiding their eyes. I don't want to be in their airstream.

Ignoring the signs plastered all over the doors and windows, they are like children. They pretend not to know a mask is meant to cover both nose and mouth. Perhaps it's because they live in the land of image, where appearance matters more than truth. They've forgotten the mask serves a health purpose and is not an accessory.

What I want to say is *what is wrong with you? Where I come from, masks are a matter of hygiene.*

No different from washing hands in the bathroom or blowing your nose in a tissue rather than clearing it out with your fingertips!

But they have many myths here. One myth is freedom. The other, choice. I know. I hear their stories. They sell themselves to engineers and doctors, lawyers, and businessmen. They have rings to prove it. Not one is happily married. Not one.

What does their bondage buy them?

Trips to the nail salon to see me. To breathe on me with pinched white noses protruding from above masks. Masks they remove in order to gossip.

Another myth; their victory in the war against my country.

As if she can read my mind, this one, her name is Joni, leans down. She assails me with her breath and taps my shoulder. Of course, because she believes immigrant means no English and hard of hearing.

"Miss," she says, loudly.

"Miss, do you know of any traditional herbs or charms that help boost immunity? Now, Marci here doesn't believe in the Coronavirus, but I do. I just think they're making too big a deal out of it."

She's forgotten me already and this next part she says to the other women sitting in a row, their feet in little tubs of warm water.

"I already take vitamins and drink celery shakes three times each day. And I wear this."

She extends her wrist, turning it side to side, jangling a bracelet covered in stones of different colors. I'll be damned if I know it from a hole in the ground but of course, she probably thinks I'm a superstitious villager. She doesn't know I'm one semester shy of completing a postgraduate degree and only here to help family with the business.

"It protects against bad vibes. It keep my vibration high, so I can rise above all the negativity," she explains. She asks if I have any such traditions in "my culture" that do the same as "we can never be too careful with so many negative people and pedophiles all around."

I recognize this talk. The white American script. The biggest bullies pretend to be the biggest victims. Those who look to others as backwards and superstitious fail to see the silliness in their own superstitions. The magical powers of jewelry. Money. Whiteness.

She waits for an answer. I respond that I do not know of anything but have found that wearing a mask *correctly* prevents illness. I slightly emphasize the word "correctly."

I don't get a tip.

* * *

Joni

"Can you believe the nerve of that woman? Shaming me in public just because I refuse to live my life in fear!" I tell Barbara as we leave the salon. I wave goodbye to Marci as we turn in the other direction. "What was her name? I am never going to that place again. We'll have to find another."

"I don't know, Lin, or Lu, or some Chinese name. Where does she get off being so rude? Considering the role China played in bringing this virus here," Barbara responds.

Anna, who has to walk faster to keep up with us as we make our way down Broadway, chimes in.

"First of all, the owners are Vietnamese, not Chinese, and second, you can't both not believe in the Coronavirus and also use it to be racist toward Asian-American people."

She's always a Debbie Downer. Anna is Barbara's younger sister. Much younger. As in, "Oops, what a surprise!" younger. So, while we are worldly and much wiser, she is almost out of college at one of those Liberal universities. That place has been filling her head with nonsense and charging a fortune to do so. I roll my eyes. If it weren't for Barbara and her insistence on spending time with Anna, I would never spend time with such a negative and rude person.

I try to be nice, as I was taught to be. After all, she may be a radical, but I am a lady. Barbara must have known where this was headed. She changes the subject.

"Let's stop here for tea?" As we approach the Bistro, tables out front are already crowded. We sit down at a vacant metal table and wait for our server.

"Have you and Dan planned a new date for the wedding?" I ask Barbara, "It's a shame your entire event had to be postponed because of that treacherous Cuomo closing everything down."

"We're going to wait until next year, that way we can see what's still open before putting more money down and losing our deposit again," Barbara tells me. Anna plays with her phone and ignores us. Just as well.

I try not to sound jealous and hope I concealed the tone creeping in around the edges. I could have been married too. Jeff was starting to talk about it. But then...

Was it really what he said? Had I really chosen them over him? At the time it seemed normal, but so much seemed normal and wasn't. How much of my past was an illusion?

I clear my throat, not wanting to come off the wrong way and finally venture to ask.

"So, have you seen Jeff around?" I cringe as soon as the question comes out of my mouth. My smile was too big, my voice too perky, it's clear I'm trying too hard. Too late, cat's out of the bag.

Barbara breaks eye contact with me and tries to smile reassuringly, but it looks patronizing. As if my boyfriend dumped me right before prom and people have to treat me with kid gloves.

"I haven't, not real recently. Though, I did see, online, a while back. It kinda looks like he may have moved on," Barbara tries her best to be honest without shattering my hopes.

It's okay, I'm an adult. I can handle it. Think positive.

"Oh, well, that's nice. For him," I blink back tears and breathe, and relax and breathe. I distract myself with happy thoughts to push it back down. Just like Lynnaeus councils us to do in our Zoom sessions. Don't give in to the negative. Visualize what you want to attract. I fan my fingers out and admire my freshly painted nails. "I have missed this!"

Barbara's face changes, as if she's relieved that I didn't have an all-out meltdown. Really, she must think I have no backbone at all.

Anna looks up from her phone then.

"So, Joni, how's life in the mobile home park?" she asks. Her question lands like a gut punch.

I look to Barbara, scowling. My eyes saying everything.

You told her?

Barbara averts my stare.

"It's temporary," I tell Anna, trying to remain steady. "But it's actually nice. I get to spend plenty of time with my niece and nephews. A rare treat since Cuomo insisted on being a home wrecker this year and keeping everyone apart. Tearing families away from each other. It's villainous! I'd say I have the best of both worlds."

She goes in for the kill.

"It must be so refreshing to not be in that NXIVM compound anymore down in Clifton Park."

I feel my cheeks turn red. Instinctively, my right hand goes to cover the brand on my upper thigh. No one can see it, but the reference to the self-help program turned sex-cult makes me automatically feel exposed. "It wasn't a compound." I try to remain level. I had been living with a member of the group who converted me. I found some of their philosophy to be empowering until it turned crazy.

Barbara had helped to get me out of the group before things got worse. But I never would have expected her to tell the entire story to her sister.

Before I can reply, Barbara kicks Anna hard under the table. I see her jump.

"Ouch. Fuck," she says.

The rest of the afternoon is awkward. Leave it to Anna to ruin a pleasant day. She's always doing things like that.

Chapter 19

Marie

Unable to concentrate on work again, I decided to clean out what used to pass for a fire pit. Jackie darts around me, trying to anticipate which way I'll launch the refuse on the shovel. She thinks it's a game. I wish it were as fun for me as it apparently is for her. The heat dissipates to a tolerable simmer from a day of humid sweltering. The fire pit is a mess.

Like the mice. A mess for someone else to deal with. I scoop the remains of soot and firecrackers. Remnants from a rowdy Fourth of July. One last hurrah for the prior residents.

Jackie pants, leans into a play bow, then lunges for me. I stumble back and spill soot onto my leg. I can't be mad. So, I set the shovel down and pat my knees. She jumps up on me and kisses the sweat off my face.

"You're bored, aren't you?" I ask her.

I promise we'll take a walk once I've leveled the pile of burnt garbage to the ground. I distract her with a ball and while she chases and bats it around in her mouth; I continue to shovel the ashes, broken bottles and... is that a baby diaper? It is.

Displacing the garbage from the fire pit to a contractor bag lined garbage barrel. Another throw of the ball, and another. Unbearable humidity now replaced by the needling of mosquitoes. It's still light out, but I can tell it's now getting late. I look to the heap of rubble. It's almost completely cleared, at least the broken glass is out of the way. The last thing I need is for Jackie to cut her pads on the waste or get into something dangerous.

"Jackie, Time for a walk."

I stop inside to wash my hands, then grab my mask and her leash. We stroll around the private road that winds around the small mobile home park. She seems so much happier to see my neighbors than I do. While she pulls forward, her tail wagging, I barely muster the enthusiasm to wave. I try to keep us both at a distance.

The kids are out playing in the road, as usual. I pull Jackie close as we walk by. I'll give them credit, children playing in real life is a rarity these days.

We turn down 9R and dodge what seems like hordes of mask-less wanderers. I've come to expect this, in this part of the world, where reality is subjective and science irrelevant.

Jackie wants to keep walking as we get to the boat launch, but I tell her it's too late now. Even with the sun setting, there are too many tourists. We head back, this time both of us sharing a reluctant, melancholy mood. Neither Jackie nor I content to not have what we want.

The kids have gone inside. Rounding the path, movement catches my eye. It's off to the side of what is arguably the most dilapidated trailer in the park. So much furniture lines the front yard that I wonder what furniture could possibly be stored inside. I tighten my grip on Jackie's leash, squinting my eyes. Never one for good eyesight at dusk, I can't be sure if I'm about to encounter a wild animal that has taken advantage of the wide array of things to feast on in the odds and ends strewn about the yard, or another child who stayed out to play alone.

Neither, it turns out. A small spark of light, then another and another. Now I'm curious.

A woman with hair so long it reaches past her knees hovers over what looks like an old card table. She's lighting tea lights and tall candles encased in glass. She sees us and her grin suggests she is not surprised to be intruded on by our presence.

"Well, hello," she says in a pack-a-day voice.

Her hair is completely white. If it weren't for the torn jeans and faded heavy metal t-shirt, I could imagine her some kind of angel or fairy.

"Hi," I say back, not wanting to be rude, but fingering my mask out of habit. I don't know whether I do this to make sure it is securely in place or to make a signal that she, too, should be wearing one. She's far more than a distance of six feet, standing in the side yard amidst the rubble.

Be rude and leave? Stick around and talk? I don't really want to do either. She answers for me.

"It's a lovely Full Moon tonight, isn't it?" she asks. I realize I hadn't noticed but instantly look up at the sky. Jackie follows my gaze. There is, indeed, a beautiful September Moon hanging low in the sky. How long has it been since I've noticed the Moon? I suddenly wonder.

"It is, yes," I respond. She continues.

"She's the Goddess, you know. Used to have a whole lot full of others who would come out every Full Moon to celebrate with me," she gives a hearty cough. Were it not for the cigarette she's been pulling on I may have jumped to other conclusions.

I look again, and it's as if I see her lawn with new eyes. These aren't random artifacts of furniture. They are little tables, stools and knick-knacks, all with a similar theme. Fairies, elves, gnomes, little crescent Moons, and Goddess statuary. Sprinkled in amidst the spare tires, old refrigerator, rusted lawn chairs. Even stacks of coolers and animal carriers. In the far corner, there's a broken armoire.

"Yeah, well, can't do that now. So, it's just me and the Goddess. That's just fine, I'm a tough old broad and I've always known it's just me and the Goddess. She gives me all the protection I need," she says this with a hearty laugh as she takes another drag from her cigarette.

There is something oddly charming about her. Though I do wish she would wear a mask. She gestures toward Jackie.

"And who is this beautiful creature?" she asks.

I smile. "Her name is Jackie. I adopted her recently."

"Well, she is a gorgeous creature, and no doubt is a lucky one too to have such a wonderful mother, now isn't she. You know, normally, I would come closer to visit, but I don't have my mask on, hate wearing it in the heat, so I'll keep my distance and admire her from afar."

"Thank you," I tell her. Then I add, hesitantly, "maybe another time."

"You have a blessed evening! And your little Wolf Friend as well!" She motions to Jackie as she says this. Of the cast of characters that make up my neighborhood, she seems the most endearing. Under other circumstances, I could see myself drinking tea on the porch with her, asking her questions about her life. Even sharing a Full Moon telling jokes and stories. Surrounded by incense and candles to set the tone. Talking about the Sacred Feminine and the meaning of dreams and Tarot cards.

But not now.

I look up again at the Moon. The Goddess is alive, indeed, but she's chosen to keep Her distance until we learn how to behave.

I wish the older woman a good evening and lead Jackie back in the direction of the trailer.

Chapter 20

Justin

Magenta globs ooze and float; suspended in liquid. I watch it through the glass of the Lava lamp; the last gift my dad gave me before he walked out. It was the week before my tenth birthday. I don't blame him. I know what he had to deal with. I've been dealing with it ever since.

I recite one, then another line, trying to think of the perfect comeback to own the lib who has been trolling me on Facebook. It comes to me and then is gone. Erased in a slam of the refrigerator door.

"God dammit!" I slam my fists on the desk. My concentration is ruined. Nothing to do now but open my door to see which of the lowlifes has done it this time. It's one of the renters, or should I say squatters. That's really what they are. My mom rents to them every year, but there's no room in the trailer, not with her boyfriend taking up the spare room with his crap.

So she lets them park their beat-up cars on the lawn out front and use the kitchen and bathroom. They come and go like crack heads. Each week a different guy. Some stay the whole summer season.

"Who are you?" I ask

"My name is Bruce," he says.

"You don't look like a Bruce," I tell him. No one is home, which means I can talk to these freaks however I want. He doesn't look like a Bruce. More like a Pedro or Jose. I think I'll call him that. Why not? God gave man the job of naming the animals...

"So, Jose, you working at the track?"

"My name is Bruce," he says. He looks scared, like I may have some kind of in with his boss at NYRA. The fuck I do. I could care less about any of those douchebags. "And yes. The backstretch," he says tentatively. He grabs his beer and a bowl of something that stinks to high Heaven, and heads out to his car to eat. Just as well. It's a wonder I can get any work done around here with all her crazy men and renters.

I hop on Signal and send a heads up to my contact whose handle is Master88.

We're putting some big plans together. Very big. I can't afford to be distracted.

Still, Pedro or Pablo or whatever his name is reminds me of the track, shut down because Cuomo the Homo has to incite fear so he can control his flock. Sheeple. All of them. It's just as well, though. Unlike the rest of the losers in this town, I could give two fucks about the racetrack. All those Chads and Stacy's sitting in the stands, dressed up like they think they're something. They won't have anyone to dress up for this summer. The track is only televised now. No spectators. Sorry, Stacy. Too bad, Chad.

I can see them all in the stands, at the picnic tables, dressed to the nines on mommy and daddy's credit cards. I know their type. Then I see the explosion.

That was last year's plan. We had it all set pretty good, too. The best part is, we could do it right under their noses and they'd never know. They'd blame it on those animal rights nuts always standing outside with signs. Hell, maybe a few of them would get arrested, go off to Prison. No one would know, until the next time we strike, and by then it would be too late.

* * *

A Message comes in from Master88. A time, a date and location. Followed by the question; Will you be there? Yes, I reply. I'll be on that like Joe Biden on a fifth grader.

Chapter 21

The Caretaker

"This is the only lot we got left. It's a prime location, being near the lake and all." I show the young couple the slab foundation surrounded by lawn and trees. It's a shady spot. I wouldn't mind it for myself if I had the option.

I don't try too hard to sell it, though. I've shown this lot more times than I can count in the past few years. No one wants it. In my estimation, if a person is going to buy a trailer and pay to have it hauled, they would likely invest in a better park.

You can't beat the lake being nearby, but most people want something a little more... refined. After all, it's still Saratoga. That isn't lost on me. It's to my advantage to have one less family to keep an eye on. So I don't complain. It's not like I'm the landlord.

Usually, by the time someone drives all the way down the road off 9R to check the place out, they're already thinking they've wasted their afternoon. Or a guy likes it but his wife scowls and pulls him away.

Not today, to my surprise.

Tom and Bianca scope out the perimeter of the lot.

They ask about permission to build a fence. I can't be certain, but I thought I heard her turn to him and whisper "build the wall" then smile and jab his side.

"Owner doesn't mind if you want to build as long as you don't break a pipe digging. He's laid back."

Indeed. Which is how I came to be living here, fresh off the streets. True of a few of us here. That's why I don't mind unclogging a toilet or shoveling or helping out with the general maintenance. Most of the people here are just trying to get by in a world that's done nothing but shit on them.

I have a feeling that's about to change. I've noticed some things. Things I don't like. About certain kinds of people. That may think they're going to cause trouble now...

"And where is my property line on this side?" Tom asks, pointing to one of several trailers festooned with trump 2020 flags. "That is, if I were to rent here?"

I walk him along the edge of the property. The neighbor's kid, Scott, is outside. He acts shy now that his brother and their friends aren't out playing with him. He's hunched over a pile of GI Joe action figures. Vintage, I recognize them from when I was a kid. Probably a garage sale find. Or eBay. As I answer more of the young couples' questions, I hear Scott making explosive sounds.

As action figures fly across the yard, I hear him chanting low, "shoot Antifa."

***

Turning through the white noise, finally, a clear reception on the Police Scanner. Routine shit so far. A report of a domestic incident, kids loitering downtown, drunk drivers. I turn the volume down low and put my feet up for the first time today. I reach for my Gibson and strum the strings. It needs a tune up.

I fiddle with the pegs and adjust the sound.

Shoot Antifa.

The kid had said. Well, I guess it's all over the news. Probably heard the president use the term...

But I can't shake the thought that Scott and the other kids spend more time outdoors than they do inside. Odd for their generation, but true. I never see their faces glued to screens. Would he really have heard the term on the news?

Or from his dad, more likely.

I strum absently, losing the desire to play. My gaze drifts out the window, back in the direction of the vacant lot.

There's something happening here.

I think to myself, strumming the riff from Buffalo Springfield and humming over the Police Scanner.

That couple just may rent it. Asked a million damn questions. Say they have a trailer ready to move. Just waiting for the owner's approval. He'll approve anyone. Which is why I live here.

He doesn't ask too many questions.

Chapter 22

Andre

Cautiously optimistic. Probably the best way to describe my friends and neighbors, the ones who stayed. Many didn't. My building looks pretty much the same. I'm not one of the more privileged people who can run away when things get bad. I see them, though. The people MAGA folks could call "Coastal Elites."

They quote NPR like it was gospel. They tolerate people like AOC. And people like me. But they don't really understand us. They would never act out the way the MAGA crowd does. They make it clear, in their subtle ways. Their actions show they wish they didn't have to deal with us. Too much baggage. Too much to unpack. Unlearn. Relearn. Too much change.

Those of us who are staying, who are ride or die NYC, we've spent the summer gradually stepping out of the shadows. People without the complexion for protection, that is to say, people who look like me, blessed with extra melanin in a society who sees this as a curse, have been bolder. We have to be out in the streets, marching for our lives. Because 'rona isn't the only thing killing us in this country.

I haven't been to a bistro since last summer. Today, I just said fuck it. Sitting on the patio, waiting for lunch to be served, watching people. Thinking about how fucked up it was to see these streets, empty.

I mean, I'm pretty sure they even throw in a few extras to wander the streets in those apocalyptic movies, just to make it look authentic. But for weeks at a time, it had been no sound but the ambulance.

I shake my head, trying to erase the memory of the constant sirens. The faces that I never got to see on Mass Cards displayed at funerals I never got to attend. Faces of people I will never see alive again. Too many.

A rustling at my feet gets my attention and I'm on alert. I look down and see the biggest, nastiest, most entitled rat. You can't even imagine. They're like the size of Yorkies by now.

Just for shits and giggles, I take a picture with my phone and send it to Marie. She needs to lighten up. I follow it with a message.

Andre: Is this one of yours?

Marie: WTF?! Where IS that?

We shoot the shit back and forth. I'm laughing out loud. I know she is too. Then the bullshit begins again.

Don't get me wrong. I know it's been hard for Marie, what with her ex turning trumpy. But girlfriend needs to get a grip. The last few times we spoke, she sounded like she was turning into one of these old cat ladies who sits by her window and spies on the neighbors.

Maybe I should be more patient, but I'm tired. I'm tired of hearing white people lament over their losses, which amount to more than Black people have ever been allowed to have. And that feeling doesn't change. Even when that white person is your friend.

What I'm really tired of, I know I shouldn't feel this way, but I can't help it...

What I'm really tired of is the onslaught of white fear always command attention. How white people's security is always paramount. When we are being shot in the street, we've got to keep our indoor voices. Don't protest the "wrong" way. Don't be too loud, don't show attitude. When white people are in danger- especially danger they themselves created, we are hostage to their feelings. Their anger, their pain, their losses. Constantly. And we're expected to just shut up about it.

Because you don't want to make a white woman cry.

I know Coronavirus is a crisis. It's taken my friends. It's taken my coworkers. It's still more likely to kill me than it is to take out Marie.

Just purely based on statistics. And yet, I'm supposed to be a good friend and listen to her fears.

Maybe it's because white people aren't equipped to handle actual fear. I mean, they go to the movies and pay to watch shit that terrifies them. At least, they used to. Whereas Black people, we just walk out the door. I know I'm supposed to empathize, but I'm running out of fucks to give to anyone but my own people.

Here she is, two or three jokes into a conversation, texting about the weirdos in the trailer park. Hell, I coulda told you what you were in for. Some of it is just too much. I wonder if she's not just projecting her own issues. Who knows?

She's going on now about the Caretaker. How he's weird. Like the kind of person you'd expect to be responsible for an underground crime ring.

I tell her, "Here you go again, what did you join Qanon now?"

That's another one. I don't know what sums up white privilege better than a bunch of people who organize armed interventions to stop imaginary pedophile rings allegedly run from the basement of a pizza restaurant that doesn't even have a basement. Especially when they have nothing to say about marginalized kids actually getting trafficked in real life.

It's like white people have it so easy, they have to invent things to worry about. Now even Marie is starting to do it.

I don't know. I have my own troubles to worry about. Even being cautiously optimistic.

Chapter 23

Marie

The medical bill, car note, and final notice on a Discover Card account await me in the mailbox. They are the misfortune of the trailer's previous owner.

Jackie pulls me impatiently as I reach around for any hidden letters or postcards that may be mine. Nothing. Could be worse, I tell myself, as I nudge Jackie to sit beside me long enough to reach in my pocket for sanitizer and squirt it into my hands. Jackie backs away from the smell. I don't like it either.

We head back to the trailer after another of our longer evening walks, the neighborhood less crowded at this time, but still enough light to see and be seen. As the sun sets, the shadows cast on the ground are almost enough to remind me of other summers. Summers spent in backyard barbecues, or sitting in front yards, talking with neighbors. Neighbors who weren't committing negligent genocide.

Summers used to be spent listening to music, going to drive-in theaters, taking vacations and staying in three-star hotels. Then two-star Air BnB's. Just to have a long weekend at the ocean. Summers I would normally have spent with friends, instead spent traveling for work, walking through strange cities, taking pictures of attractive graffiti, dining alone, video messaging back home. Promising that someday when the book tour was over, things would get back to normal.

Angela Kaufman

I miss the strangest things. The library and the smell of books. Festivals.

Jackie stops to sniff around as we enter the community garden. It isn't bad, actually. I've never been able to keep a cactus alive. This doesn't bode well for Jackie, but I promise her I will do better and thank goodness she's a dog and not a succulent.

The littlest things. Festivals and greasy food that I have no intention of eating. I couldn't afford the process. Remember how we would try to find the healthiest thing on the menu, then split it? Remember how we would laugh about finding out how to get away with spending the least amount possible and still trying to cover all the food groups? Even if we had to count Ketchup as a vegetable? We could joke about our Reaganesque diet then. Before you developed an appetite for radical right-wing politics. I picture you now, pointing to tiny, chopped onions, and peppers on some kind of hotdog or sausage with French fries, pretending the grease laden meal counted as an assortment of vegetables.

That was what summer was for. Wandering through festivals in the sweltering heat. Wearing completely impractical dresses made for such occasion and little else. Stopping at the booths and pawing through jewelry, clothing, handicrafts.

I see myself in the mirage touching scarves, handbags, necklaces. Then I shudder at the thought of my hands on objects touched by so many people.

No, I tell myself. It was okay then, remember?

Just like it was okay to stand and talk for too long with the bored-looking vendors who were happy to have company just as long as no one was lining up to make purchases.

Jackie pulls me toward a tomato bush. She seems more excited by the juicy plants than I ever was.

"Leave it, not for you. Good girl," I tell her.

We walk deeper into the garden. Thank goodness no one else is around. I can breathe easier.

I remember past summers, back in the beginning. Being a vendor at farmer's markets, conferences, festivals, anyplace I could afford a table. Surrounded by stacks of books. Happy to make five sales in an entire day. Making the most of the sun and a chance to travel some place new when there were no sales.

Always assuming that, like summer, there would be another chance. If I had known. What? Would I have insisted we each had our own lunch? Would I have thrown in some Cotton Candy? Would it have even mattered?

Now it is getting harder to see. I tell Jackie it's time to go home. "Home, girl. To Jackie's house."

She looks up at me and focuses one eye, then the other, in a dog expression of curiosity and interest.

The word home sticks. I've started using it. Trying it on. Not sure how it fits. How easily we adapt. From a life together, to a life lived out of a suitcase, a night or two in different homes, in bus stations, in Pilot parking lots, how easy life on the road became natural. How easily we acclimate to tensions building. Nights spent in separate rooms, different playlists on YouTube and different newsfeeds on Facebook, feeding us two different realities. Until we can no longer even speak the same language. How easily we adjust to the rising tide until we no longer know what drowning feels like.

I look at the trump flags. The debris. The place I'll get used to. Is that how Jackie sees her home with me? Does she refer to me, in her mind, as the person she ended up with? While dreaming of a family she can no longer go home to? Does she talk to them, in her mind, the way I still find myself talking to you?

Does she wake from dreams and feel her heart sinking? Or is it just me?

Jackie scents the air and I follow her gaze. As I do, I hear it. I know the song. I've never heard this recording of it. The bizarre contrast between the Byrd's melodic fuck you to Ralph Emery and the melody of a grunge ballad catches my attention.

It can't be the same song.

I pull at my mask to make sure it's securely in place and guide Jackie, who seldom is allowed off the trail, in the direction of the music. It's not a recording after all.

The Caretaker sits on his front steps, strumming a guitar. A small fire burns a few feet from him. They all burn their garbage here. I hesitate to approach further. I wonder if he sees me.

He continues to play, giving me a glance I can't decode. I don't want to interrupt. When he stops, I applaud. Surprised at myself. I don't want to make friends with anyone here, but I have to know.

"Was that what I think it was?"

"This one's for you, Ralph." He mimics a southern drawl. I laugh in spite of myself. I walk closer, Jackie follows behind me, sits behind my legs and stares cautiously at the stranger.

"Some nerve playing a song like that in a place like this," I'm still not sure I trust this guy.

"I think it's a perfect song, all things considered," he responds, letting his fingers slide down the strings in an open chord.

"Clearly your neighbors don't recognize it then," I suggest.

"Our neighbors," he corrects me, "and not when I play it like this," he winks. He then adds, "not that I give two shits whether they recognize it or not."

"What else is on the playlist tonight?" I ask, curious to see what other rabbits he can pull out of his hat.

He thinks for a moment, then begins another. It's slow but familiar. I cock my head to the side, squinting as if narrowing my eyes will jog my memory. Then I hear it.

"Joe South. Don't It Make You Wanna Go Home?" I ask.

"Is that your thing? To slow down even slow songs? Turn everything into a lullaby?"

"Maybe I'm just tired," he says, then asks, "what's your favorite, I probably know it."

"No favorite, but I like key changes."

He begins another. This one I don't know. As if to rebuke my comment about slow songs, it's more moderate. I don't realize I'm leaning in, stretching my mind, irrationally hoping proximity will help me name that tune. The music soothes Jackie. She emerges from behind my legs and sniffs the ground in a trail until she is nose to foot with the Caretaker. I tense, not sure how she will do with strangers, but she seems calm, and he doesn't seem to mind.

I try to guess. "Metallica maybe? I don't know this one."

He chuckles. "I wonder if Buffy Sainte-Marie would be insulted or James Hatfield would be flattered, to hear you say that."

"Who?"

"Goodnight," he tells me.

"Oh, right, it's getting late," I turn to leave.

He stops playing.

"No, that's the name of the song. Goodnight. By Buffy Sainte-Marie. I took some liberties with it."

"Never heard of her."

"Bet you have," he says, eyeing me wryly.

"Um, no, I haven't"

"Pretty sure you have," he insists. Then he changes tunes. Another slow melody with an unmistakable 80s love song opening. I do know this. It was in a movie, and probably the wedding song du jour when I was a kid.

"Up where we belong?" I didn't mean it as a question, but it came out that way.

He nods. "That was Buffy. So were a good number of other songs. Amazing, white people couldn't get enough of that one, but wouldn't play her songs for a while in this country."

"Why?"

"Native woman, activist, very outspoken in the 70s. Antiwar songs, songs that called out AIM and the FBI's treatment of Native people. Just to name a few reasons."

"So, you're really not like the rest of these people here?" I ask, not sure I'm forming the question correctly even as it escapes my lips.

"Perhaps."

"How can you stand it?"

He strums low now and stares into space. I wonder if he's going to answer at all. I can't tell if he's mad. I feel myself becoming more frustrated by the labyrinth that is communicating with this man whose name I am pretty sure I still don't know.

As I am about to turn and leave, tiring of the staring contest, he responds.

"I had no other options for a good long while. This was the option I was given. My career, my income, my money, all of it was stolen from me by your government,"

"My government?" I ask. He ignores my question and continues.

"I've given up my citizenship. I just exist now. Among you. I was given this," he gestures to the trailer, and I realize for the first time it is one of the better kept in the park. Not fancy, but well maintained.

"Given is not accurate," he corrects himself, "I was offered an opportunity to live here under reasonable terms, in exchange for my many skills. That is how I came to be the Caretaker. It is not my chosen career. It is not the best use of my skills. It is what I can now do to get by. To exist."

I think back to where I started. My education, my prospects only a few years ago, and the many trap doors that slipped open beneath my feet resulting in where I am now. His talk makes me think he may be crazy, but I can relate to what he's saying. I wouldn't call my career stolen, but I can understand the disappointment. The feeling of a swift drop. But whose fault is it? When an economy changes, when a book doesn't sell? When a pandemic upends any future prospects of a second chance? When writing mindless blogs is what remains of a career that started out writing literary fiction?

I don't know how to respond so I just say "oh."

He laughs.

"But how do you stand, all of this?" I gesture to the trump flags that wave like the markers of poison on a label.

He stares into space again. "Things are being set into motion," he begins, "I see it now. In time, you'll see it too. So will they. You may think you know better than a lot of them," he gestures to the trump flags, "but judging people because of the way they talk, the place they live, or the way they look is part of what got trump in office, right? Take a look around. This is generations of class war. In every war, you run the risk of people falling prey to demagogues."

I consider this. He's not wrong. I still hate it here. He continues. "The biggest mistake that both conservatives and moderate liberals made is to give the average person nothing to lose. People who think they're out of options, they're a demagogue's dream. These people didn't get to be desperate, fearful and hateful overnight. It's been cultivated in 'em for generations. Fueled as much by ignorance as by neglect. Neglect by institutions and politicians that allow this to happen," as he says this, he gestures to the deep potholes in the road. The collapsing roofs. The trailers with missing windows.

* * *

Walking back to the trailer, I replay the conversation. I feel relieved to know there is one ally in the park. Don't fool yourself, a voice in my head breaks in. He's crazy. He's a good musician, though. Good taste in music too. Smart, and not one of them.

That doesn't mean he's one of you.

He has a foot in reality.

Does he?

I argue with myself as Jackie pulls me through the front door and jumps up for a hug.

"You seemed to like him. Are you a good judge of character? Because apparently, I'm not."

Chapter 24

Jess

I haven't seen the new lady, Marie, since my mom acted a fool and embarrassed me, again. I want her to know I'm not like them. My mom doesn't speak for me. My dad certainly doesn't.

She's probably avoiding me. I don't blame her. My parents suck. I run a hand over my head, now stubble. I always thought it was bad ass for women to rock a bald head, to be honest. Until I saw Marie do it, I just never saw it in real life. It was pretty hot. Not that I'm gay. I'm not. But it made me think maybe I could get away with shaving my head, too.

The next day, I borrowed my dad's clippers. Well, to be fair, I didn't ask. I just tried them out. First thing I did was text a selfie to Eric.

"What d'ya think?" I asked him.

"Who's that hottie?" he texted back. He likes it, I like it, that's all I care about.

Mom shit a brick. Dad flipped out. He went on and on about how no dykes allowed in his house or his family. Aunt Joni tried to smooth things over by talking about how it could be symbolic of starting over and new energy, and all that woo-woo shit she's into. At least she tried to have my back. Not that it worked.

Dad doesn't want her here either, but he's keeping that under wraps for now.

I wander out onto the path. The neighbors stare. The few that are out. But no one says anything. Then there's Justin. I swear that guy is a fucking loser. He takes one look at me, scrunches up his nose, gives me the finger and then goes back inside, slamming the door. Good. Maybe now he'll stop trying to get in my pants.

I swear, one of these days that dumbass is gonna be on the front page for shooting up a Walmart because no one will blow him.

I don't see Marie. I know she has to come out sometime. I mean, she's gotta walk her dog. Her dog is awesome. The kind of dog I want to have someday. She lives by herself. No husband, no kids, that's pretty badass too. I wish my mom was strong enough to do that. Instead of shacking up for life with my idiot dad.

But no, she would rather stay married to keep a roof over her head, which is no different than prostitution, when you think about it. I wander further down to the garden, by now not expecting to find her, just out for the sunshine.

So I'm surprised when I turn a corner and see the big fluffy dog, with the newly baldheaded woman holding the leash.

"Hey!" I say, trying to not be too loud and startle her. She turns and sees me. She doesn't run, doesn't look mad. I breathe a tentative sigh of relief. I walk closer. She steps back. Then I remember. "Oh, sorry," I tell her, pulling my t-shirt over my nose to make a mask. She seems to relax.

"Hello," she says, eyeing her dog as if to make sure I'm not going to steal her. She's weird as hell sometimes, but it's all good.

"Listen, I just wanted to say, I'm sorry my mom was a douche."

She laughs at first, then does the adult thing where she tries to look stern, but I know she's a marshmallow.

"I don't appreciate you taking my book."

She would suck at being a parent. Her kids would walk all over her. There's no real gravity to what she's saying. It almost sounds like she's joking. I apologize anyway. I was wrong.

She adds, "it's fine. I have a feeling I understand why you had to be sneaky about it."

"Yeah, my parents are, intense."

"Look, I don't want to make trouble for you or with your family. Your mom made it pretty clear she doesn't want me talking to you."

"What do you think about that?" I ask, afraid of what she might say.

"I think neighbors sometimes cross each other's paths and it's polite to greet each other and make small talk."

I smile. She continues.

"And sometimes, in the summer, neighbors like to stroll by the lake. It's a good place to walk a dog, for instance. And sometimes, when people do this, they run in to people they know."

She looks at me as she says this, like we're sharing an inside joke.

"Sometimes, people then end up exchanging a few words," she adds.

I nod to show her I get her meaning. She smiles and then adds, "as long as their neighbors are wearing masks."

I laugh and shake my head. "Done deal," I tell her.

"Nice haircut," she changes the subject.

I feel the sandpaper stubble with my palm again. "Thanks," I tell her, "you inspired me, not to sound like a fangirl and shit, but I saw you and then thought fuck it, I've always wanted to try it too. What made you do it?"

And then you'll never believe what she said.

"My shower broke, and I couldn't afford to pay a plumber."

I nearly died laughing. She wasn't offended. At least, I don't think so. She laughed too.

"There's a lot of things my parents think," I try to explain to her, "that aren't me. I just want you to know. I may live with them and all, and they're family, but I'm not one of them."

"We're born where we're born," she says, "but we decide who we want to be, we don't have to follow what we're taught as kids. It's okay."

I nod.

She continues. "Reading opens so many doors. I have other books. Sometimes I come here to read them. Sometimes, Jackie here distracts me, and I leave without them. Just so you know," She winks as she says this last part.

"Gotcha. I'd have to hide them from my mom. She goes through my room and everything."

"I understand," she says, "my mom used to be the same exact way. I got so sick of her reading my diary, I started writing in a secret code."

Now, I'm totally intrigued. "Really? What kind?"

She tells me, and it's fucking brilliant. Makes me think of a way Eric and I can write to each other. Even in text. I'm liking this new lady more and more. Even if she is a little weird.

She let me pet her dog, too. Jackie, I think she said the dog's name was? The Dog climbed right into my lap when I sat on the ground and started kissing all over my face. My shirt collar fell off my nose and I noticed the new lady, Marie, didn't seem to freak out.

Back home, I try out Marie's code; I call Eric and tell him how it works, then we test it out on each other. This is going to change everything.

Chapter 25

Jackie

I pull toward the smell of fish and weed and duck. It's a "No." She walks the other way. The way of dirt and grass and worms and vegetables.

I follow, and we walk, and we walk, and I sniff at the food. It's there on the ground. Tomatoes and lettuce and carrots and eggplant.

I sniff and I lick at a tomato. And it's a "No."

I don't eat, and neither does she.

We just look at them.

It's okay, I try to show her, you can eat, and I chomp. And it bursts and red and sweet and juices fill my tongue. I chomp and I chomp, and I taste the bit of stem before I gulp, and it's gone. I look to her. It's her turn. She just looks.

It's okay. She pets me and pet and a scratch behind the ear so good that I thump, and I thump, and I thump with my paw.

I smell someone new.

She smells like the smoke and the burger and the chocolate. Chocolate is a "No." But I smell her and underneath it all I smell she is good. A pup. No fur on her head, like the one on my leash.

She is good; I try to teach; she is good! She is good! And I arf, and I jump side to side, side to side, side to side and She holds the leash but relaxes because the pup is a good girl. So, She knows because I show her.

I introduce us to the pup. She kneels down and pets my head, and she pets, and I kiss, and I sit on her lap.

I look back and I show; I show how to smile and arf, and love and kiss. She seems to understand. She kisses me too, but with her mouth closed. And not inside my ears.

It's okay, I teach.

The pup stands and they speak, and I sniff, and I sniff.

I squat and I spray, right on the edge of the tomatoes. I leave my smell over the smell of squirrels and cats and hedgehogs.

Then we walk and we walk, and we walk to the home. Then we walk and we walk, and we walk back to the tomato and cucumber and dirt and worms and-

The cats were here again! And I squat and I spray, and I sniff, and I leave my scent.

This time, She leaves Hers too. She leans, and She drops the papers that smell like Her.

Don't chew the papers! Don't step on the papers! The special papers, all bound together. Not toys. Not for play. She leaves them with Her smell by the vegetables. She doesn't pee.

She leaves the stacks of papers by the eggplant and tomato and the worms and the dirt and the cats better stay away! And I arf, and we walk, and we go to the home and we play, and we sleep and then the next day, we walk back to the buffet and I sniff, and I sniff, and I smell Her. I smell Her and I smell the pup, but the papers are gone.

Chapter 26

Jess

"Where're you going?'" Dad asks as I pocket my phone and head for the door.

"Out."

"Yeah, I know what's on the other side of the door, smartass, I wasn't born yesterday. I mean where in the outdoors are you going?"

"Around. To the lake maybe. It's not like I can get anywhere since I don't have a car."

He hates when I say this. Maybe as much as I hate being stuck here. He slams his fist on the table and turns away from the TV now. Then he makes a gesture that has annoyed me for as long as I can remember. He makes a fist with his hand and holds his index finger, extended up by his eyes, which now look like they're going to leap out of his head, which is now turning red.

"Show some respect. If you want a car, get a job, and earn one. This isn't communist Russia where people are just handing out cars!"

I try to stifle a laugh, imagining sensible sedans being handed out as people stand freezing in bread lines. Where does he get this shit? Am I the only person in this household who isn't fucking crazy?

I don't want him to think he's won, so I say, not nicely, "I'm going to go for a walk, probably around the lake because I'm bored and have nothing to do, and on foot, I won't be getting far even if I did have some place to go."

I don't wait for an answer. Just get a job? Where? Everyplace has been closed all year and now I'm competing with people his age, people with college degrees, and everyone in between just to flip burgers. I try not to think about this. I really try.

I mean, what is there to plan for? Will there be colleges to go to in two years, when it's my turn? Will there be any jobs left? I try to not ask myself these questions. The only logical answers lead me back to a reality I desperately don't want to believe in.

That I'll be stuck here. Forever. Like Aunt Joni. Except not crazy. I'll be the only one in the trailer with a foot in reality. Until the day I die. I look around the neighborhood, wondering if I can mow some lawns for a few bucks, but it seems the majority of overgrown weeds and lawns strewn with furniture and nick knacks this side of the bridge answer that question for me. On the other side of the bridge? Forget it. Those people hire a crew to keep up with their neighbors. They don't want a gas mower stinking up their front yard for a few hours. They want the full works.

I walk past the Stewart's on the corner. I could probably get a job there. Someday, when someone dies. Since the same people have been working there for as long as I can remember. One of them, Misty, lives in the park. She's older. She was in college at one point. Then, I saw her walking to work, that's the best part of working down the block from your house. She was sporting a baby bump, walking down the road with her schoolbooks in hand. Probably planning to do homework on her break.

Then, I saw her without the baby bump. I never saw her with a baby. I never saw her with the schoolbooks again. As if I've summoned her, she steps out the door, nods in my direction, pulls down her mask and lights up. I nod back from across the parking lot and keep heading toward the lake.

Has my dad always been such a jerk?

Maybe that's not the right word. I mean, he didn't go to college. A lot of people his age didn't. He also didn't do so well in school. He never told me that, but it just shows now. I look out at the dock and remember the days when we used to have so much fun. Even though he was working then, before he hurt his back, he would still make sure every Sunday was family day. Once, during the Christmas season, I was like eight; The phone was ringing off the hook. It was a busy time for his manufacturing plant. They needed so much overtime. I didn't know that then. I just knew his boss kept calling. He wouldn't answer. He said its family day and his boss couldn't have a piece of his life today.

That's the dad I miss. I sit on one of the benches and stare at the water. It's still plenty hot out. People are rolling their boats into the water, fishing, wandering around, laughing. Dad would bring us here as well. We'd take the boat out on the lake for an entire day. Picnic lunch and everything. Mom wasn't crazy about the boat, but she would cave just to make him happy.

This is where he taught me how to fish and talk about his opinions on everything. He was only trying to teach me. Except, as I now know, some of those things weren't true. Like when I asked him about the Indians, sorry, Native Americans, who used to live here. He said that was none of our concern, that they just died off. He actually told me- and believed it- that they just died off. A long time ago. Like the dinosaurs.

So, you can imagine my reaction when a friend at my school told me he was part Native. And what did I say? "You can't be, they all died off. A long time ago."

Can you believe that?

He always had some backwards ideas. And some that were downright embarrassing. Like the stuff he says about Black people. Even worse, when he imitates them, or what he thinks they sound like. I've started to wonder if he's ever seen a Black person in real life.

I hate it when he does that shit.

Even that used to be only when he would get together with Uncle Bill. After they both had a few beers. The past few years, maybe five or six years or so, he's just been... different. Maybe I just notice it now.

Golden Apple

I hear a kid's voice squealing with laughter. I turn my head and see a family loading onto their boat. Their family day. See, this is what I mean. This nice family. A man, three kids, and a woman, they've got their lunch, their drinks, their towels, and life jackets.

And you know what my dad would say if he was here?

Loud as hell, for everyone to hear, if my dad was here right now, he would point his finger in their direction and say, to me, but louder than he needs to say, "They're a long way from home."

Because they aren't white. He would announce this kind of thing. Just to point them out. To make them feel like they don't belong. To ruin their day. Something he never had to worry about. He could just ignore the phone to keep anyone from ruining his family day.

Not able to just see that this is a family. Trying to enjoy what may be only one day off. Why couldn't he relate to that?

The crazy has gotten worse. Take the whole Russian free-car-communism thing. Now, my dad's not the smartest guy. But the stuff that has been coming out of his mouth, especially in the last few years, it's just, like any smarts he had went in reverse.

Maybe I was just as bad, and it seemed normal to me. Like the things he said about Native Americans, or even what he used to say about Black people. I shudder, thinking of the things I picked up from him. Some of the things I even repeated to my friends at school. Before I learned better. And the kicker?

Kids heard me and laughed right along with the jokes. The stupid statements. Hell, teachers even heard. No one corrected me. For years.

An engine revving breaks my concentration, it sounds like people racing their cars over the bridge. But I don't see any cars. The sound is farther, then closer.

I walk over to the bridge and cross the street, following the sound. The sun bears down on my face. I raise a hand to shield my eyes and squint to get a glimpse of the commotion. People are yelling now. Laughing. Jeering.

I look out past the marina. I see the source of the commotion; Two motorboats loaded with guys who appear to be in their twenties. They're hooting and cheering, but it isn't a fun noise. I know this noise. It's the kind of cheering my dad and Uncle Bill do when they're drunk and hollering about "Owning the Libs."

I lean as far over the rail of the bridge as I'm comfortable leaning. Holy shit.

Something waves from both of the boats. Red. White. Blue. But it isn't an American flag. It's the same exact flag my Dad flies at home. Each of the two boats is trailed by at least two spiraling trump 2020 flags and one Blue Lives Matter flag on the one boat. The flags convulse violently in the wind, like the tales of some kind of dragon.

They've had a few too many. I think to myself. They're boating like assholes. I try to imagine what it would be like if I was out on the lake now, with Dad, Don and Scott. I imagine how our boat would rock side to side with the wake these clowns are making. How it would ruin our time together, how it would scare Scott, who isn't a strong swimmer.

Then I see something else. They aren't just speeding in circles. They're circling a smaller boat between them. The wake is rocking over the side of this boat. Others sail by outside of the scene they created. They honk in support. Some yell "trump 2020." Others yell, "Build the Wall!"

In the middle of the fuss, aboard the smaller boat, a family is huddled together. The family I watched board their boat moments ago. My father's imaginary insult no longer the issue. Nothing compared to the spectacle that has now been created.

"Hey!" I yell, though I don't know who I am calling for. "Hey! Knock it off!"

There's no way anyone can hear me.

Another boat approaches. This one labelled Saratoga County Sheriff. Thank goodness.

Any hope is short-lived. The boat pulls to the periphery of where the two trump Boats circle like sharks. Then it stops. I can see the Boat Police Officer watching. He's grinning. That's all he's doing.

The chant of "Build the Wall" now turns even more sinister, "Sink the Boat!"

Someone needs to stop them. But no one will. I panic. Who do you call when the police are the bad guys? I think of the footage I've seen in recent months. Maybe this is why no one pulled the cop off of George Floyd's neck. Maybe this is why people just take videos instead of intervening. There is no other way to intervene.

I take my phone out of my pocket and start filming. It will make no difference. It won't stop them. I don't know what else to do.

The laughing dies down. The revving motor slows. One of the trump boats comes to a halt, a guy on board motions to his buddies. He points to me. Screams, "Fuck you," and speeds under the bridge and off in the opposite direction.

I don't wait to see what happens next, though maybe I should have. I run in the opposite direction of home. Purposely darting away from 9R. As if anyone is going to jump out of their boat and chase me.

As if I was ever the one who was really in danger.

When I'm convinced it's safe to head back home, I realize I've been gone much longer than I intended to be. Dad will probably be pissed, so I swing by the community garden to grab something off a vine to make him happy. Some cucumbers or some shit.

That's when I remember. That new lady. She indicated she may leave some for me to read. If I had been thinking, I would have stopped by here first. Grabbed the book, and then gone to the lake to read in peace. Ignoring the commotion on the lake because I can. But it didn't occur to me to check for a book until now.

I wander through the garden, wondering if she kept her word, or maybe was just talking shit. Sure enough, at the end of a row of tomatoes, I see a paperback casually tossed to the side. Philip Roth. *The Plot Against America*.

I pick it up and manage to hide it in the yard before entering the house through the same door I slammed shut hours ago.

Chapter 27

Marie

I pull Jackie's leash. She responds by returning to my side. I don't want to knock on anyone's door. I don't want to talk to anyone here. I don't want to deal with anyone, anymore. Shaved head or not, having no running water is not as easy as I imagined. He seemed friendly. All things considered.

We approach the steps. No car in the drive. Had there been a car before? I don't remember. I knock on the door, then step back immediately and douse my hands with sanitizer. The smell hits Jackie and she makes a face.

"Sorry, girl. I have to do it."

A few minutes later, the door opens. The Caretaker looks surprised to see me.

"Hey, I'm sorry to bother you, but, my pipe broke. I don't have running water in the shower. I can't afford to pay a professional, but I could give you a little money or make dinner or something if you happen to be able to fix it?"

"Yeah. I can fix it. Be over later. And I'll wear a mask."

* * *

I stay as far away as possible, but Jackie takes no such precautions. Even with half the Caretaker's body lodged in the corner of the bathroom, metal clanging as he replaces the faulty plumbing, she thinks it is a game and tries to wedge herself into the space with him.

"Jackie, no!" I call after her.

He just laughs.

"Sorry," I tell him, pulling at her harness to pry her away from him. "She really seems to like you."

"She's not a good judge of character," he winks and slides back into position. It takes a few hours and trips to and from his trailer. I try to pass the time with Jackie in the yard, trying desperately to get some work done on my laptop.

"You have water," he announces finally.

"Thank you! If I had known you were able to fix it, I may have spared my hair!" I rub a hand over the stubble.

"Well, it suits you," he says.

"How much do I owe you?"

"Don't worry about it. It's what I do here."

"Thank you. Do you want anything, seltzer, water, tea, or anything?"

"Will work for seltzer, sure."

Jackie stares into his eyes like she's found a long-lost lover. It's weird actually. He seems to notice.

"I think she likes you better than she likes me."

"Nah," he takes a long chug of seltzer, "she likes you just fine. She's just glad to have running water again. Now before you chop off any other body parts, next time something breaks, just let me know, okay?"

I agree and watch as he leaves. He's not so bad. Then again, neither is Jess. The people next door seem pretty decent. Another woman, Josephine, she seemed friendly enough. Not so sure about her son Justin, though.

I take my mask off and wash my hands. Jackie leans on my legs. Maybe I was being too judgmental. There are a few off the wall characters here, sure. When I add them up, most of them are alright. Just trying to get by. Harmless.

Chapter 28

Joni

I adjust my pantyhose with a tug on the waist and slip into my new Christian Louboutin shoes, a gift I manifested for myself. Ok, I used my stimulus check to buy them, but the positive vibes certainly didn't hurt. These reveal my newly pedicured (finally!) toes with a high heel that adds just the height I need to rock the fabulous dress I bought. I didn't feel bad splurging. It was on sale at a Boutique on Broadway, only five-hundred dollars. Besides, what with the shutdown and whatnot, I figure I'm shopping local and supporting Main street. I'm just doing my patriotic duty.

I don't know why I still feel the need to justify my decisions to myself. It's like I don't trust myself and have to explain things to get my own permission. I work hard, or used to, and if I want to get dolled up for an afternoon with the girls, then so be it. I deserve it!

I throw my more comfortable shoes, the ones I drove here in, into the trunk of the car, out of sight. It's a good neighborhood, but with all the rioting and Antifa threatening to take the suburbs, you just never can be too careful. From the trunk, I retrieve the pièce de resistance: my hat. It matches the shoes, of course. The entire thing towers so high, with silk lilacs and ribbons; lace and peacock feathers; that it wouldn't fit on my head inside the car. I brush my bangs, getting uncontrollably long, out of my eyes and adjust the hat to my head with bobby pins. "Thank you very much, Mr. Governor, for not allowing me to get my hair done," I tell myself.

GOLDEN APPLE

It's potluck as usual though if I know Barbara, she's gotten a caterer as well. Anyhoo, I grab my little contribution, a Pina Colada ice box cake. I found the recipe on Pinterest. I check the car windows to make sure I look decent before heading for the gate to the yard. Barbara lives on Campion Dr., where the houses begin at half a million dollars. Her home, mansion I should say, is spacious. All new features. It's gigantic, actually. I can't imagine how much work it takes to keep clean. Traffic was unusually light for track season, but it is to be expected this year. That's one good thing about the drop in tourism.

Though looking around on the way here, the restaurants don't seem to be hurting. Their business is outside rather than indoors, but that's nothing new on Broadway. Luckily, the people here also have the sense not to fret over that silly mask business.

The thought occurs to me then, that I'm not wearing mine. I usually at least keep it in my pocket, but of course this dress doesn't have pockets. I left mine in my car. After all the trouble I went to in order to find a perfect match!

I resign myself to leave it be unless someone asks me to put it on. Like if someone has an oxygen machine, or something like that.

Barbara sees me enter through the gate. She looks dazzling, as always. She waves to me from across the sizable and perfectly manicured lawn. I'm fashionably late, but only slightly, and already the party is in full swing. But there aren't as many of us here as in past years.

Barbara is dressed in bright red; her hat is adorned with dramatic burgundy and yellow feathers. Her cleavage, which I happen to know is not all hers, at least not all organic, if you know what I mean, seems on the verge of spilling out of her dress. Self-consciously, I look down to make sure my girls are behaving themselves and staying indoors.

We're good on that front.

I walk to one of several tables where she is arranging food. To my relief, no one is wearing masks. In fact, I don't even see any. Barbara gives me air kisses and I air kiss her back. She takes the

Angela Kaufman

dessert from my hand and sets it on the table next to a few, which look disappointingly similar.

"Joe, here, is helping me with the party. He's been just an absolute lifesaver, and he's done the lawn and kept up with the pool as well!" she tells me, gesturing to a young man who I can only guess is from Mexico.

"Oh, well, that's nice that you were able to give him a job," I smile at Joe, adding, "what with the track being closed down and all of you back stretch workers out of a job this summer."

I see his face turn and before he can respond, Barbara puts a hand on his shoulder and clarifies "No, no, he's one of my tenants. I rent to him. The place in Latham I inherited from my grandmother? I've converted it into five different units. He's just been so extremely helpful since Robby has to work so much overtime at the office lately."

Barbara then turns to Joe, who I am sure I have accidentally offended, and says, "Backstretch worker! Oh no, Joe, here," She looks back at me and continues, "is a professor over at Skidmore. He's had a lot of time off this year and has been so good to lend me a hand."

"I'm sorry, Joe, it's nice to meet you," I offer an apology. I don't want him to think I'm racist, of course. Then again, these days you can't do anything without someone thinking you're racist. I swear it's like white people have become the most persecuted of anyone, just like the man on the radio says.

Joe smiles and gives a brief nod before walking away to do whatever it is he's doing. I feel my cheeks turn hot and Barbara must know this because she gives me a hug and says, "Don't worry, he's not one of those cancel culture types. It's an easy mistake. He's probably already over it."

We catch up briefly and then I hear squealing and laughter, we both turn to see what the fuss is all about. In walks Vanessa and I swear she's won the day. She's won the year. Her hat is going to win this year, and don't we both just know it?

She knows it too. She flings open the gate and lets it close behind her. Then she saunters in just enough to let the gathering of women flocking to take her photo have a better look. She turns once, twice, then strikes a pose like a model on a runway.

Her dress is of course gorgeous. White with red edging, a deep v-neck, and spaghetti straps. But her hat. It's her hat that everyone gathers around to oooh and aaah over. And now they're leaning in for selfies with her. Or with her hat.

It's a ball, almost the size of her head, with what in any other year would appear to be little red spikes with round nubs on the end. This is 2020, and we all know what that is supposed to be.

The now universal symbol for COVID-19.

Barbara walks over to join the reverie and embraces Vanessa, and I trail behind her. The excitement eventually dies down and the stereo, blasting but far enough away to not be too disruptive, is playing dance music. I catch up with Barbara again. "Where is everyone? Such a small crowd this year!" I mention.

"You're telling me. And after I hired a caterer and everything. But they're all drinking the Kool Aid and afraid to come out and live their lives, can you believe it?"

"All the lame stream media," I agree with her.

The gate opens again. This time it's Jocelyn. She reads Tarot at all our annual events. We absolutely adore Jocelyn. She's not like one of those fortune tellers you see in the movies. She's such an enlightened soul and always gives such great advice.

***

"Joni, you're up!" Vanessa calls to me, as she comes back out to the pool after having her cards read. I excuse myself from the group I was chatting with and scurry down to Barbara's sunroom where Jocelyn is set up. We exchange a hug and air kisses, and then she hands me the cards.

"You know what to do!" she tells me.

"I sure do!" I tell her. As I shuffle, I consider all the big questions on my mind. When will I get another job? Will my business making CBD infused candles and selling them online finally take off?

I mean, when I get into a house or apartment so I can set up shop again? And will I be successful as an influencer? I want to go back to teaching yoga and meditation classes, and when will I fall in love and well, you know, all the usual questions.

I lay the cards down and sit with anticipation as she sets up the spread.

"I tell you, this was supposed to be my year, and look at all what's happened!"

"Well," she says, "this is a great time of awakening, but you have to trust the plan and not get caught up in what the media wants you to believe. All the fear mongering."

"That's what I say, exactly!" I tell her.

She lays down the cards and tells me that she sees a future for me on a spiritual path, which is amazing because that's exactly what I was thinking! Then she tells me she sees me leading big retreats and workshops, like Brene Brown and Elizabeth Gilbert, and I remember why I love this woman!

She said I'm going to meet someone new real soon and we will have our own home by early next year. I couldn't be happier!

"That is, if this COVID craziness ever gets under control."

"Don't you worry," she tells me, "my intuition has told me from the beginning it is being blown way out of proportion. My guides have shown me. trump will win in a landslide, and he'll put a stop to all this insanity and get us back to business as usual. I've seen it all."

That's the best news I've heard all day.

I leave her a tip and walk back out to the lawn, sending in the next woman on the list. I resume my spot around the fire pit by the pool, Barbara emerges and hands me a glass of something that looks pink and sweet and alcoholic. My favorites.

Our group has expanded now, but just slightly. Anna has arrived, to my dismay.

"And how is your family doing?" Barbara asks me.

"She's doing great, thanks. It's so nice to spend time with her and the kids."

"Oh, you should have brought her along today!" Barbara responds.

I look around awkwardly, trying to picture Shari in this group that is clearly above her station. "Well, thank you, that's nice of you, but my sister, she probably wouldn't fit in, exactly. She lives in a trailer park." I explain, eyeing the group who seem to understand.

Except Anna, who says, "but if you live with her, then don't you live in a trailer park too?"

Damn her.

"It's temporary. I'm staying with her. She has so many kids and all." I try to cover. Luckily, someone changes the subject.

A woman I vaguely remember, named Carol, I think, asks Barbara how business has been this year. "Well, considering how hard Cuomo has tried to destroy us, we're getting by. I would say thank God for our rental income, but we can't count on that right now. It's a wonder we can even put food on the table with all this craziness!" she says, passing around a tray of hotdogs wrapped in bacon.

"It really is ridiculous," another woman adds. I don't recall her name. She attended the party last year as well. She continues, "I mean, gyms and churches had to close but liquor stores could stay open?"

"It's because," Anna says, and I realize she's pushed her chair back a ways from the rest of us, "liquor stores aren't a gathering place. Also, people with alcohol problems would need to avoid going into serious withdrawal and overwhelming the detox units."

"Well, it's still terrible," the woman argues back, "I mean, cutting people off from church and banning Alcoholics Anonymous, but leaving people to the mercy of liquor stores, what kind of message does that send?"

"Actually," Anna continues, God, why won't she just let it go? "AA and NA have continued to function online. As many religious services have."

The woman makes a noise in her throat to show her annoyance. "Really? You're going to ruin a nice afternoon with your self-righteousness and toxic negativity?"

"I'm actually using the same tone you are, and simply correcting an incorrect statement you made," Anna tries to say more, but Barbara, who looks annoyed, cuts in and asks her to refill the ice in the cooler. She obliges. Thank God.

The last thing I want is her ruining my afternoon. Especially after such an inspiring reading.

Part II The Suburbs

Chapter 29

Jordan

I forgot to silence my phone. Notifications distract me as I broadcast live on YouTube. I try to play it off, but my momentum is fucked. I glance down. It's Feldman. That fake-Jew. The hard part of having so many fans is that you get the fan boys.

I look at the screen on my laptop. They don't seem to notice. The comments are pouring in.

"Preach!" and "Jordan88!"

I wish they wouldn't. Even now, midflow, as I'm telling them about how we have to work harder to break the stereotypes of all this nazi crap. They just don't get it. They want the flashy, *heil hitler* bullshit.

They're going to cost us if they keep this up.

"Do you dress like it's the 1930s?" I ask. "Do you want to get paid what someone got paid to do your job in the 1930s? Hell no. So, why are you stuck in the slogans and references from the 1930s?"

I try to press on, hoping they'll get it finally.

"We, our movement, has no future if we remain stuck in the past. It isn't good enough to repeat nazi slogans and salutes. If anything, it hurts our cause. So, I do implore you, help me bring this movement in to the present. Our white children and white grandchildren are counting on us. We need to make our efforts count. Playing WWII re-enactment isn't a movement."

The comments are still pouring in. A few Antifa scum trolling my page as usual. It's all good. Means I'm having an impact.

I wrap it up with my signature closing. About getting back to American values. Christian values. I roll the outro. I never cared for this song, and my mom is no doubt rolling in her grave to know I'm using one of her favorite hippie songs from her Libtard commune days.

The people need an anthem, even if it is only a few lines from the days when stoners believed they were stardust.

Golden.

And had to get back to the Garden.

I sign off just after loading the signature Golden Apple logo.

Now, to my phone. Feldman sent a message on Signal. I hate it when he does that. Dumbass doesn't realize that no communication is really off grid, no matter what his fanboy friends may think. That's why he's never going to come up through the ranks, even though he kisses my ass constantly.

It's a link to a video posted on YouTube. I click it, even though I really don't have time for these childish things. It loads. Damn. And what had I just spent time trying to explain?

"Stupid fucks!" I slam my hand down on my desk. Thor jumps down from the corner where he always sits, licking his paws and purring when I do my recordings.

"Sorry, bud. Not you," I tell him. He's not forgiving me for interrupting his happy thoughts. Well, life sucks for us all, doesn't it?

I click Feldman's number and he's there in one ring. Fanboy was probably sitting there staring at his phone ever since he sent me this crap. Just waiting for me to respond.

"Hey!" he says.

"What the fuck is this?" I pull no punches. It's what they've come to expect from me. It's why I'm the leader of this movement. Any pride in his voice is gone now. He's trying to squirm out of this mess, I can tell.

"What? Me and some guys, we were out boating. Then we saw some other dudes, they had the same kinda flags, and it just happened."

"It just happened?"

"Yeah, you know it was a spontaneous thing. Our boat, the other boat with flags like ours, we just started chasing down those spics. They had no business being on our lake. We were just messing with them. Teaching them a lesson. You should have seen their faces."

"Listen, Feldman,"

"It's Fieldman,"

That's the only time he'll correct me. He hates it when I insinuate he's Jewish.

"Yeah, Feldman, this is not the kind of shit our movement needs, don't you get it?"

"What? We were just having a little fun!"

"Yeah, right. Where did it get you?"

"No one is gonna do anything. They know we're right. Even the cops were on our side."

"Yeah," I continue, "For now. Until some idiot takes things too far, gets on their radar, and not with the kind of attention we want. Look. How many times do I have to tell you, there is a plan in place. Trust the plan. But for now, we can't have this kind of high-profile shit. I mean, whoever took the footage got a clear shot of your face!"

"So? They don't know who I am, it's your face everyone sees."

"True, but that can change. Especially since you're trying so hard to move up in rank. Your face, associated with Golden Apple, is now going to be associated with this sophomoric clown shit. Is that all you want? You want to harass some people on a boat? Or do you want to save the future of the white race?"

Silence. I continue, calmer now, no need to further berate him.

"Look, this kind of stunt, it's just a distraction. When we get our hold, when the plan goes into place, we're going to have plenty of time for fun. For now, though, focus on the goal. Keep your eye on the prize."

"The Golden Apple," he says.

"Damn right."

Chapter 30

Jordan

It's not that I give credence to this whole "social distancing" thing. No more than I give a shit about the white power line. It's just a means to an end. Give the people what they want. Zoom reaches more people and I don't have to deal with the logistics. It's ten to two and already we've got fifty people logged in. Make that fifty-one, two, three.

I watch as the chat fills up with introductions. Bob from Canajoharie. Steve from Catskill. Drake from Albany, yeah, sure, that's your actual name.

Justin from Saratoga is familiar, he's been to every meeting so far. Some of the other guys, and they are mostly guys, through no intended exclusion of women, come and go. Some pop in every few weeks, others show up once and decide we're not for them.

Whatever. I don't want people flaking out, anyway. Justin doesn't seem like the brightest bulb, but he's devoted. That's what we need. There are a few women in our midsts. Most are finally taking the Red Pill and learning the truth.

That feminism destroyed their prospects of a decent life. Ruined the family unit, turned them into a bunch of hairy legged screaming banshees. Then they find us. We help them remember the natural order of things. They are relieved and find their purpose.

That's what we all really want, isn't it?

Five minutes to showtime, now sixty-three participants, sixty-eight. This may just be our biggest turnout yet. And who can blame them, with communists and looters running through the streets. Even right here. Saratoga Springs, Troy, Albany.

Some are wearing Back the Blue shirts. Others wear trump shirts. Some just look like they've left the office for the day. A few looked like they never got the memo that the heavy metal scene is all dried up.

Whatever floats your boat.

This is a recruiting meeting, as the last few have been, but there are some repeat participants. I encourage them to come when they can for solidarity. So, people can see they aren't alone and so people who recognize each other from the community can feel safe again, knowing they aren't as alone as the lame-stream media likes to make it sound.

I check the stats on my spreadsheet on another screen. All in all I have three set up today. Thor, left without a place to sit on my desk, is instead curled up on the chair. Sulking.

According to my stats, we've had a forty percent conversion rate from each meeting. That only includes new members. Not repeats like Justin. Still, as the numbers climb, I run the calculations in my head. We aren't on target yet but getting closer.

It's two on the dot. I mute everyone except myself.

"Good afternoon, fellow aryans. I'm Jordan Tennyson. Thanks for joining me. Please hold your questions 'til the end or drop them into the chat."

Today is not for delving deep into the plan. That will come in time. This is still the first phase. It takes time to weed people out and see who is for real. Like Justin and even Feldman, as much as I bust his balls.

I look at the faces, mostly strangers, on my screen. I require videos to be on and I record every meeting in case I ever need it for… strategic… purposes. I have a feeling these people would leave their videos on, anyway. Happy for a place where they can see and be seen for who we are and what we believe, with no one shaming us or shouting over our message.

"Plans are being set into motion," I tell them. "You can each have a part if you want one. If you're not ready, though, if you're not committed, if you're not ready to do your part, then I'll be frank, we don't want you and we don't need you."

I let this hang in the air for a moment, then continue.

"But if you've got what it takes, and if you aren't going to pussy out, if you're serious about making America great again," God I hate even using that line, but they eat it up every time, "then this is the movement for you."

They know they're muted, but as I look into the faces on the screen, no one can contain themselves. They cheer and holler soundlessly. Some give that ridiculous nazi salute. Others pump their fists in the air and scream, silently.

They can't hear each other. I pause so they can hear what I say next.

"Something big is coming. You can be a part of it, if you're worthy."

Chapter 31

Justin

Mom says I don't apply myself. What the fuck does she know? If she could see me now. I try to imagine the look on her face if she knew what I was doing. But then that would be ridiculous. She would never understand the mission. Clearly, saving the Aryan race is not her prerogative, what with all the creeps she lets live here.

Don't apply myself.

I've been to every single meeting since they started in February. Sometimes, I'm the second or third one to sign in. I know Jordan has noticed. He has to have. I haven't counted one other guy who's been on as much as me.

I even brought a few people and got them registered up and everything. He talked about there being a place in the organization. For the devoted. Oh, hells yeah, I'm in!

So I tell him, I send him a private chat, and I tell him, yes. I'm ready. Put me to use. I tell him all about what I can do. How I hacked into the school's computer system and fucked up everyone's grades back when I was in middle school.

Of course, the school caught me and changed the grades back and I got suspended, again. But that's not the point. The point is that for a good solid month; I had them by the balls. They didn't even know what to do. And I had done it all myself.

I know he's a busy guy and all, so when I got a message later that day, I was like "Damn! Here we go! Ready for liftoff!"

I kept it real cool and was professional. He asked if I was ready for my first assignment and I was like "Ready!"

So he asks if he can call me and I'm like "Yes!" only not that excited, playing it cool and all, and he calls me and it's just like in the movies. Like a spy movie. He gives me the assignment and the whole call is less than five minutes, but my heart races because this is the real shit.

The real shit.

Fuck school, fuck this trailer park, fuck everything. This is like Navy Seals level, what we're gonna do. And I have my first assignment now.

I wrote down the names like he told me. All the new recruits. And when I'm done, I'll burn the paper, like he told me. But for now, I turn up the anthem, headphones in, guitars screaming. I play air guitar along with the old farts, and when the time comes, I sing out loud. About getting back to the garden.

I enter the first name into search. Will Dexter. I start with the obvious. Google, Facebook, Reddit, all the social media apps. One by one. Mike Ontario, Cyrus Dixon, not far from here in Ballston Spa, Wayne Gilligan, Howard Jeffries, some of these names are fucking crazy.

Search every single one, he said. And I know why.

Don't apply myself, bullshit. How do ya like me now, Ma?

Chapter 32

FBI headquarters

Cliff

Howard Jeffries, I type into the online form. These people would kill me if they knew my real name was Cliff Rosen, so it is Howard Jeffries for now. I know this alias like the back of my hand now. Have to know it at first reaction. Can't afford to hesitate even for a minute. I continue to fill in the form. Place of birth, date of birth. Would they really do a search for my birth certificate?

A scene flashes in my mind. The current president, years before anyone would have imagined him in the Whitehouse. "Just show us your birth certificate," he had said. And birtherism had been born.

To make a good first impression, I've gone to at least three of this bastard's Zoom meetings. His recruitment days.

Address, got it covered. That is, unless they take the time to drive out and find that the address I've given on Hollbrook Drive is a soon to be condemned barn being taken over by weeds and rats.

Reason for joining the movement. Got that reheared, too. These guys love to hear all this "preservation of the white race" bullshit.

A few more details, and I sit, hand on the mouse, hovering, I can hear my heart in my chest. The guys think this group is nothing but a bunch of cub scouts turned angry incels, ignorant, angry, but toothless. Something tells me otherwise. Their leader, Jordan, is more sophisticated than people want to give him credit for.

Before I can technically get agency approval, I need something more concrete than his vague promises of "something coming." But without agency approval, I'm really putting my balls in a vice.

Click.

Now it's done. Approval may take forty-eight to seventy-two hours. So be it.

Out of my hands for now.

Chapter 33

Cyrus

Ballston Spa

I don't really do online meetings. But Chad and Rick were going to this one, I saw it on their newsfeed, so I said, what the hell? It's not like I have anywhere else to go.

I pull the curtains back and instantly regret it. I've forgotten what sunlight feels like. My eyes adjust. I look down at the sidewalks below. Normally I'd take a walk over to Kelley Park and shoot the breeze or hang out by the pool. Just not feeling it now. Even though lockdowns have ended, and the ice cream place is open. No motivation.

I pace around my room. Bored with watching YouTube videos. Bored with playing video games. Not interested in going out. I shouldn't even be here today.

If it weren't for Emperor Cuomo, my family would be on vacation now. The cruise I've been looking forward to. Just like the high school prom, graduation and pretty much everything else that was supposed to happen this year, only to be canceled. Well, the cruise wasn't cancelled, but now that Dad's rental income is fucked, he had to sell off our tickets.

The real kicker is, even with everything closing, then opening, then closing again, it will be who knows how long before we can even afford to go to Lake George, let alone go on a real cruise. I heard my dad talking last night. On the phone. With his lawyer. He doesn't know I heard him.

It was about his tenants. The ones who stopped paying him months ago. Mooching, because they can get away with it now. Meanwhile, hardworking guys like my dad, who inherited two properties and decided to show initiative and rent them out, are left with the short end of the stick.

The restaurant he and my uncle were supposed to open this year? Didn't even get to have the grand opening they sunk their money into. They're stuck with the lease, but no customers for the first few quarters of the year.

It's a slap in the face. It's not fair. It wouldn't be happening if it weren't for all these Marxists and intersectional feminists trying to tell everyone what they can and can't do. Shutting down for a virus that only kills one percent of the population, and the weak part at that.

People like Marisa. I think of her last words to me, when she dumped me.

"You've become a despicable human being. I can't be with you anymore if you believe these things."

Persecuted for my beliefs. Talk about nazi Germany. I wasn't sure about this Jordan guy at first. But what he says makes sense. I watched one video on YouTube, then another, then another. This guy is saying exactly what I'm thinking. What no one else will say.

Still, I don't like joining groups. I may just listen. It's like therapy or like the way drunks go to AA just to hear people they can relate to. Maybe that's all I'll do for now.

It's hot. It's sunny. I sit in my room. Why bother going out? Everything I looked forward to has been taken away. I stare at my weight set on the floor. It's been months since I lifted. Mark's gotten buff during lockdown. I tried, but lost interest. Truth be told, I worry about my parents. Even more than me. They got screwed. And they are still getting screwed.

From what I could hear of my dad's side of the conversation, he's out of luck. Can't evict his tenants, and they're not paying him. What's he supposed to do?

You know what kills me? He came home with a Biden-Harris sign for the lawn. After what they've done to him. I'll be able to vote this year. For the first time. I can't tell him, but no way in hell I would vote for the democrats. They failed on the stimulus, failed on the pandemic, failed to control Antifa and stop the violence in the streets.

If he wants to ruin his own prospects, that's his business. But still, I worry about him. I'm not supposed to know it, but I know he took a second mortgage out on the house to invest in the restaurant. For nothing.

The music plays in my head again and again. Getting back to the garden, I like it. Back to basics. Values. Decency. Everything I've been trying to tell people. I'm hungry. I roll out of bed and go downstairs. Dad's facetiming with his girlfriend. She's afraid to come over because she thinks he has COVID cooties or something. And he just puts up with it. Talk about being a cuck. I know I'm not supposed to say that about my own dad, but it's true.

No dinner yet. I open the fridge. A lot of containers, mostly empty. I find canned pasta in the cabinet. Processed pasta. From a can. Like we're white trash or something. Even though we live in one of the richest neighborhoods in the area. Fucking Cuomo. I wonder what he's eating for dinner. With his daughters and the daughter's boyfriend. Probably out at a restaurant. With no mask on. It didn't escape my notice that he never wore one out in public. People put it on Facebook. Cuomo, walking his dog with no mask. If he has tenants, I bet he makes them pay.

Dad comes in the room now. I don't ask what he has in mind for dinner. It's a fend for yourself night more often than not these days. I grab a bag of chips.

"Hey what's up today?"

There are a million sarcastic retorts I could make I mean what could possibly be new?

"Nothing. Going upstairs to talk with Mark."

I may or may not do this, but it gives me an excuse to leave the room. The more I see how weak, what a cuck, my Dad can be, the less I know what to say to him. I mean, I feel bad... but he backs the people who put him in this position. I bet you anything, if someone different was in charge, none of this would have happened.

I don't know exactly who I'll vote for. Probably not into trump. Biden's a pussy though. Maybe I'll go Libertarian. Makes sense. Personal responsibility. Pick yourself up by your bootstraps and all.

I pull the bag of chips open once I'm back in my room, sinking onto my bed with a heavy flop. Maybe I'll chat with Mark after all. I hit him up on messenger and the voice call rings. He doesn't answer. Weird. Like he's got anywhere to go.

A few minutes later, though, he dials me back. I turn on my camera. My hair's a mess. Too late now. I'm sure he doesn't care.

"Hey, what's up?" I ask him.

"What's up, Cy? Sorry I missed your call just now," he begins. I can't put my finger on it, but something is off. He isn't looking directly at me. I know sometimes people look off to the side on video when they're doing other things, texting, doing homework, even driving, but this is different. It's like he's avoiding looking at me.

"No worries," I tell him, then, "hey what did you think of the meeting?"

"Golden Apple?" As he asks this, his eyes dart around. Maybe his mom walked into the room or something.

"Yeah."

The background behind him shakes and I know he's carrying the camera somewhere else. I wait to give him a chance to go someplace private. Then he answers.

"Look, Cy, not going to tell you what to do, but it's not for me," he says.

"It's all good," I tell him.

But there's something more. Something he's not saying. Not right away. He looks like he's a girl about to dump me. It's really weird.

Then he totally surprises me, like out of nowhere. He says, "Cy, I got to be honest with you, as a friend, this stuff you're into, it's really not cool."

Like that. Just like that. Like he's caught me in the bathroom smoking crack and wants to have an "intervention" or something.

"What stuff?" I ask him, really not sure what he's getting at.

"This white supremacy, Alt. Right crap."

Now I wonder who is smoking crack. "What are you talking about?" I ask him.

"Golden Apple."

"They're not white supremacists, Mark. I mean there's a lot of white guys but you know, maybe that's just who is online these days. I mean who is it getting screwed out of jobs and stuck home on lockdown because of the liberal agenda."

"Cy, have you looked into this Jordan guy? Because I did. I watched his podcasts. People are always giving him nazi salutations in the chats, he never chastises them. If anything, he gives a lot of dog whistles and stuff. It's like he tries to tone it down to not hurt his reputation."

"I think you need to take the mask off and get some fresh air, my friend," I tell him. But then I really do get mad. Where does he get off with this self-righteousness? So I push back harder to make my point.

"See, this is exactly what guys like Jordan are talking about. You've been brainwashed to think anyone who isn't ashamed of being white is a racist. What he's talking about is real values, law and order and being proud of your heritage, rather than always apologizing for the contributions of our ancestors. I mean, do you know how many people would be scratching around in the mud if it wasn't for what our ancestors built? Why should we erase our history and be apologists?"

He actually looks hurt. Like genuinely hurt. Like I just told him I ran over his cat or something. But there's something else. He looks at me like he's feeling sorry for me. That really pisses me off.

I want to yell at him, to curse him out. Something I've never done in all the years we've known each other. And I mean, it's been since kindergarten.

"Cy, I... I don't know what to say. The people you're following, I don't agree with them. If you can't see it, then I don't know how else to tell you. Except to say, I can't be part of this."

"Okay, whatever, I got it. Golden Apple isn't for you."

"It's not just that," he says then, "I can't be friends with someone who doesn't see how bad, how dangerous these ideas are."

My defenses go up so fast I don't really register exactly what he's saying.

"Dangerous ideas?" I snap back. "See, that's the thing, how can an idea be dangerous? I mean, there are Antifa and thugs rioting in the streets, and you're worried that an idea is gonna hurt someone? This is how brainwashed the media's got you!"

"That's just it, Cy," he begins. He sounds too calm. I'm annoyed at what he's saying and how calm he can be while saying it. He continues. "We've reached this point where, no matter what, we're both just going to look at each other and see the other as brainwashed. As a tool. There is nowhere to go forward from there. I just don't see what we have in common now."

I suddenly want to cry, but I push it down until it's regurgitated up as anger. "No, Mark," I tell him, "I don't see you as a tool. Brainwashed, yeah, all those Libs you've been hanging around with to impress the girls. But I don't see you as a tool. I see you as a friend, but I guess I'm alone in that!"

He doesn't say anything and now I'm really pissed. So I dig in and twist the knife.

"I bet you never tell them the jokes we used to tell. The jokes we both used to laugh at? The Helen Keller jokes and the whole Blackface thing at that party, that whole thing that was your idea. And the holocaust jokes? You don't tell your new girlfriend that shit, do you? What, you want to erase that part of your history just like you want to erase history now? Was it not racist and politically incorrect then? Or are you not the white knight you're pretending to be now?"

Argue back! I try to will him to fight back. Give me a reason to keep pounding harder, because I have plenty more. The time we beat up that faggy kid, Shawn. The times he used to make fun of the Chinese kid in gym class. It wasn't nice, but it happened. And now he's accusing me of being a white supremacist.

Fuck him. Argue back. Argue back so I can-

"Bye, Cyrus," he says, and hangs up. That's it. That's all. Just that.

I go to message him and he's already blocked me on social. And on IG and on text. I throw my phone and then wince, remembering neither me or my dad can replace it. Luckily, it hits a chair and doesn't break.

White supremacist.

What a cuck. Has everyone drunk the damn Kool-Aid?

Chapter 34

Dottie

"Two in one summer. We haven't had this many neighbors since, well, I don't know when, come to think of it! But then again, I've been here so long, I'm an original!" I call across the road to young Jess, now not so little anymore. I've been here before her family moved in. I've watched her grow up. Thank Goddess, I've got some hope she won't end up like her father.

I know when I see a man walking around, beer bottle in hand like it was his binkie. And I know what I hear when I hear yelling and hollering and a slam and a woman crying. And then when I see her walking around in sunglasses and a hat and it's not even summer. So yeah, Crazy Old Dottie knows a thing or two.

Jess smiles and follows my gesture down to the empty lot where the moving truck is parked.

"Should be interesting to see who lands here," she says, now walking closer, but not too close. Though no one in her family seems to be too concerned about the virus, she stands in the middle of the road while I flick my cigarette butt off the edge of my lawn.

"I see you've been making friends with the new lady," I mention. Something in her face changes, as if she's suddenly scared. She looks side to side, over the back of her shoulders toward her parents' place.

"I'm not supposed to be," she mouths and gives the universal "keep quiet" sign, finger up to her lips and all.

I bring my hand to my mouth by reflex. "I'm sorry, hon, I'll keep it to myself. Not like your folks come my way for conversation anyway. Only to accuse me of stealing the mail!"

We both laugh at this. "But don't you worry," I reassure her, "our secret."

Fuck, I figure she's practically a young woman and can make her own mind up about what is and isn't good for her. Who cares if her neanderthal daddy has something to say about it.

Turning back to face the empty lot, well, not empty any more, I say to her, I say, "Pretty impressive new place they got there. What do you 'spose a clean-cut young couple with the cash to afford such a nice mobile home wants with this park?"

She chuckles and shrugs. "It's by the lake?" she offers as an explanation.

"I guess, but hell if I had the money to dump into a place like that, I'd just as soon get the hell outta here. Then again, I've been saying that since before you were born."

"Are you back to work at the store?" she asks.

That's what I love about Jess, she's one of the few people who pays attention to Crazy Old Dottie and even knows where I work.

"I am indeed. But I tell you what, for all I don't wish this pandemic on no one, it was quite a treat for me to get stay home with income for a whole two months while it was closed. Do you know, I'm seventy years old and in my entire adult life I've never had so much as a week off with pay? It was glorious! I mean circumstances aside."

I look back to the new place, a doublewide, must have about three bedrooms. Only one in the park to be so big. Newer model too, I can tell. New roof, nice looking windows.

"Well," I say to Jess, taking a puff of my cigarette, "maybe our property values will go up now!"

"Yeah, I don't know who in their right mind would want to be the first to gentrify a trailer park, though," we laugh again.

I like Jess. If I had a daughter, I would imagine she would be just like her. That would have been nice. But I never found a man I could stand for more than five minutes and that ain't long enough to get the deed done if you know what I mean.

Came close once. Childhood sweetheart. My sidekick. Until he got old enough for high school. Suddenly I wasn't cool, even though I used to play Dungeons and Dragons with him. Nope, suddenly a feminist witch for a girlfriend wasn't cool, and living on the other side of the tracks definitely wasn't cool.

We say our goodbyes. As I turn to head back into the house I see one of the people in the group helping to unload the truck into that high falootin' new trailer. He's just about to get in his car to leave and he turns to the guy who's moving in, the husband I assume, and does some kind of crazy hand signal.

And I'm the weirdo.

Chapter 35

Vinny

My Mother taught me how to be a gentleman. No matter how far we've fallen as a country, I still keep my manners. I haven't forgotten how to give a warm welcome to a new family in the neighborhood.

That's why I left that new girl alone, I mean, it wouldn't'a been proper for me to go cozying up to a single woman, though from the way she looks now, either she has cancer, or she don't go to my church. If you know what I mean.

What I mean to say, is, when it's proper, I will be the first to extend a friendly, neighborly welcome. Like when you take the case of a nice, young family. Man and woman, so there isn't gonna be no gossip or people getting the wrong idea. It's like the Vice President says, you don't want to be alone with a woman who isn't your wife. I don't have a wife, so that means I have to be careful to avoid gossip.

Can't be alone with a woman these days without risking your reputation, even your career, if she decides to MeToo you. Not that I have a career anymore. Still, a man's gotta protect his reputation, especially these days. Give a nice girl a compliment and she'll take you to court.

So, I don't mess with the single girls, but instead, I've got a lasagna that Ma made and a nice welcome to the neighborhood spread with some wine, leftover from last Christmas. I don't drink much anymore so I never got around to it and they'll never know it was regifted.

Here she comes, the little lady of the house.

"Hello, ma'am, I'm Vinny. I live just down the way here."

I hand her the lasagna and the wine. Her face looks surprised. Guess people aren't used to their neighbors having old-fashioned American values anymore.

"Thank you! I'm Bianca. My husband, Tom, he's around somewhere, probably fiddling around in the shed putting things together. How nice of you!"

She pauses. I don't want to be forward and invite myself in, so I wait to see if she extends an invitation.

"Well," I finally say, because what are we going to do, stand and stare at each other? "I'm right down here at lot 9 if you or your husband need anything. I've lived here some years now, it's a pretty quiet neighborhood, no drama around here and we like that."

"Well, that's reassuring." She's smiling and looks about the park. I notice her eyes fix on the Donnolly's place. White Trash, that's what they are. Ain't nice to say it but it's true.

"Ah, yeah, that there, that's the Donnolly's Josephine and her son, Justin. They don't bring no trouble, but as you can see, we tolerate some people who, ah, don't share our standards of living."

She nods, sympathetically.

"At least you won't have any thugs or riffraff moving next door, if you know what I mean."

"What makes you so sure?"

"Well, first off, this is a place that, ah, attracts a certain, uh, type of people, like," I try to be discreet, these days you can't just say what you mean because everybody takes offense. I try again, "What I mean to say is, the park is full. This was the last empty lot, and the people who come here tend to be, old-fashioned. Americans. Patriots, hard-working people. You catch my drift? We have a few weirdos, but they're harmless. No rabble rousers or Antifa, Black Lives Matter flags or that kinda thing." I took a risk there, I know it. She didn't flinch.

"Oh, well yes, we don't want any of that," she says.

Indeed, we don't. Park owner, he'll let anyone move in and he don't care what. Could have anarchists and drug dealers and whoever and he won't care. It's only by the grace of God no one like that has found our little park. Except the people at the end of the park, before the new lady moved in, they seemed suspicious. Had visitors all hours of the night. Maybe some drug activity, marijuana most likely, no crack and police busts or things like you get down in Schenectady or Troy. I don't tell her this, though. No need to bring it up in polite company.

"Well, I just wanted to ah, welcome you to the neighborhood, and if you or your husband needs help with anything, don't be a stranger."

"Will do, and thank you again," she says, lifting the casserole dish and wine in emphasis before turning back in and closing the door.

I peek over her shoulder, habit. Couldn't help myself. The inside of her home is sparse, from what I could see. Big marker board hanging on the living room wall. Odd placement, not exactly a homey look, but what with Emperor Cuomo making people work from home on a whim, maybe they just aim to be prepared.

CHAPTER 36

Derrick

I pop the microwave door shut and hit a few buttons. Dee sits across the room, finally focusing on the markers and paper I found for her. It seems like she's been extra antsy today. Maybe she's run out of steam now. Maybe she'll just sit and amuse herself. She's usually good at that. But I guess it gets old after a while when you're her age and can't go anywhere.

"Mac, Cheese, French fries, no lettuce," she instructs me on how to perfectly create her meal, as if it is the first time I've cooked for her.

It isn't.

"Yes, I know," I tell her.

I don't care that I've been cooking for her since she was old enough to eat, I mean, if you can really call microwaving cooking. Although back in the day I did cook. Back when we had the house and had money. Before my scumbag sperm donor father threw all my mom's savings, and his own, out the window on his mistress.

I'm not supposed to know about that part, but I have a way of finding things out. Back then we had a house in Ballston Spa. We had a yard and a pool. Dee barely remembers it, she was so small. But we had enough that even with Mom and Dad working all the time, and Dad doing other things that aren't exactly work but still meant he wasn't home, I had the whole kitchen to myself after school. I cooked for the whole family then.

They didn't mind. One less thing they had to do.

Since we've been here, just Mom and Dee and I, the dinners have gotten steadily more boxed and frozen. I know Dee's special requests by heart, but she still recites them. She's got a special menu that she'll eat for weeks at a time. Then she'll switch to another, and another. I think it may be a mood thing. Or a Dee thing. I don't know. I just mix and microwave.

It doesn't bother me anymore that we no longer live in Ballston Spa. Those kids are mostly wannabes who don't realize they aren't shit anyway. The Saratoga kids look down on the Ballston Spa kids who feel superior to, well, kids like me.

And we all, well most of us, look down on the kids from the cities. I don't though, because I've hung out in Albany and Troy with friends I met through my mom's work at the hospital.

I'm over the sperm donor walking out. If Mom forgives him for ruining her life, I can let it go. I'm not upset about cooking and the cleaning. I don't mind taking care of Dee while mom works a million hours.

What does worry me is I never know until she comes home if she's going to be alright now. Other kids don't believe it, they're in their own little bubble. But I know better. I fight with them constantly on Facebook when they say the virus is a hoax.

"You're putting my mom in danger, you selfish shithead!" I tell them. I'm not supposed to swear, but I don't care.

It's true.

And they don't care.

"My research shows it isn't even real" they post back. Then I usually post something like "Maybe you should spend less time reading conspiracies and actually talk to real people, you'd know!" and we go back and forth until I'm exhausted. Then I try to do my homework. I could fake it and get by a lot better when we went to school in the classroom. But now, I hardly have any time for homework. My grades are slipping. Doesn't matter anyway. Mom has a college degree. Look where it got her.

I worry every day.

I never know until the car pulls in the driveway, if Mom is going to come home. Or if this is going to be the day she calls and says "Derrek, it's time to enact the emergency plan."

We talked about the emergency plan back in March before school even shut down. Back when everyone was thinking it was just like the flu, no big deal, will go away when the weather breaks, or whatever delusions they had.

The emergency plan is that if mom gets sick, she's going to sleep in her car until she gets better so that she won't bring COVID home to me and Dee.

I dread it every time the phone notification goes off because it may be that message. This time, it may be the day I get the news that Mom isn't coming home. If she has COVID and is sleeping in her car in a parking lot somewhere, she's probably not coming home, ever.

But we don't talk about that part.

The microwave beeps and I open the door. Steam rolls off of a plate with a little of this and that from a few different TV dinners. It sucks, but Dee loves it.

She sits on the couch in front of her favorite show. *I Love Lucy*, of all things. She watches the reruns. I have no idea what she sees in Lucy or how much of the show she even understands, but she watches it nonstop.

I bring the plate to her, along with a napkin and fork.

Returning to the kitchen, my turn to eat, I open the fridge. Leftover pizza, a ton of condiments in the doors, and a few odds and ends from the vegetable garden, but nothing that stands out to me. I could make a tomato and mayo sandwich, again, but tonight I'm not feeling it.

I pull a container off the shelf and scoop some powdered potatoes into a bowl and add hot water from the tap. Opening the door to the fridge again, my eyes pass between barbecue sauce, ketchup, and a few other dressings. I decide to live large and use the taco sauce packets left in the margarine drawer. Throwbacks from our last big hurrah for Mexican take out, back before the shutdown in the spring.

Since then, we haven't gone to any restaurants.

"It doesn't matter if they're open for business," Mom says, "that was a financial decision, not a health and safety one."

I know she's right, but the meal I've thrown together is also a matter of financial decisions. No one would call this mess healthy.

Six of one, half a dozen of another.

I sit down at the the far side of the couch next to Dee and dig in to my lumpy, taco sauce laden, lukewarm potatoes. I glance at my phone on the table. It's seven in the evening now, Mom still has another four hours to play COVID roulette before she is in the clear. At least for tonight.

Chapter 37

Marie

Jackie pulls me at a slow trot as we head back home from the mailbox. I try to keep the small stack of letters from flying out of my grip while also trying to slow her to my pace.

I look up and see what has her so excited. One of the free-range kids has kicked a ball out into the road and darts out in hot pursuit of it. Not even bothering to look either way before running into the road. I pull Jackie back on instinct, though I'm sure she's fine with kids. She's been only friendly toward strangers, which is more than I can say for myself.

But she's big and clumsy and could accidentally hurt one of the smaller kids without meaning to, so I take precautions. Still without looking up at me, the smaller boy, the one who was being tormented by his older peers last time we saw him, walks confidently back to the lawn where toys and bikes are strewn about.

A few days ago, Jess had asked for a mask and I had given her a few of my extras, but I have yet to see any of the kids wearing one, except for her on occasion.

"You better watch out with that dog! He's a menace!" I hear the woman shriek in an unpleasantly familiar tone. I don't need to turn my face to know it's Jess's mom, who has mostly kept to herself since insinuating I was trying to bring her daughter over to the dark side.

Does she know I've been leaving books for Jess? If she did, she'd probably come right out and say it. Must be one of those Hatfield and McCoy neighborly grudge situations, people with small lives addicted to drama.

"She," I correct, "was nowhere near him, and being this close to 9R, you may want to teach your kid to watch both ways before he runs into a road," I shoot back.

She makes a face like she's smelling shit, but she doesn't argue back. As we walk past, I hear her muttering to the kids to look out for "that crazy lady" and her "mean dog."

Now that was uncalled for. I may be crazy, but Jackie is anything but mean. There's no sense making kids excessively afraid of a friendly dog when she should be teaching them to have a shred of common sense and look out for real dangers.

An otherwise beautiful late summer afternoon is now ruined. I've grown used to expecting that will happen every time I leave the house.

Nearing home, Jackie once again gets excited and pulls forward on the leash. I look up and see the kids next door and their little rabbit caravan, still a few feet away. I pull Jackie and I over to the far side of the road to wait while they pass. I smile, though they can't see it under my mask.

"Hello," I regard the older brother, I think he said his name was Derrick. Past encounters have taught me the little girl isn't much for socializing. That's alright. Neither am I in most cases.

He nods his head and gives a "Howdy."

Then he does something unexpected. He brings the wagon to a halt and motions for his sister to wait there. He approaches Jackie and I, but not too close. One of the only other people here to wear a mask, I suspect he has an idea of which way the wind blows.

I've seen his mom get in the car early in the morning wearing scrubs and can deduce why.

"Hey," he says and glances over his shoulder in the direction of the scene that just transpired, a nervous look on his face. "That lady, well, her and the guy who live there, they're really nuts. Be careful of them, between you and me."

"Thank you," I tell him, "yeah, we had a run in before. She seems to think she's Queen of the Trailer Park, huh?"

He laughs nervously, then looks left and right before continuing. "Earlier this year, before you moved here, my mom, she's a nurse. She handed out masks to everyone, or at least she tried to. Gave them to the kids, too. They got so pissed. Excuse me, mad."

His face turned serious then.

"I'm sorry. That's ridiculous. She was only trying to help them out."

"Yeah, and it wasn't just that the lady told my mom off. Right in our own driveway, she threatened my mom too. She's got a big mouth and all, but it's her husband who's the real bully. I've seen him in action before. After that happened, like two days later, CPS showed up at the door. They were threatening to take Dee, my sister."

"Oh my God."

"Yeah, someone reported her for working all day and leaving us alone. CPS closed the case as unfounded, but not before they had their caseworkers checking out the place day and night for months, dropping in for random visits. My mom had to jump through all kinds of hoops. We know it was them, the guy, Dave, we just can't prove it."

"I have no doubt either," I say, outraged on their behalf. Then I add "well, I will keep an eye out for them, thanks. In the future, when your mom is working late, if you need anything or have any problems, I'm right next door, so you can knock any time."

He nods, and I can tell by the expression around his mask that he's relieved.

I turn to head back to the house and almost trip over Jackie, who is firmly planted on her behind, patiently sitting as little Dee caresses her head, her loose pointy ears, and her neck. I look up at Derrick who says, "She's selective about who she gets close to. She loves all animals, but I guess you're alright in her book as well."

"Well, that makes my day."

I kneel down to be on level with Dee. I tell her "Dee, you are more than welcome to come over and play with Jackie any time you want. As long as you have permission from your mother or brother."

"Okay," is all she says.

Chapter 38

Dave

I gotta hand it to the new couple. With the help of a few friends, they had the concrete poured, home loaded in, and moving truck unpacked in record time. Ambitious. Nice place, too. Look like reasonable people.

Then they set to work building a nice big fence, and that's alright with me. I don't need people nosing around my property. They seem alright. Haven't gotten to really meet with them yet, only saw them in passing a few times. Just long enough to hear the guy, Tom I think he said his name was, listening to some radio show. Talking things I don't understand about "ethno-state." Maybe he's a biologist. At the end of the show, you know what song they played? That hippie song from Woodstock.

They don't look like hippies. As far as I can tell, they look like good, God fearing Patriots. Even got a few flags outside of their trailer. I like it. I like to know where people stand.

Part III Downhill

Chapter 39

Protzeg Village Estates

Saratoga Springs

Jordan

The heat greets me as I step out into the late afternoon sun. Slowly but surely, the cul-de-sac is coming back to life. For months, lonely balloons and do-it-yourself #518rainbow posters had been the only signs of life in the area. Then pandemic restlessness had set in. My neighbors began celebrating the onset of spring long before the Governor officially eased lockdown restrictions.

I notice the collections of new bicycles- all the rage now- lining the lawns along with toy cars. The kind kids can pretend to drive, Fred Flintstone style. Across the street, Tracey is walking her little dog. Some breed that has enough shih and poo to sound like a bowel movement and not something that descended from wolves. She waves and smiles.

I smile back and nod my head. It's important to make people think you're their friend.

"How are you?" she asks. I don't want to hang out and talk. Just came to get my mail, not to make friends. But I humor her.

"I'm doing well. Working out now that the gym is open again." I flex a little. I know she likes it.

"Better not let Emperor Cuomo see those guns you got on you!" she teases. I laugh. Even though it wasn't funny. Nor was it original.

Angela Kaufman

She walks her oversized rat down the block. I walk down the winding lane to my mailbox. Keeping a low profile in a place like this means making small talk. Smiling. Waving. Listening to trite conversations about Jayden's soccer game or Maxxon's award for achievement in his class for gifted and advanced kids.

I unlock my mailbox and retrieve the envelopes and packages inside. Concealing them as best I can. I look from side to side. Some kids are playing. Neal is watering his lawn. Again. Even though it's rained almost every day for a week. Let him water away. It means he won't notice me.

I smile to myself, thinking of how little any of these people knows about the guy they invite to their barbecues. The guy they brag about their kids to. The guy who lives right next door.

They don't know me. I, on the other hand, know plenty about them. One of the best things I learned, dare I say, the only thing I learned in school that has any bearing on real life, is the importance of maintaining one's vantage point.

The less I say, the more they talk. I just make a few mental notes. Listen first, then talk. And I do listen. I listen to their casual comments, their passing remarks, I hear their grievances, I hear what they say and what they don't say.

I do a lot of listening before I respond. A strategy that has never steered me wrong. When it's time to talk, I already know what to say. And I've been talking to a lot of people online. My neighbors take great pains to curate an image to the outside world. They curate an appearance. I curate content.

I look from home to home, sizing up what I know of just this little microcosm of a bigger universe. SUVs in the driveway, their bumper stickers boasting of what kind of exceptional genius is on board. But I know when the man- or woman- of the house is slipping out at odd hours or coming home from work late.

Balloons hang from the porch of another fine structure. If I didn't know from the oversized electric grill in the driveway, the banner announcing Madeline's birthday is all the announcement I need.

They'll celebrate today, but I know the ambulance has been there monthly, bringing little Maddie to detox. Doesn't stop Mom and Dad from drinking, though, they're already planning for quite a birthday bash. Next to the grill is a cooler stacked to overflowing with ice and booze.

I watch. I listen, and that's how I know exactly what to say. I talk to a number of their sons, and a growing number of their daughters, through my Zoom meetings. Their husbands, assistants, nephews and nieces, their best friends, their roommates, I feed their minds. They eat it up. People like Tracey, walker of the designer-poo dog, would have a coronary if she knew what I could get people like Bill, the guy next door to her, an avid Golden Apple foot soldier, to do. With just a suggestion.

And when we're really ready to make it rain, I think to myself as I lock the door behind me, no one will believe it.

The group's influence is spreading. Membership is racking up nationwide. In the suburbs, the cities, and of course, in the sticks. The timing is right. Someday, people may ask why? The real question is, why not? People are desperate. Looking for direction. They're hollowed out. Empty. Even in my little community, inside the half-million-dollar homes, they can't fill the emptiness. Their desperation is fuel. They just need someone with the right ideas to light the match.

Maybe a few guys from neighborhoods like this will be picked off here or there. Sure, I'm careful. I know what's at stake. I also know the foot soldiers in places that don't look like this are the ones who will be picked off first if anything goes wrong. Even the Libs love to blame the rural poor. They'll never look close enough to see who really started this war.

Chapter 40

Marie

"Time to go home." I inform Jackie, directing her away from the lake. The sun is setting. It's a rare evening cool enough this time of year that tourists have stayed away. She gives a tug and lunges toward the bridge, the opposite direction of my intended destination.

Traffic is minimal. No pedestrians, mask-less or otherwise, in sight.

"Okay," I indulge her.

She jumps in excitement and darts off toward the sidewalk, leading me over Saratoga Lake on a bridge along Route 9R. I try to not look at the waves beneath, running at perpendicular angles to the lines on the sidewalk, creating a dizzying effect. I hate walking over bridges, but she seldom gets the opportunity for a sizable walk. Her sixty pounds of fluff and muscle are eager for additional exercise tonight, and I all but jog to keep up with her.

Once across the bridge, she directs me up the hill. The difference is astounding.

Cookie cutter mansions along a designer neighborhood. A stone sign reads "Regatta View Road."

Of course, I think.

Each house is opulent. Too big to easily clean and maintain without exploiting some unfortunate soul to do the dirty work for you. I look down at Jackie, who is sniffing at a lawn sign. On the sign is a picture of a dog squatting with a circle around and line through it. I secretly hope she squats right here. She doesn't.

A few paces ahead, she ambles up alongside a trump 2020 sign, circles three times, and then hunches down to make this stranger's lawn great again.

"Good girl," I tell her as she looks up at me nervously. I suppose there is no appropriate face to make while trying to relieve yourself in public while someone has you on a leash. I try to avert my gaze, feeling guilty for embarrassing her. When she's done, I contemplate leaving the present right where it is but think better of it.

"One of these bastards is liable to shoot you. We have to be careful," I tell her.

"It's a bad world for animals."

We round a corner and find a bench. I'm getting tired. I approach the bench overlooking the grand view of the lake from on high.

"Excuse me…" I hear a woman's voice calling to me.

I turn to look, and Jackie pulls toward the middle-aged woman, eager to make friends.

The woman's face tells me she wants no such thing. She scowls at me sans mask and points to a sign. "Bench and Park are For Residents of Regatta View Only," it reads.

I should have known.

I hoist myself up and lead Jackie back to the sidewalk. It's getting darker now. Once again, I tell Jackie it's time to go home.

She ignores me, pulling me to a heap of garbage on the side of the road. Before the pandemic, I would have welcomed a treasure hunt. I think of my first and only house. Purchased when I was fresh out of college and barely able to afford it. Furnished from other people's refuse save for the bed.

People throw away the best things.

She sniffs and scratches, and I cautiously remove a layer of discarded boxes with my foot to see what's gotten her attention. Inside a large Rubbermaid tub, an ornate wooden doll house, in a Victorian style, in perfect condition.

I've never had a dollhouse. Never even liked dolls. My favorite toy had been a stuffed dog named Puppy. But something about this doll house calls to me. It's the most ridiculous thing. But it's free. And discarded. And I want it.

"Jackie, let's go get the car. If it's still here, it's ours."

I return a short while later, driving cautiously through the cul-de-sac with a very confused Jackie, no doubt wondering why we returned home to just go out again.

It's still there.

"Stay," I instruct her.

I jump from the car, rubber gloves in one hand, rubbing alcohol and a washcloth in the other. Wiping it down thoroughly, every window and tiny room, I hoist it into the back of the car, and we return home.

What the hell are you even doing with this ridiculous thing?

I ask myself, wiping it down again and placing it gently atop the table in my living room. I don't know how to answer. With a closer look now, I surmise this was not a child's toy. More like a craft created by a hobbyist, perhaps from the estate of some now dead old lady who was its creator and caretaker. The little bathroom has a claw-foot tub, just like the bathroom in my house. The one I had to sell earlier this year.

The spare bathroom I could never afford to repair. The claw-foot tub I never got to use.

The dollhouse bedroom has a four-poster bed with curtains around it. Charming but bougie. A tiny toy cuckoo clock hangs in the living room.

And the clock stopped, never to run again, when the old... man... died ...

I hear the song and remember my grandmother's cuckoo clock. Hand carved. An ornate wooden bird would emerge and cry the hours, and the chime was as haunting as it was jarring.

The dollhouse has windows with shutters that open and close. It even has a tiny attic, like the small attic room in my grandmother's house where alternating cousins, siblings and parents lived at various points when they fell on hard times.

I have no use for this thing in a trailer too small for clutter, but perhaps it is the closest thing to a house I will ever have again.

Jackie sighs.

"And besides," I tell her, "it was free."

The next morning, Jackie licks me awake. First by swathing her tongue across my closed eyes, then by plunging it into my ear. It tickles and I squirm and laugh.

"Let's go out," I tell her. She jumps from the bed and I throw my robe over the t-shirt and shorts that serve as pajamas. We head to the back door, but I stop short in front of the dollhouse. My nose is assailed with the rank smell of mouse urine. Jackie notices it too.

She looks up and growls. I follow her gaze.

Two grey mice, giants in the world of doll houses, dart from room to room. One climbs from the tiny attic down to the bedroom, peeing on the four-poster bed. The other gnaws at a wall between the bedroom and bathroom, its feet perched on the side of the clawfoot tub. Feces and urine are strewn throughout the dollhouse. The painted interior now filled with scratches. Holes chewed on the walls.

I grab the entire thing, toss it into a garbage bag, and throw it in the trash.

2020 strikes again.

Chapter 41

Jackie

I know She wouldn't like it. But She was asleep for a nap and I smelled on the breeze, something tart and exciting. A cat. In the yard! I didn't want to Arf! and wake her, so I pulled, and I pulled, and I pulled, and I lunge through the screen and onto the lawn.

Cat didn't expect me, and he ran, and he ran, and I chase.

I leap over the fence. So many cats!

I run! I Arf! I come so close, so close, and I open my mouth and he slash! He scratches me.

No bother, plenty more!

I run, and I run, and I chase through the grass through the trees onto the hot ground into the streets where cars blast "Outta my way!" and I run, and I run.

I stop by the lake. No cats. Only people.

She wouldn't like it. We have to stay away from the people. She says. This is a bad world, She says.

I smile and I Arf, and my tongue lags in the wind.

I see the bridge and I run.

The people must want me to run because they leap out of my way and clear the path.

I run, and I run, and I Arf! And I run up the hill.

She was sad when the mice chewed her toy. I will find Her another.

I sniff, and I sniff, and I run, and I roll in the leaves and then sniff again.

Golden Apple

There are no more toys. The lawns are all empty. They smell sharp and sour.

I run, and I sniff, and I play, and I smell something new. Burning wood. I let my shadow get long. The dark is coming up. She will worry. When the dark comes up, it's time for Her to worry. I don't want Her to worry alone. I'll go home.

I turn back to the smell of ducks and fish and weeds, and I run. I run, and I run, and I jump away from a car.

I run down the hill. I run back over the bridge.

I run through the gravel, past the honking, to the shrubs that smell familiar. I run to the side now, turning at an angle.

It's dark.

I'm almost home.

I hear her howling my signal.

"Jaaaaackkkkiie!" She yells.

"I'm here!" I wooooof!

I run and I see Her, in the distance. I see the light at our home.

I'm almost there.

Almost there.

Almost home.

I run, and I run, and I

"Jackie!!!"

Run and I....

Sharpness stabs through my shoulder. It rings into my ears with a bang. It pierces me. I try to breathe and taste blood. It gurgles up in my throat. It chokes me and rolls through my mouth.

My head screams, "No!" A command. Like "Sit!" or "Stay!"

I fall to the ground.

Blood spills from me. It's warm, but I tingle. Paws weak.

I see work boots and a smoke. The smell of metal.

I hear Her scream closer, see Her drop to her knees. It's getting dark. Time to worry.

I'm almost home. I'm almost home.. I'm...

Chapter 42

The Caretaker

Gunshots aren't unusual in hunting country. Especially in trump country. But this time, it was close. Right here in the park close.

I look out the window, someone's screaming. Hysterical. Swearing. Not making sense. I could go take a look, but sometimes you learn more by staying in the background. I've learned that being where I've been.

I turn on the scanner. Whatever is going on, I'll hear about it soon.

Suspected drunk driver on Broadway, what else is new?

Domestic incident on Phila Street. Yep. No surprise there. Patriarchy is alive and well in Saratoga. This ain't no one horse town, the old advertisement jingle used to say.

And they were right. We've also got all kinds of vice and debauchery. You can dress some people up, but you can't take 'em out. No matter how tempting the thought.

Suspicious person loitering, I take a long gulp of lemonade, fresh squeezed, perfect for a sweltering evening. Loitering, in these parts, means someone don't like the look of someone else, don't want 'em in the neighborhood, and can hardly do shit about it.

Except call the police and make some exaggerated claim about feeling intimidated.

I hear the dispatcher now give a familiar address. Anonymous caller someone shot the neighbor's dog. Distressed woman at the scene.

The new lady, and that big fluffy shepherd mix she keeps glued to her hip.

"Jesus fucking Christ, really? You shot her fucking dog?" I ask no one in particular. If I had to guess, I would say it was Vinny. Or Dave. Probably plan to use some bullshit excuse too. He'll probably say he thought it was a burglar or whatever excuse people like him make to fire off their damn guns. At least, Dave would do that. If it was Vinny, he'll probably just slink into the shadows and hide.

I know the new lady about as well as I know anyone else, and that is to say, not at all. She's high strung. A fucking train wreck, matter of fact. Lives alone. No one visits.

Only person in the park to wear a damn mask. She's either got health problems or is much more concerned about the pandemic than anyone else for miles around.

She never leaves the house without that dog. This isn't gonna be pretty. Haven't seen her speak more than a few sentences to anyone in this park, but she talks to the dog. I don't know if she knows she does it.

Did it.

If she still talks to the dog now that he's dead, well, that would definitely be fucked up. I rub my forehead. Wondering what that stupid fuck, and I bet it was Dave. Wondering what the fuck he's gone and done now. And what kind of headache it's gonna cause me in the long run.

That poor dog.

Chapter 43

Dottie

Now that the cats have all been fed, I sit down to enjoy my dinner. Well, if you want to call pop-tarts dinner. Two bites and I nearly choke, the loud bang is close enough to make me jump. Scares the shit out of the cats too! Run right under the couch, behind the table and every which way.

"What the fuck?!" I yell to whoever it is this time. I've heard them shooting off their guns before, but not usually this close. That sounded like it was right here in the park.

I put my pop-tart down and make for the window, pulling back the curtain, not expecting to see anything when, holy shit would you fuck me twice there it is.

It was here alright. I hear a woman screaming to wake the bloody dead and I'm sure she was the one who's been shot. I grab my phone and call 911.

"Someone's shooting off a gun. One of my neighbors is screaming, I'm not out there yet but she may have been shot," I give the address and now I'm pissed because I hate calling the fucking cops but it sounds like someone's hurt. I run out the door in the direction of the screaming.

Whoever it is, they must not be dying. Not if they can scream like that. I see the silhouettes now. Big guy standing, gun at his side, one hand up like he's trying to explain something.

"Thought it was a coyote is all, ma'am." It's Dave.

And on the ground, I see the pale fur and I know what's happened now. Marie ain't screaming because she's been shot.

"You sick fucking son of a bitch!" she screams, and then wails, face down on the dog's lifeless body, her shoulders heaving with sobs.

Christ on a fucking cracker, he's shot her dog. He's killed her beautiful dog.

"What the fuck did you do that for?" I yell to him but Marie is screaming and I doubt either of them can hear me. With all the carrying on, I didn't hear the car finally pull up.

The police come and go. A lot of good that did. And didn't they all come out to their doorways to gawk? Not one of them stood up to him, though. Only me. Bunch of cowards. I don't know how long it took to get her to go home, and when she did, she was clutching that dog's body like it was her safety raft. Like she would drown if she let it go. Sun was already setting when it happened, but by the time the fuss was over it was full dark. Still, on the way home I could see that bastard Dave, smiling. Joking. Mimicking the way she was crying as he stood talking to his buddies, the cops who had responded. Made my blood boil.

"I don't know who your parents were," I said to them, "but if I could, I would slap them across their faces for their failure to teach you better morals." And with that, I went home.

Chapter 44

Marie

I cry until my throat is hoarse. Cry and scream. I don't care how late it is. I don't care who is trying to sleep. "You no good, racist, cracker, pieces of shit!" I scream out every name in the book, pacing the house.

I open cabinet doors but there's nothing good to throw. Nothing loud and breakable. I have two dishes. They're plastic. No glasses. I've already lost everything.

For days I walk through the house crying, screaming, ranting. Eventually, I remember a little girl lives next door. Has she been terrorized by the screaming lunatic who forgot she existed?

She'll have to learn that this is the world we live in, at some point. The world she will inherit. Where her ability to just exist, to live peacefully and go about her business doesn't matter. I just didn't want to be the one to teach her this.

I try to eat instant potatoes. After two spoons, I see Jackie running. I hear the gunshots. I throw up and dump the rest out the window. Let the cats eat it. I try to work. Stare at the screen, cry and flip the lid down on the laptop. I hold Jackie's favorite toy and cry into it, breathing out her doggie smell.

I see Jackie, jumping playfully, smiling, and then I see the blood. I see her midair when the red erupts in her fur. I see Dave with his gun. And I see you.

You did this.

He's one of your people, isn't he? Even has the flags around his house to prove it. Part of your club. Is this what you voted for? To cage children. To let a pandemic run wild. To terrorize Black people. To kill dogs.

How are you sleeping at night? Can you keep your breakfast down? Knowing you did this?

* * *

Andre tells me again, trying to be soothing.

"I wouldn't put it past some trumpy fool to do a lot of fucked up shit. But you can't prove it. As far as you know it was just an accident."

I don't believe it. I saw how he looked at us through the screen on his front porch, Back the Blue and trump flags swirling around his neck-bearded face. I've tried to tell Andre. And my parents, and my sister. But no one believes me.

"He did it on purpose. I knew one of these fuckers would do it and he did it on purpose." I repeat.

"Do you need me to come visit? I will if you need me there," Andre offers.

"No." I answer, too quickly, and then, "They'll shoot you too,"

"Marie. Do you hear yourself?"

I don't answer.

"Marie, I'm worried about you. Maybe living with the Beverly Hillbillies is getting to you. Do you want to come down to the city? Stay with me for a little while?"

I consider this.

"Not a good idea. It's too dangerous to travel."

"The numbers in NY are going down, you'll be fine. The offer stands. Whenever you need it."

I don't argue with them. The numbers are stagnant at a high level. No one is taking it seriously. People are taking vacations because they're tired of living with COVID, not because the virus has become less of a threat.

People say we've gone through a wave. Not a wave. A tidal wave suspended in air, hovering over us. Like the repeated nightmares I used to have as a kid. Dream after dream, I would see myself walking down a beach on a beautiful day, and then a tidal wave would rise up. It would cover miles, hovering in the air. Everyone could see it, but no one could do anything about it. I couldn't outrun it and would wake drenched as if I had in fact been overcome by the sea's long arms.

"Marie?" they ask. I remember where I am now. How long was I silent?

"Sorry, brain fart." I tell them, then, "thank you for the offer, but I'm going to wait to see what happens with the virus."

Another pause.

"You should have seen this guy," I tell them, "when the cops showed up, it was like a reunion of old buddies. They knew each other by name. How fucking sick is that?"

"I know, it's creepy. In a million ways. But that doesn't mean he killed your dog on purpose." Andre pauses.

"And if he did… Marie, how well do these people in the park know you?"

I laugh sarcastically. "Not at all. The one lady, I think she's his wife, accused me of being a lesbian who was out to convert her daughter to homosexuality because she stole one of my books…"

"What? She stole your book?"

I explain how my book went missing. How the crazy woman came to my house, accusing me of influencing her daughter. How Jess and I had become covert friends of sorts. How Jess seems like such a lost soul trapped in that horrible family.

"You may be overstepping there, Marie. Though I know your intentions are good. Maybe they found out you're still talking to their kid."

"I doubt it. And I haven't been able to leave any books for her. Not since it happened. I know it's not her fault, but I can't even look at them. I can't even leave the trailer."

"Be careful, Marie. Look, I don't think this was intentional. But if it was, maybe it's best to tone it down. Don't be too.... Open. With any of them. For a few weeks maybe?"

No need to worry about that. This place can burn to the ground, I won't lift a finger. Not even to dial 911.

Chapter

Marie

I pour powdered potato flakes into a bowl and add the steaming water.

Did you ever make colcannon... with lovely, pickled cream?

I hear a woman's voice singing, her Irish accent echoing in my head. The lilting of whistles, the guitar, and of course, the drumming.

Oh, you did, yes you did, yes you did and so did I...

I mix the powder that passes for potatoes today.

I hear you singing along in the tavern on the smallest of the Aran Islands. Long past my bedtime, everyone from the little old ladies to the four-year-old kids sat around the table filling the pub and nearby streets with music.

Oh, you did, so you did, so did he....

Before you did it. And the following year they asked you, "what happened to your country? How could this happen to America?"

You didn't tell them, right away, that you voted for him. You hinted at it. You defended him. You drifted farther and farther away.

Oh, you did and so you did, so did he and so did I...

I've made it too thick and strain to push the spoon through the white flakey mix.

Oh, weren't them the happy days, when troubles we knew not...

I hear the drums. They're nearer now. They're at the door. I don't know why they're at the door until I hear someone call my name.

Knocking, not drumming.

I grab my mask and put it on quickly.

"Krissy?" I ask, confused. Feeling like a child who's just seen their teacher in the store and realizes they, too, mingle in the community and aren't confined to the school.

She's wearing a purple mask, and it took me a moment to recognize her.

"Can I come in?" she asks.

"Why don't we sit in the yard." I glance over both shoulders, the coast is clear, no neighbors in sight, and walk her through the gate to the back patio.

"This is a nice place," she says, but she sounds like she's trying too hard to convince herself.

We sit down. She pulls her mask down slightly and must have seen something in my face because she adjusts it back over her nose again.

"Marie," she begins, "we need to talk."

"You're breaking up with me?" I ask, facetiously. We both laugh.

"No. I talked to Andre last night."

I remain silent. She continues.

"They're worried. We're all really worried about you."

The look on her face is pitying. Condescending. Fuck her.

"Well, nothing can be done. I'm fine. He murdered my dog. I'm stuck here, but hey at the rate we're going, we'll all be dead soon. So, it's all relative."

"This isn't like you."

"It is now."

"I don't think you're being rational…"

"This sounds familiar," I snap, sounding harsher than I intended. I continue, no longer caring. "It wasn't rational when I told you trump was going to win, right? I was just being paranoid? When I told you about the dreams? About the dreams of nazis marching through the streets? Back in 2014… I was crazy, right? When I quit my job the next week because someone spray painted swastikas in the parking lot. I was over-reacting, remember?"

"Marie…" she tries to cut in.

I don't let her finish.

"And when I said this virus was something more than just a flu, that it wouldn't just be gone after a four-week shutdown, that it was only going to escalate, I was paranoid then, too, right?"

I'm on a roll now, I feel myself shaking.

"And when we were in middle school, and I told you that NAFTA was going to seriously fuck over the working class, but you were too busy crushing on Bill Clinton? Or when I told you that Columbus was guilty of genocide and rape and you wouldn't hear it because he's an Italian American hero? And when…."

"So what?" she finally yelled back. "Damn, Marie, so what? You get to have an I told you so. You saw it, you knew it, you told me so. So what? What does any of this do?"

Nothing, I think to myself. No one ever listens until it's too late.

"I just came to check on you. You don't look like yourself, Marie. I came to see if you need anything."

I need a lot of things. I realize this suddenly.

"Nothing you can do," I tell her, calm again.

Chapter 46

Jess

"Pastor Mark is here."

My dad says, after not speaking a word to me for days. He just opens the door, barges in, and announces it. I wish I had been masturbating. That would teach him to knock.

"So?" I ask him.

"So, I called him here to take time out of his busy day, to talk to you."

I don't look at either of them. I stare at my phone, scrolling Insta. His hand comes down hard and snatches the phone right out of my hands. "What the- that's my phone!" I scream.

"Actually, I bought it, so it's mine." He makes that smug fucking face.

He turns to Pastor Mark who stands in the bedroom doorway. Pastor's eyes shift side to side like he wishes he was anywhere but here. I'm glad he feels awkward. Serves him right for agreeing to stick his nose where it doesn't belong.

My dad tells the Pastor, like I'm not here, "she's been a rude, disrespectful and petulant girl this past week."

"That's better than being a murderer!" I turn on him and stare him right in the face, yelling back. I feel my cheeks getting hotter. I know where this is heading. This is the part where I tell myself to chill the fuck out, all while ignoring my own internal advice.

I don't have time to lash out further. My father's voice thunders down from the doorway, his self-righteous directives emphasized with a pointed finger, aiming right at me.

The way he aimed his stupid gun at that poor dog.

I barely even hear what he's saying now. I see Pastor Mark put his hands up in an attempt to calm my father down.

"Perhaps I can just talk to her for a moment," he finally says.

My dad agrees and walks away, but knowing him, I'm sure he hasn't gone too far.

I no longer feel like being a bitch to Pastor Mark. He's just doing his crumby job. I'm not really mad at him after all. He pulls up a chair from my desk across the room. I think it's pretty fucking rude to have a seat without being invited to do so, but I don't bother pointing this out to him.

"Jess, we go back a long way, right?" he asks, doing the grown up trying-too-hard-to-be-your-pal thing. It's cheesy as fuck, but I feel it working. I don't want to be rude to him. I remember how he used to teach the kids' Bible class. He wasn't the biggest asshole in the world, just a typical out of touch adult.

"I guess." I try to remain aloof. I don't want him to think we're buddies, even if I'm not mad at him.

"You can tell me if something's going on. Right?"

I shrug. This is so lame.

"I see you've gone for a new haircut."

I shrug again. What does he want me to say in response to stating the obvious?

"Can you tell me why you're so angry?" he asks.

Fine, Dad, I think to myself; you want to bring a stranger into this; you got it. So much for *what goes on in this house…*

"Did he tell you he killed a dog?" I turn on Pastor Mark. I know I'm making my best Linda Blair I-dare-you-to-throw-some-holy-water-on-me face.

Pastor Mark looks surprised, and skeptical. As if he already has it figured out that I'm doing the "adolescent exaggeration" thing but isn't entirely sure. Because maybe I'm telling the truth.

I imagine it's the reaction he has when little kids come to him in confession and tell him that daddy drinks too much, or does bad touches to them, or beats mommy. Cautious, and neutral just in case. Playing the middle of the road because he doesn't want to pick a side.

"I haven't heard about that incident. Can you tell me your side of what happened?"

Strike one.

"There is no *my side*. I said it. He killed a dog. New neighbor had a dog. She really liked it, always walking it and talking to it. I heard my dad say he was going to teach her a lesson. Next night, dog got loose, he shot it. Just a few feet away from her front door."

I wait to see what he says.

He makes his mouth into a grimace. Now he definitely looks like he wishes he didn't agree to put himself in the middle of this cluster fuck.

"I can see," he begins, "how it may seem like your dad's anger at the neighbor makes this accident look like-" he goes on, putting his words together slowly, like he's piecing together a puzzle. I don't wait for him to choose the rest of his words.

"No accident. He wasn't sorry either. He was laughing about it. But, hey, whatever, if you want to pick and choose what commandments are important to follow, who am I to tell you you're wrong?"

His face turns red. He pulls in his lips like he's trying to fight back a bitter taste or hold back on what he really wants to say.

"Speaking of commandments," he begins, "honor thy father and thy mother is also one of God's most important commandments."

"Oh, sure. Obey your father, the murderer who obeys his boss, the worthless sack of shit who dumps on him constantly, who's responsible for him being out on disability half the year, so he can honor his boss, so we can all honor the big daddy in the sky. Right. I forgot."

We go back and forth like this until I get bored with him. And annoyed. I need to find a way to get my phone back. It's the only way I can talk to Eric. No way could I let Mom and Dad find out about him.

I need to get my phone and get this asshole out of my room.

This guy is wasting my time. I throw him a bone. Nodding my head, pretending to agree to play nice and be respectful. Pretending to give a shit.

I don't know if it worked or if it was just easier for Pastor Mark to pretend so that he could cut bait and get out of here as well. But eventually, I have my room back to myself.

Then I have the trailer back to myself. I find the phone on top of the fridge. The same place they used to keep our Halloween candy when we were kids, and they didn't want us to eat it all at once. Do they really think I'm still five?

I unlock it and call Callie.

"We make phone calls now? What is this, 1997?" She asks.

"They confiscated phone. I got it back now. I wanted to tell you, we've got to be extra careful about how we… arrange things. Meeting tomorrow as planned?"

"Yeah. Your parents are over the top, by the way."

"Tell me about it."

Chapter 47

Jess

"Sorry I took so long," I tell Eric, hugging him as he lifts me off the ground. Out of habit, I look over my shoulder. No one from the park would hang out here, but I can't help it. I turn to Callie, who is pulling her mask over her ears. Eric and I kiss before he covers his face with a mask. Another reason we would never be able to meet near my place. That is the least of the reasons we don't meet up anywhere near my parent's place. Even though we go to the same school and he lives across the bridge and on the other side of the city.

Callie's boyfriend's name is Andy, but we call him Dragon because he's a nerd who likes to play D&D. In a few minutes, I catch sight of him coming down the alley, checking his phone for her texts before he sees her.

I shouldn't bitch about Callie being slow to pick me up. She's doing me a favor. I can't even afford to give her money for gas since my job closed down and decided to not hire so many people again when it opened back up.

"I got you here, didn't I?" she said. I can't get her to understand. I appreciate her sneaking me down to Troy. I hardly get to see Eric all year since school was locked down.

I try not to let it bother me. Instead, Eric and I have a great time. Like the old days. But as the sun starts to set, I realize how much I don't want to go back home.

"Can't we just live together? I can't go back home to them!"

"Right, your racist ass dad is gonna be fine with you living with me. You're trying to get me killed, aren't you?"

He's got a point. Only a few more years, then we'll be ready.

* * *

"I'm sorry, babe. I'll kick Callie's ass I promise." It's way past time I needed to head home, and she never came to pick me back up.

"No worries, but I can't drop you off exactly at your dad's place," Eric tells me. I know this already and wouldn't want him to risk it. I can't believe she ditched us like that. Probably off getting high somewhere.

We're almost at Exit 13N when the sound of sirens erupts behind us, piercing the air.

"Aw fuck," Eric slaps the dashboard with his hand and pulls over. My heart races.

"Just stay calm, don't mouth off to them, I can't get away with that like you can," he tells me.

I've been in cars that have been pulled over before, not usually any big deal. So I'm surprised when the cops roll up on us, yelling.

They practically drag Eric out of the car. "You can't do that!" I yell and reach for my phone to start taking a video.

"Turn it off," another cop pulls his gun on me. They search his car, illegally. And can't find anything. Before they let us go, the one cop says, "what's wrong with white guys?"

I want to go down the list, but that won't help.

"Are you okay?" I ask Eric. He's sweating, and not just because it's warm out.

"No, but it's just another day."

Chapter 48

Dave

"'Could you not smoke your cigar near my crystals? They're sensitive to environmental toxins, 'k, thanks.' Those were actual words. She said 'em. Just as she walked out the door of my trailer. Where I've been letting her stay." I tell my wife.

Shar turns her back on me and acts like chopping up carrots for dinner is more important than what I got to say. I take another puff on my cigar.

"It ain't like I smoke 'em every day, Shar. You know that. Even if I did, this is my house. Some people around here forgot that."

Shar sighs and turns back to me, one hand on her hip, like she thinks she's gonna lecture me, "I know you two don't get along. But it's only temporary. She's going to get her own place soon."

"That's what I've been hearing for months."

I blow a smoke ring and smile. I still got the talent.

"She's really trying," Shar whines now. God, I hate it when she whines.

"I don't see her trying. I hear her in there chanting morning, noon and night," I tell her, pointing to the sunroom door. "But I don't hear her making phone calls, talking to landlords, nothing. I think she's getting too comfortable here. And she's annoying. What is she contributing? Nothing."

Shari doesn't respond. She turns back to her damn carrots. At least she cooks, unlike her useless sister. Finally, she responds, "it's hard to find a place right now. She lost everything to that cult, and she can't just go get a job somewhere."

"Stewart's is hiring."

"Shari won't work at Stewart's, hon, she's working on trying to get a new business started it just takes a little time. She showed me her plans. She's going to be a life coach, an influencer. Online."

Influencer, what the fuck is that? I think to myself.

Shari keeps going on about it. "She's building up a following, but in order to do it she has to post videos and photos and it's hard with all the noise and the kids and all."

"Oh, so now staying in my home for free isn't good enough because I'm ruining her ability to influence?" I let out a fart for emphasis. Another puff on my cigar. Shari acts like she's done with the conversation. But I'm not.

What's the matter with these women? My wife, making demands, trying to undermine my authority. Her sister, following one crackpot guru after another. My daughter, trying to take after that broad who moved in. Showed her. I sure did. No one is going to get away with disrespecting me. This is my home, and I'm not going to roll over for no one. I blow another smoke ring and turn back to Shar.

"I want her out of here. By the winter."

Chapter 49

Tom

"Honey, where did we put the boxes for the office?" I hear her calling me from the other room. The place is finally coming along, just as we imagined. I walk through the hall and into the living room. The ratio of boxes to furniture is decreasing. Just what I like to see. Speaking of what I like to see, I put both hands on her hips and kiss her neck.

"The boxes for the office are on the stack in the kitchen. I'm going to get to those next. Just trying to finish setting up the computer first, then the jammer, then the books and all can come later."

I spin her around and hold her face with both hands. She smiles up at me and I brush her soft hair away from her eyes. I think, not for the first time, my wife is the picture of American beauty and purity. The perfect match for a man with a special destiny. The Eve to my Adam.

"I can't believe it. I just can't believe it's really happening. Finally, we're going to have what we've always wanted." Her eyes sparkle as she says this.

"Yeah," I agree, "the place is perfect. Couldn't have asked for a better spot. The higher ups know what they're doing. Like I've been telling you, trust the plan."

I kiss her on the mouth. All this hard work puts me in the mood for a different kind of hard work.

When I lean back, she's smiling, but I see tears in her eyes.

"What's wrong?"

"Nothing, I'm happy. All we've worked toward is finally paying off." She wipes a tear away and then says, "and when they write the history books, your name will be there."

I laugh. "Well, my name and yours as my devoted wife. The midwife of the movement. We couldn't do it without you. Women are the key to our success. Don't we always say that?"

Her smile widens. She nods her head.

"I know you weren't crazy about him at first, but now what do you think?" I ask her.

"I never said I didn't like Jordan. I just thought you were spending a lot of time in all of those meetings is all. But I understand why."

"This is our future, right? For us, for all of us. We're going to make history." I tell her. She smiles at me like an excited kid. I see she's set up the electronics. Not bad, for a woman. Not bad at all.

"I see you got the electronics set up all by yourself." I plug in my phone and scroll through my playlist. "How about some mood music?" I ask her.

The sound of the guitar's opening riffs fills the trailer. I couldn't stand this old shit at first. Somehow it got under my skin and grew on me.

"Got to get back to the land and set my sooooul freeeee!" I sing along. Bianca grabs my arms, and we dance like a couple of lovestruck fools who have finally found our way home.

Chapter 50

Dottie

I don't like to intrude, but when the Goddess sends me on a mission, who am I to question it? Half a century in this crazy world and I've had zero fucks to give what anyone thinks of me for all but maybe the first ten years. So I go to the last home on the road. The lawn's up to my knees practically. Not off to a good start. Who around here is going to complain?

A butterfly dances past me. Change is coming, yes indeed. We've got to get ready. I start to head toward the front door, when I see a grasshopper hopping toward the gate to the yard. So, this is where I go instead.

"Whatever you say," I tell Her out loud. Who cares if anyone can hear? They think I'm crazy, anyway. I knock on the wooden gate. The fence is high, and I can't see over, but I wouldn't snoop anyhow.

The door opens a crack and I see red eyes on the other side. Just about my height. She pulls up her shirt to cover her nose and mouth. Dammit, it didn't occur to me to bring my mask, so I do the same. Out of respect. Just like I would take off my shoes in someone else's home. If anyone ever invited me in, if that is what they did. When in Rome and all of that shit.

"Hello," she sounds surprised, and I don't blame her. I didn't think I'd be coming here today either.

"Good afternoon, Dear. I don't want to bother you, but I was worried about you and just wanted to come by to see how you are doing."

She nods her head. Little specks of pointy stubble are growing in. Reminds me of the chia pet sitting on my windowsill back home. After a pause she says to me, she says, "I don't know. I hate it here. I don't know what to do. I can't concentrate. I keep seeing her and I try to push it away."

I don't mean to interrupt, but I can't help it.

"No, no, don't do that. She's been visiting you, you know. When you see her, welcome her."

"Do you really think so?"

"I know so. I know she's here now. She came into your life for a reason. Death doesn't end that. Death isn't the end, honey. In fact, she's part of the reason I came here to see you. She's been coming into my dreams pretty insistent. She's worried about you. She didn't come all this way to see you flounder, missy. I know you're hurting and believe me when I tell you I would love nothing more than to wrap both my bony hands around Dave's neck and choke the life out of that pompous asshole. But until the Goddess tells me that is my mission, I'm gonna hold back and let Her tell me what to do."

She laughs and a few tears come out, but I can tell she's gotten my meaning.

"It's awful what happened, but that can't be the end for you. The Goddess brought you here for a reason. Not to hide in the shadows. I don't know what that reason is, it isn't to waste away like this. Do you understand?"

She nods, then says, "yes, thank you."

"Don't mention it, and if you need anything come on down and give a holler any time, day or night, okay? I don't do the cellphone thing, don't want the government keeping tabs on me. You just come down to my place anytime."

"Okay, thank you."

I'm just about to leave. I want her to sit with this. Really sit with it. Then you would just have to appear there, wouldn't you?

What? You want me to tell her?

I don't know if she's ready for this. True, true, she did take to hearing her dog talks to me in dreams. Okay, if you say so.

"One more thing."

Marie had started back to the yard, but the sound of my voice makes her turn back toward me. She's farther away now and keeps her shirt down. I see her face for the first time. All the lines of worry like a road map. I wonder if she had them before this year.

I take a breath, not sure how she'll take this. "Jackie is still here. And so is your grandmother. She hears you. She wasn't alone when she died. Her sisters and brothers, they were in Spirit, but she saw them. In the days before she died. She was already closer to them than she was to the nurses and aids and whatnot. She wants you to know. She wasn't alone."

Marie cries for real now. Actually slumps to the ground and puts her face in her hands. I stand back, watching. I reckon it's best to let her. In the old days, I would have offered a hug. But under the circumstances, I just stand and wait.

"It's alright. You've got a job to do and she's going to help you. You've already started it. You may not know. It's written in the *Book of Discordia*, we're going to need all hands on deck this year. You get yourself strong again, okay?"

"Yes," she says finally, clearing tears off her face.

Chapter 51

Marie

I sit in a folding chair by the window. Taking a break from writing, or rather, from not writing. Still nothing. Still drawing blanks. Fortunately, no one will read it one way or the other, I tell myself.

I hold a fuzzy stuffed lambchop on my lap. What's left of the toy, anyway, squeaker now extracted. Threads shredded and one eye gone. Jackie's favorite. I pet it mindlessly as tears roll down my face.

When you feel her, welcome her. Dottie had said. But I don't feel her now. Just emptiness.

I'm sorry. Some rescue this was. I'm sorry... I tell her over and over.

That's when I heard it.

* * *

Dee

Fiver wants to go for a walk. I know he's bored because I'm bored. We usually get bored at exactly the same time.

"Derrick Torrey," I call down the hallway. I hear him moving his chair around. The music he was listening to goes away. He's getting ready. He just does everything so slow.

I open the door and start down the steps. I hear something. Children singing.

Maybe they're having a birthday party.

I wasn't invited. We couldn't afford a present anyway.

* * *

Derrick

I unlock the latch and Dee scoops Fiver into her arms. She hugs him and dances side to side, humming a song I don't recognize. She leans her mouth close to his long floppy ear as if singing to him.

"Dee, what are you humming?" I ask her. She picks things up from TV sometimes, but this tune is new. She clearly doesn't know the words. Fiver is secure in his wagon now. She grabs the wagon handle. We stroll down the path.

Then I hear it for myself. The same song Dee was humming, now being sung by the neighborhood kids. But that's too many voices. Who are these kids? And what are they singing?

* * *

The Caretaker

I drag the mower into the shed, close it up and secure the lock. My ears are buzzing from the sound of the mower. Something new, maybe it's broken. My head throbs. I hear the buzzing. It isn't the mower. It's the voices of... children?

I turn toward the road and as I reach the tree at the edge of my lot, a chill goes up my spine. It's begun. These no-good bastards. It's begun.

I expected this. I just thought there would be more time.

* * *

Justin

What is that fucking noise?

I imagine my mom, dozing on the couch on her lazy ass. One of her renters watching some bullshit Telemundo channel with screechy little kids singing bullshit songs.

I open my bedroom door. The living room is empty. The TV off.

The singing is coming from outside.

I step out of the trailer and my eyes squint on habit. So fucking bright out. I shield my eyes with my hand. The sound is coming from the newly occupied lot. Weird motherfuckers.

And what is that fucking song?

* * *

Dave

I smile at Shari. "Isn't this great?" I whisper. For once, we got some decent neighbors. I've been spending a lot of time getting to know them. Upstanding folks. Patriots. Not like that whiny snowflake dyke moved in this summer. Nope.

Scott and Don found fast friends with their kids. I look now at Scott and Donny in their little uniforms. Navy blue pants and Golden t-shirt. A small price to pay for membership in the Bible class the new neighbors offer.

There must be twenty kids here today. In military formation, marching across the lawn, then proudly parading onto the road. My Scott, holding an American flag, looks at me and winks. Don carries a cross. They sing the song again and a tear comes to my eye.

I may never march in the cavalry.

* * *

Vinny

"Hey, Ma, how those burgers cooked? Just the way you like them?" I lean over to ask. I don't like the way Ma looks. She's getting thinner in her old age. Some of it came when she lost her balance, couldn't walk as easily. My sister made the executive decision, that's what she said, to put Ma in one of those homes. Not a nursing home, thank God, but a, whatd'ya call it? Assisted living home.

I bring her out for long weekends whenever I can. I hate those old people's homes. If it were up to me, she never would've gone. My sister is power of attorney and no sooner was Ma confined to the old people's home then didn't she and her husband start cleaning the place out.

To save time later, she said. Yeah, right.

Ma knows who takes care of her. She ain't been to see my sister or her husband, or her grandkids or great grandbaby in over a year. And they can't blame that on the pandemic. They're just selfish is all.

I bring over another diet soda, the Waist Watchers kind, like she always likes.

"Here ya go, Ma," I tell her as I pour it into her glass.

"Thank you, Vinny," she says, mid-chew, then adds, "burger's good Vinny."

"Cooked all the way through?"

"Just right."

I close the lid on the grill and smoke escapes out the sides as I do. Slumping down at the chair near her at the table, I crack open a beer. She used to nag me about the occasional beer, but she don't anymore. I guess when you get old you pick your battles.

"It's a nice day, ain't it, Ma?"

She looks kinda foggy, like she may not have heard me at first, then she says, "Yeah, nice day." And it is. Some days it's just too hot for her. But today is just right. Sunshine, but not too humid since that crazy rain let up, remember that?

"So, what do they have going on over at the home, Ma? You getting to play Bingo or anything?" I ask, seeing how my sister said socialization was one of the reasons she needed to be in that place.

"No, not Bingo. We have to keep to ourselves, and, what d'ya call it? Social distance," she tells me.

"What? Why? You're not in a Nursing Home."

"Well, we have to meet outdoors, not in our apartments. They had an outdoor concert the other day, but it was chilly to have it outdoors, on the lawn. And all the mosquitoes. I didn't go."

"So, what, what're you doing then?"

I'm pissed now but I try not to get a tone with my mother. Instead, I take it out on an unsuspecting mosquito who made the mistake of landing on my forearm. She stops to think again. Everything is so slow at her age now. Then she says, "Well, Denise helped program my TV so I get all the shows I like that Tucker Carlson. I do crosswords and I color with the coloring books Denise brought me."

My sister buying our mother coloring books! And she could have watched TV and done crosswords at her home. I grit my teeth, imagining the words I'm gonna have with Denise when she bothers to call me again.

Ma scoops up a forkful of macaroni salad with a shaking hand and brings it to her mouth, then she stops and turns her head.

"Vinny," she says to me, "you hear that?"

It takes me by surprise because usually I'm the one who hears everything, not her. I almost blow it off. Then I hear it. Singing, like kids, singing in a chorus.

Not on the radio either, but here, in the park.

* * *

Marie

The new neighbors. I knew they were fucking creepy! They've got row upon row of kids marching through the park singing.... Carrying flags. The new Youth for hitler, it appears.

I may never shoot in the infantry...

My blood turns to ice. Their faces are vacant. Children of the Corn vacant. I'm transported back in time. It's 1985.

I smell coffee. The church always smelled like roasting coffee. The worn turquoise carpet is flattened and stained. The smells of coffee and woodwork in churches, what is it that makes all churches smell the same?

I hold my cousin's hand. She's here for the summer, from out of town, and I finally get to pretend to have a sister.

We swing our arms back and forth, marching as we've been instructed to.

I may never shoot for the enemy, but I'm in the Lord's Army...

I remember how the song had meant nothing to me. Just another of the songs we were taught at summer Bible school, an offering in the neighborhood church. We didn't even attend masses there normally, but Bible School was free for a few weeks. We made crafts, and they told us Bible stories. One day, the teacher asked us to close our eyes.

"What do you see?" she asked.

I raised my hand and told her the many things I could see with my eyes closed. She yelled at me in front of everyone. It had been a trick question. I was supposed to say I didn't see anything. But that wasn't the truth. I also wasn't supposed to lie.

That was my first hint that the church may be bullshit.

And that night, it was family night, we dressed up and sang the songs we learned. Including the battle hymn about being in the Lord's army. It would be years before I realized what we were actually singing and the thought of it now makes me sick.

That was also the night my father had gotten mad.

The church gave prizes to kids whose families donated the most money. My family was not among the top donors, of course. We couldn't afford to make the donations.

I didn't understand why he was mad, then.

"The church is a bank, that's all it is, is a bank."

I didn't understand then. I was four and my cousin was five.

Now, seeing the neighborhood kids, dressed alike, marching in formation, singing I'm in the Lord's Army, I want to vomit.

I turn to leave the spectacle and head back to the trailer when it occurs to me...

Who the fuck are all these children?

Chapter 52

Joni

"You kids going to your class today?" I ask Donny and Scott as they rush for the door.

"Uh huh!" Scott barely answers. Donny was already down the front steps, not even acknowledging my question. They have their father's manners. No matter, the new neighbors and their little school has been good for the kids. I think. I'm not really sure what they're teaching.

"It's like a Sunday school, but also with manners and civics," Shari told me when I asked her about it. They wear the cutest little uniforms, and the other day were marching in a parade with all the other little Golden Appleseeds. That's the kids portion of the group. It was cute.

Plus, I have to say, I'm enjoying a little extra peace and quiet without them here during the day as much. The other evening, they both fought over who was going to help Shari with dishes after dinner. Said it was homework and they could earn points for helping.

Imagine that.

Now if only they had a class for Dave. I've barely seen him lift a finger to help Shari since I've been here. Who am I to judge if she's happy, right?

I test the front door to make sure it closed. In their haste they slammed it shut. Retreating back to my converted sunroom, time to prepare for my own morning class. I click on the Zoom link and am about to agree to join the group with video when I hear a knock at the door.

I figure it's Scott or Donny coming back for a notebook or cellphone or something. So, when I pull the door open and see a woman my age standing there, I was taken by surprise.

"Oh," I said, by habit of shock, fully expecting to see a little person in formal pants and a gold shirt.

"Is this a bad time?" she asks.

"Oh, not at all, I just assumed it was one of the kids."

I step outside into the early morning sun. The air is crisp, and I hug my arms.

"I didn't want to bother you. Just making the rounds to introduce myself to the neighbors. I'm Bianca, my husband and I just moved in and we've been running the Golden Appleseed program down the way there from our yard."

I recognize her then and extend a hand. "Oh, it's so nice to meet you. I was just thinking what a big difference it's making they've become eager to help their mom suddenly. I'm Joni, Shari's sister. I'm just staying here temporarily."

She nods and smiles, handing me a business card.

"Well, if there's anything you need, don't be a stranger. One of the things our group likes to do is to be of service. We are thinking about starting some committees to try to better those in need, do some charity, philanthropy, that kind of thing. So if you have any ideas or want to get involved, we're having our first meeting next week, Wednesday, over at our place."

She points to the trailer down the road, but by now I recognize which one is hers. In fact, after months of almost no one coming down this lonely road off 9R, suddenly most of the visitors have been to her place. They're not noise or disruptive, just different for such a quiet park.

"Sure," I tell her. "I may just stop by, thanks."

Chapter 53

Marie

How long has it been since I've checked the mail? It doesn't seem to matter. Without Jackie, there are few reasons to leave the house. I don't even really buy groceries anymore. Just an occasional trudge to Stewart's for vegan ice cream and a few snacks.

I wonder if the box will be overflowing with envelops as I haul ass down the path, hoping I don't see anyone. I don't want their questions. Their pity. Their stares. Not a single fucking one of them.

The box is full. Most of it crap. And a bill.

Goody.

In a rare twist of fate, there is almost no one out. Not in the park, not in the rest of the road. It's going for six. Usually people are meandering about, spreading disease and doing whatever else they do around here.

I decide to take advantage of the lull and head over to Stewart's. The tourist season is winding down. I wonder if this desolation is what remains here in the fall. If so, sign me up.

Walking across the parking lot, I notice the Marina is almost empty. My eyes wander momentarily toward the bridge. I wonder how deep the water beneath is.

One way to find out.

A voice whispers from somewhere in my own head.

I pull my eyes away from the bridge and head into Stewart's.

They're all out of vegan ice cream. No surprise. I probably bought the last of it last time I was here. Pretty sure there isn't a big demand in this neighborhood. Surprised they even carry it.

With a wad of mostly junk mail in my hand, I turn to leave the store. Before I do, I see the small section in the back. Dog treats and food, marked up from the supermarket prices, of course. A dog on one of the boxes looks just like Jackie. I'm glad no one can see my face between the sunglasses and the mask. I'm well versed in crying quietly.

Back out in the soon to be setting sun, the tears disappear as quickly as they had come on. In their place, something else. I clench my fists so tightly that feel my fingernails pierce into the palm of one hand and tear into the mail in the other hand. My teeth clench and all I can see, again and again, is that ugly bastard, Dave. Holding his gun. Smiling.

"Oops, coulda sworn it was a coyote."

I see him grinning at the officer who arrived on the scene. The two of them talking as if I wasn't there. As if my dog's corpse wasn't lying on the ground because of him.

"It's an easy enough mistake, hoss, don't you lose sleep over it now. Anyone coulda made the same mistake."

I think of how they had palled around and knew each other by name. And then my suspicion was confirmed.

"You coming to the PBA fundraiser barbecue next weekend?" The cop had asked. I don't remember if Dave confirmed his plans to attend or not. By then I was on my feet, screaming at them both. It was the first time I had taken my hands off of Jackie's body. I don't even remember exactly what I had yelled.

I just remember someone had come out, then, I don't even know who. Someone had taken me by the arm, someone had led me away, saying, "Nothing good is going to come from this now. What's done is done."

Someone had taken Jackie's body away before I even knew what was happening.

You know how people say they saw red?

Well, I saw red that night. I see it now. The mailboxes, all on their posts in a row, the empty road, one leading into Saratoga Springs and the smaller leading to a dead end, and my trailer.

That night, I saw everything as if through a filter. Through a glass, darkly, as they say. The far end of the park where the garden is, distorted by a filter of crimson. The trump flags waving as if on fire.

Screaming brings me back to the present. The red filter is gone. I don't know where the sound is coming from.

I thought it was me at first.

But it didn't throb inside my head the way my own screams do. And after a moment, I realize it's the voice of a child. High-pitched wails. Howls of pain or fear; I don't know.

I see him. On the ground, holding his stomach, I think. He's hunched over, screaming to wake the dead.

Scott.

Dave's son.

Over his curled-up body, his brother, hovers. He's yelling for Scott to shut up, to not get him in trouble. Then he sees me and his expression changes to panic.

I should ask what happened. I should take out the cellphone I carry out of habit and dial 911, especially now that I can see blood.

I should get closer, try to calm them both down.

I should do something.

But.

But. It had been their father. Maybe it would just serve them right.

I shake the thought away. My stomach is in knots. Had I really just contemplated letting this kid suffer out of spite?

Go on, a voice in the back of my head replies. *Just keep walking. Not your problem. Maybe his brother thought he was a coyote.*

Shut up! I almost say out loud and before I can hear that voice again, I lock eyes with the uninjured brother, Don.

"What happened here?" I ask him.

The boy starts to cry too, slowly, not like his brother's hysterics. "It was an accident! We were playing siege and I accidentally shot him! It's in his arm!"

My stomach sinks.

I drop to the ground, resisting the urge to move Scott so as to assess the damage. I realize it's not his stomach he's holding, but his left arm.

I take out my phone while asking, "where are your parents?"

"They're out. They had to go get groceries. Aunt Joni is out for a walk. Don't get me in trouble!" Don yells.

I try to make the universal signal for "be quiet" as the dispatcher answers the phone.

"This is 911, what is your emergency?"

I wait while the ambulance arrives and by then Scott is calm and Donny has chilled out a little. Down the road, Derrick approaches. He must have heard the screaming. He turns and runs back toward his place, returning with his mom, who appears as if she was awakened from a nap. Probably sleeping before her next shift. She looks him over and asks some initial questions. She's only just started to look him over when the ambulance pulls up. Joni, the kid's aunt, comes running down the road, eyes widening as she realizes the ambulance is pulling up to their place. She can take it from here, I tell myself.

Back at the house, I reach for my key and unlock the door. I hear Donny's voice again, "we were playing siege."

Chapter 54

Marie

I can't get beyond a few chapters, but I need to. No ambition left. I can't remember when I've ever been this far behind deadlines.

For once I've kept everything off. No radio, no podcasts, not even the Young Turks daily newscasts on a YouTube loop in the background.

My phone rings and I cringe. Fully expecting it to be a bogus call about my car's warranty being close to expiring. But it's Andre's number that appears on the screen.

I haven't spoken to them in a while and was likely an ass when we last spoke. I answer.

"Hey, how are you? I miss you!" I say, all the words pouring out faster than I intended them to.

"Hey, I'm good. Have you seen the news?"

"Is the president dead?" I ask, a little too enthusiastically.

They grunt in amusement. "Nope, it's 2020, we can't hope for news that good this year!" Andre shoots back.

I missed them more than I realized.

"In all seriousness, I've been ignoring the world for a while, just trying to get work done and not having any luck."

"Well, this isn't going to help. Maybe I shouldn't tell you."

"What? Aw, come on, you know I hate suspense. Go ahead, tell me."

"You sitting down?"

"Yes, what is it already? Don't make me hop on Google and find it out for myself!"

Andre drops the bomb.

"RBG is dead."

"Oh, fuck." My eyes tear up. My heart sinks. How much more can we take? Then I instantly feel selfish. Fuck, my loss? What about her family?

"Yeah, and they're going to rush through a new nominee, mark my words."

"Fuck." I can think of nothing else to say. But I feel like I have to say something. I'm crushed, but for Andre, this is more than a loss of an ideological role model. This could be life and death.

I muster up the best response I can think of, knowing it falls short. "Andre, are you okay?"

"I'm just in shock. And no, not really. But what can we do? If the left is too demoralized, we've already lost. And for people like me, that means…" What is unspoken stick in the air.

I take a deep breath and sigh. "What does that say about an entire political wing, if all we have to cling to are a few select heroes?"

"Some of whom aren't even really that heroic." Andre responds, "she did a lot of good, but her track record wasn't great. It took her too long to recant her statement on Kaepernick, but if they get a pick in the Supreme Court. We're fucked. For a long time. And it's inevitable."

"You're right, and who is going to stop them?"

"Hey, maybe some of those white ladies in Pussy Hats will save the day." Andre's sarcasm breaks the tension and we both chuckle. What else can we do?

"Even the squad," Andre goes on, "the party doesn't back them, doesn't take them seriously, and as much love as I have for them, you know a handful or people aren't going to put us on the right track."

We talk about all the things that would need to happen, that we would love to see happen, and how it will never happen. Andre then says, "Welcome to 'Murica, where the chances of a full Fascist takeover are more likely than the chances of a proper progressive agenda."

Chapter 55

Marie

Not even a day after the news broke, not even a full day after my conversation with Andre, and I'm back to being glued to the news. Videos play on a loop, all points left of NPR. *Democracy Now, the Young Turks* and a handful of other podcasts. Sure enough, the GOP is trying to push through a handful of new nominees for Supreme Court.

She's not even in the ground yet.

Almost a week later, all is stagnant.

I'm still pretending to work, still staring at the screen, writing a fraction of what I used to. My mind racing, crying, then staring into space, then crying again, my news binge finally paid off.

A breadcrumb, amidst what has been a famine of a year.

I copy the link and paste it into DM and then send it to Andre with the message "Christmas coming early this year, enjoy!"

I turn back to YouTube and watch the clip for what must be at least the tenth time.

On the screen, a crowd is gathered to mourn Ruth Bader Ginsburg. The president and first lady approach. They're wearing masks. Too little and far too late to change the message of the past seven months or so, that masks are for the weak, not patriotic.

They face the crowd. Standing before a flag-draped casket. He rocks back and forth slightly, as if it is painful for him to stand still and focus on anything other than himself.

A soft buzzing becomes a louder and louder sound of dismay. They're booing him. The sound carries, now, louder, as if they are howling. Then something else. A few voices become many and then the booing gives way to a chant. In a familiar cadence. The one his disciples used to insist that Hillary Clinton be locked up. It's barely audible at first, then growing in a steady crescendo, louder.

"Vote him out! Vote him out! Vote him out!"

I smile broader than I have in months. Lost in this moment of enjoyment captured on film and the slight glimmer of hope that maybe enough people will be mobilized to defeat him. I hope you're seeing this. Wherever you are. I hope this tiny snapshot of reality has found its way to your newsfeed.

I hope you're happy with what you helped to unleash.

The knock on the back door startles me.

It takes me a moment to catch my breath. Who would be in the backyard?

I grab my mask and loop the straps around my ears then slowly pull the back door open.

Jess is standing on the back steps, looking nervously side to side, then at me.

I step outside. "Hey, what's up? Are you okay?"

"I just wanted to say thank you for what you did for my brother. Scott told me it was you who called 911. I wanted to tell you I'm sorry for what my dad did."

She can't look me in the eye and instantly my heart is broken for her.

"There is nothing you need to apologize for." I tell her, and then, trying to soften the mood, "you know, every time you've come over here it's to apologize for the adults in your family, now what does that tell you?"

We both laugh. Then she hugs me. I don't push her away. I can shower later.

"Don't apologize for other people," I tell her again. "I know you're not your family. And I'm not mad at you."

"I can't stay too long. They're gone for now. I just needed to tell you, and to see how you are doing."

"I'm okay," I lie. No need to further upset her, my reassurances aside I know she'll still feel bad for what her dad did. No need to make it worse.

"What do you think of the new people?" Her change in topic catches me off guard.

"Haven't really met them, what about you?"

"My brothers and dad are obsessed with them. Think they're the greatest thing. My aunt Joni, too. My mom likes them."

"What do you think?" I ask her again.

She pauses and looks around nervously again. "Nothing I can put my finger on, but, did you ever just get a feeling someone was… a little off?"

I can't tell her that was the exact feeling I got about most people in this park, including her dad, so instead I just nod.

"Well," she goes on, "they seem alright, like nothing I can put my finger on, but I don't trust them. Who knows? Maybe just something stupid, like maybe they're just weird swingers or something, but something seems off, I don't know."

She shakes her head as if dismissing the idea. I shrug. "Time will tell. But always trust your instincts."

Something passes over her face when I say that, and I wonder if I've upset her.

"What's wrong?" I ask.

"You just made me think of this dream I had, last night, it was about the park. There was this apple tree, and we were all going to get the apples to make pies and stuff, but then I picked one, and it was rotten, like right in my hand. And all full of maggots and stuff." She shudders. "It was gross. Gave me a bad feeling when I woke up, like a feeling that something bad might happen. I know it sounds crazy…"

"Not crazy at all. Be careful," I tell her. "Always trust your dreams."

Chapter 56

Marie

Today, I don't care who is out. I don't care who is mulling around making small talk. I stare straight ahead, squinting in the afternoon sun, and intentionally looking through anyone who happens to be wandering the private road now. I don't even try as hard to conceal the book I'm carrying.

No one's at the garden and I can enjoy a slower walk through the rows of vegetables. I can feel the empty space where Jackie would have walked beside me. Missing her is like realizing I lack something essential. Like I've left the house without shoes or pants. Or without a mask.

I look left and right and then let my arm loosen and the book drop to the ground by the tomatoes. *It Can't Happen Here*, by Sinclair Lewis.

Headed back home, relief floods down from my forehead to my shoulders, where I didn't know I had been holding clenched muscles. A weight has been lifted in this return to the smallest routine, for whatever purpose it will serve. The kids are out playing. Scott has a bandage, but wasn't seriously injured, all things considered.

I hear their mother call them in to get ready for the meeting. Who knows what she's talking about. Rounding the curve and almost home, I see my gate is open.

My blood freezes. I remember what Jess said. About her dream. An apple, rotting on the tree, something bad coming. I instinctively reach a hand into my bag, but I didn't bring anything substantial to use as a weapon. At the bottom of the bag, I've got a can of spray. I started carrying it around back when Jackie and I encountered one too many loose dogs on our walks. Non-lethal, but distracting. Still, whoever is in the yard may not be deterred.

I walk as silently as possible as I get closer to the gate. I stand off to the side and hold my breath. It's so quiet I can hear the frogs in the pond on the far side of the yard. I can hear the murmuring of the kids far behind me now. And something else.

A little girl's voice.

I start to ease my tensed shoulders and loosen my grip on the can of repellent in my purse. I let myself peer into the yard.

Leaves pile up where they've fallen. The garbage and recycling bins remain in their vigil, not having been moved in weeks. A squirrel scurries across the fence and the movement makes me jump in over reaction.

Then, I see a shadow flit across the yard, closer to the pond.

It's the girl next door. Dee. She's alone. I walk into the yard, letting my breath out fully now, relieved. But also worried. She could have fallen in the pond.

What's she saying?

I approach with soft steps, not wanting to scare her.

She's got one of Jackie's old tennis balls in her hand. I start to choke up and reach to adjust my mask.

She's either oblivious to my presence, or just doesn't care.

"Go get it!" she yells and throws the ball. Then waits and laughs.

"Hello," I say, just above a whisper so as not to scare her. She doesn't turn. Instead, she retrieves the ball and throws it again.

"I like to play with Jackie," she says. I don't know if this is a question or a statement.

"Honey, I'm sorry, Jackie can't play anymore."

"Jackie plays now."

She's determined, and I can't break the news to her, but I try again.

"Dee, Jackie died. She can't play anymore. Jackie's," I stumble. What are you supposed to tell kids again? "Jackie's in Heaven," I try. It sounds weak.

She turns and looks at me then, and points to a sunny spot in the middle of the yard. I follow her gaze.

"Jackie's there, she likes it there."

My whole body freezes.

Jackie loved to play ball. But what she loved, more than anything, to sit in that exact sunny spot in the yard. Had Dee seen her through the fence?

Dee repeats again, "she loves it there. She visits me. I play with her. She visits you too."

The gate squeaks and I turn to see Derrick walking across the yard, lifting his shirt to cover his nose in the absence of a mask.

"I'm so sorry, Miss. She got away from me," he says to me and then to his sister, "Dee! You're not supposed to wander off and you're definitely not supposed to let yourself into other people's yards!"

"It's fine, I mean yes she should not wander off, but it's no bother." I see him relax, now that he knows I won't go off on him.

"Derrick," I begin, "Dee was just telling me that she was playing with Jackie. She knew all of Jackie's favorite things. Interesting, huh?" I purposely leave it open-ended, not wanting to sound judgmental. After the visit from Dottie, I'm sure Jackie's still around. But how did this child know?

"Yeah, Dee's got some interesting talents. She knew when we had to put our cat to sleep even though she wasn't there, and Mom tried to lie to her about it. She still talks to Coco, that was the cat's name." Then he catches himself, as if he's just remembered something, and adds, "and I'm sorry about Jackie. That guy is a real douche, excuse my French."

"Well," I tell him, "she is more than welcome to come and play with Jackie whenever she wants," then I look at Dee, "as long as she has permission and lets you know where she is, deal, Dee?"

"Deal," she agrees.

As they leave, Derrick lingers before closing the gate behind him. "Thank you" he mouths silently after his sister has darted off toward their home.

***

Pulling the garbage out from the yard, I'm just about to head back inside when movement out of the corner of my eye catches my attention. I look over the lawn into the open lot next door, where Dee and Derrick have their patio set up. Also home to their rabbit, Fiver.

There's a young man there, no, a boy. He can't be older than fourteen, I realize as my eyes adjust. He's standing on the lawn, on my side, staring at the cage, staring at the rabbit, I realize. Drool puddles on his lips. He reaches through the cage, trying to unlatch the door.

"Hey!" I call to him. He freezes and looks at me. I want to offer him some food, to tell him to leave the rabbit alone, but he's already bolted toward the back of the park, into what I thought was woods and perhaps a fence somewhere. I don't even know what's on the other side, come to think of it. He's too fast for me to chase.

He's gone for now, but I don't know how safe Fiver is. I pull my mask over my face and head over to Derrick and Dee's place, knocking on the door.

"Hey," Derrick seems surprised to see me when he answers.

"Sorry to bother you, but the weirdest thing just happened."

I tell him about the sad sight of the hungry kid who almost snatched his sister's rabbit for dinner. Then I help him relocate Fiver into the house.

"It'll be a tight squeeze, but I'll make it work. Mom will understand. If anything happens to that bunny, Dee will flip. So, thank you."

"No problem."

Chapter 57

The Caretaker

I can't even stand to smell myself by the time I finished setting out the drilled pipe to irrigate the back side of the park. Days of heavy rains left a swamp that will soon become a mosquito haven, My sweat and the late fall heat mingle, and the smell fills my nose. In the kind of way that I know will linger even after a good shower. I wipe the sweat off my face with the back of one forearm.

That's when I see her. For the first time since that old blowhard shot her dog. I haven't wanted to be intrusive, but I haven't seen her around much and was getting concerned.

Stepping out from the mud and leaves, I head toward the road so she can see me. I give a friendly nod and gauge her reaction. She slows down and waves, then halts as if she's waiting to see if I will say any more.

"Hey," I begin, not sure what to say next, "I won't get too much closer, been working on irrigating this glorious pond all afternoon, but, I wanted to ask how you were holding up."

Her face relaxes slightly.

"I'm doing okay. I mean, by 2020 standards, I guess."

"I know about what happened to your dog. Not to bring up something painful again, but I wanted to say, I'm sorry."

"Yeah, well, thanks, I guess. I mean instead of apologizing, maybe you can be the trump whisperer and talk sense to your people."

I laugh at what she's insinuating. "My people? No."

"So, you're not one of them? Do they know that?"

"They know I'm the guy that gets a knock on his door when their toilets break, or their yard is flooded. But no, I don't get invited to the barbecues. And just as well."

She seems satisfied with this explanation, but still eyes me suspiciously.

"How can you stand it here?" she asks. I wonder if she remembers we've had this conversation.

"What, this paradise? You mean it's not the Garden of Eden?" I try to lighten the mood.

"No, seriously. If you're not like them, how can you stand to live here, knowing this is what your neighbors are all about." As she says this, she gestures toward the trump 2020 flags.

"Do I need to remind you that you live here too?"

"I know. But how do you stand it?"

"When your options have been limited, you learn to make do with what you have. It's better than some places I've lived. This place may be a step down for you. For some of us, it's a step up from nothing. Try to remember that."

She nods her head, as if she's considering it.

If looks could kill. She's giving me a laser beam right in the eyes.

"I fucking hate it here."

She says it as if it's my fault. Like I made her come here. Like I'm responsible for what happens here. Which, in a way, I am.

"I can imagine. Not everyone here is like Dave. Give it time. You'll see."

As I say these words, something churns in my stomach, a gut sense that I may have spoken too soon.

"Right," she says, and then heads back toward her place. I didn't mean to come across as an asshole. It's the truth. I take off my work gloves and shake them off against a tree to dislodge the layers of caked on mud and leaves. Walking back to my place, I notice the fence that went up quick. Surrounding the lot where the new people moved in.

It's not like most of the fences here. It's taller. You can't even see the trailer on the other side. Excessive, far too high for a kid to climb over or a dog to jump over. I guess it's a good privacy fence. If you're really serious about your privacy.

Someone left the gate open just slightly.

Curiosity gets the better of me. After all, I'm the Caretaker. It's my job to keep an eye on the place. If anyone sees me, I'll pretend I was heading in to check in on them.

I approach the gate, left ajar, and peer inside. Plastic totes are piled up in one corner outside the trailer. And in the far corner of the lot, a figure's silhouette. I jump back on instinct, but something wasn't right.

Silently, I lean in, holding my breath, and adjust my eyes. No, not a figure. At least not a person.

A full scale outline. In the shape of a person. The kind you use for target practice.

Chapter 58

Justin

If I had known the hot new lady was gonna knock on my door, I would have taken time to check out how I looked before I opened it. Here she is, on my doorstep, looking fine.

"Hello!" She says to me, "I'm Bianca. My husband and I moved in recently over there," she points to what used to be an empty lot but has since been fully set up with a new trailer, fencing, the works.

"Yeah, I've seen you guys moving in."

"And your name is?" She asks. I feel like an idiot.

"Justin, I'm Justin. My mom and her friend Stu live here, but they're not home now."

I figure I would give her a hint. I know she's married but come on, don't you find it a little funny that she would show up on my doorstep in the middle of the day all dressed nice and whatnot?

She doesn't take the bait. Playing hard to get, I guess. Instead, she says, "well, that's fine. I'm just introducing myself and letting everyone know we are offering some casual get-togethers in the coming week. I know it's been a rough year, everyone being forced to stay alone, so we are putting together some activities for people who believe in patriotic American values."

She hands me her card. She's got a business card with her name and number. Real slick, a real clever way to get around her husband. I'll give her that. There's something else. Her card has the same logo as Jordan's group. The Golden Apple.

I smile. We're part of the same club already. Things just keep getting better. I wonder if Jordan has told her about me, and then I realize Jordan is probably not the kind of guy that would give a woman access to such elite secrets. Not even a hot woman.

"Oh, I see you're part of Jordan's group. So am I." I let the words hang in the air, waiting to see her reaction. She plays coy.

"There are many patriots among us. You may be surprised," she says.

Lady, you have no idea; I think to myself.

Chapter 59

Marie

I look out over the lake. The sun is setting, and tourist season is mostly over. I'm glad for the break. It makes it easier to enjoy the scenery. Maybe, under different circumstances, if it was less contagious out and if this place hadn't become a haven for racists and fools, maybe I would actually enjoy it here.

I look up at the bridge and think of Jackie bounding across it on our walks, then back to the water, where I imagined we'd go swimming next summer. Maybe there will be a next summer, at least for some of us. And maybe it won't be that bad.

Maybe by then there will even be another dog.

I shake the thought away. It's too soon.

I walk along the lake, then through the marina parking lot. The RV park on the other side of a chain link fence is all packed up and officially closed for the season.

Bob's Park. The sign reads.

The light is fading, but I swear I see someone in there. Maybe a chicken or two. They wander around down here, I've seen them before, and Jackie used to try to chase them.

This isn't a chicken.

I lean in closer and walk along the fence to get a better view. No one is supposed to be in there. Then again, why would anyone follow rules?

From this closer vantage point, my eyes adjust. I see a woman. And beside her a kid. He looks familiar, and it takes a moment, but I place him as the kid who tried to eat Dee's rabbit. The woman, I suspect, is his mom. The third, I recognize instantly. The Caretaker.

Before I can complete the question of what he's doing here, he hands them a cloth bag filled with what I recognize as vegetables from the community garden. I see him pointing in the direction of the park.

I head back to the park before they are finished, wanting to make it home before our paths cross so I can avoid conversation. Still puzzled by how he found them, I recall a scene from a few months ago. Police, kicking down tents, destroying an encampment.

I wonder if this family had always lived in Bob's Park, or if it is the latest safe spot they've found. Where they assume no one will bother them.

Chapter 60

October 27, 2020

Early Voting Day

Marie

So much for getting an early start. I pull into the Clifton Park Library, realizing too late that I wasn't the only one who had this idea today. The lot is already full. It's a half hour before early voting starts for New York. I take a deep breath and let it out slowly. Creeping through the lot, my foot hovering over the brake pedal, I finally find an empty space.

It's cold. Of all the days for it to feel like fall, this is not the one. Some people, no doubt expecting to run in and out as we normally do when voting, are wearing shorts. No jackets. A bunch of people throughout the line that now snakes around the lot give up and leave, perhaps deciding to try their luck another time.

It's so fucking cold. But I'm here. And I'm not leaving. I walk toward what seems like it's the end of the line, but a woman informs me I'm mistaken. She points toward the very far corner of the parking lot, by the dumpster. That is the end of the line. I'm still early. Even as I claim my spot, more and more people are piling in. Luckily, they are all wearing masks.

After chatting with the woman in line ahead of me, I'm not sure whether to be relieved or annoyed. We're on the same mission, but here she is, wide eyed and idealistic. Talking about how we have to "pray for the best outcome."

"You know what Mother Jones said," I begin, "pray for the dead and fight like hell for the living."

"Mother who?" she asks, before waving a hand dismissively. "I don't like to feed into the negativity. I'm just going to cast my vote for Biden and pray for the best."

Figures, I think to myself. I can picture her in a modest overpriced house. Maybe in one of the more crowded cul-de-sacs. I imagine her talking to her friends. Criticizing people on the ground who have actually been, doing the work as she sits in the comfort of her living room sofa, I imagine her sharing all the right progressive memes, but not lifting a finger to do anything else. Other than voting every four years. And convincing herself she's done all she possibly can.

I take a breath, not wanting to pick a fight.

"Your thoughts and prayers got us here!" I want to scream.

Instead, I turn my back and survey the growing line.

The crowd is tame. No trump caravans, no armed Proud Boys. In fact, for all the people I can see very few of them actually have trump hats or flags. If they are here en masse, they aren't making it obvious.

Still, I'm vigilant.

The line fills in behind me. A young lady approaches, library book in hand.

"If you just needed to drop your book off, you don't have to wait in line," I joke with her.

"I've got an absentee ballot and a book to return. Then I have to go pick up my son. His father's gonna freak out if I'm late. I didn't expect there to be so many people."

"I've never seen anything like this, and I've been voting for twenty years," I tell her.

I wonder if this is her first election.

"I wasn't going to miss this for anything. I don't care if my son's dad is mad. We need to get this crazy asshole out of the Whitehouse."

Well, that answers that question. I look around and notice some of the well-dressed white women farther up ahead in the line. They

Angela Kaufman

look down their noses at us. Apparently they won't announce themselves here, but their body language tells me in other settings they'd be wearing red hats.

"I tried to order a mail in ballot, but it never came, so here I am," I tell her.

We make small talk. How old is your son? How has he been adjusting to the pandemic and being home from school?

Thoughts and Prayers, it turns out, is a nice liberal self-employed woman who runs a Yoga Studio in the area. I wonder which one of the dozen or so she is referring to, but I don't ask.

Absentee Ballot Lady works the overnight shift at Saratoga Hospital. I tell her she should get an honorary cut-the-line-pass as a thank you for doing that job, especially now.

We exchange friendly banter of the polite but politically progressive nature. After twenty minutes, a guy with a lanyard and nametag, clipboard in hand, comes walking down the line to tell us the news. There was a problem with the machines, and they are only now opening the doors.

"Sabotage much?" I ask no one in particular.

A few people behind me, including an older woman, watch intently. Her long gray hair waves in the wind. She wears a Tie-dyed shirt that she's probably had for a half a century. I can't tell if she's smiling or scowling because her mask covers the lower half of her face, as it should.

Still, I get the feeling that maybe she doesn't agree with our discourse. I wonder if she's glaring at us because she wants to curse us out.

After a while of our collective yammering about who we want to win, what we think should be done about the economy, the virus, the police, she chimes in.

"My arthritis is killing me, but I'm gonna stick this out because this may be our last election, if you know what I mean."

"Oh yes, I know what you mean," I reassure her.

A few more minutes into the conversation and it's clear, Tie Dye is definitely the woman I would want to be holed up with in a ditch somewhere when the revolution comes. Absentee Ballot Lady has the right ideas, but I don't know if she fully comprehends the seriousness of the situation. As for Thoughts and Prayers, well, I have a feeling she has been praying for the last four years that trump gets voted out so she can go back to hosting pool parties without her conscience bothering her.

I pull out my phone, my battery is low. I can't help texting Andre. "Hey, you voting today? Crazy long line here, be safe!"

They text back a few minutes later, "ya, been in line for a half hour, don't know if I'll make it today. May have to come back. No trump trains yet, though."

Even here, people are walking away, discouraged. Some have to leave for work. Others are obviously past their comfort zone, lips turning blue, physically shivering. I know Andre will vote, be it today, tomorrow, the next day.

The local news is here setting cameras on tripods; no doubt surprised by the spectacle.

I think of my grandmother. Four years ago, she had ambled around the corner from her home to her polling place. All four feet eight of her held up by a walker. She had gone to cast her vote. A local news channel had interviewed her. She looked directly into the camera and declared that she wouldn't miss election day because it was her civic responsibility to vote.

She didn't know it would be her last vote. She didn't know then that the man one of her sons helped put into office would fail her during a pandemic that she also couldn't have imagined. The pandemic she wouldn't survive.

I can see her talking about her time working as a nurse. Sitting in a wheelchair, recounting her many travels across the country. I think of her talking of her many friends, and slowly counting away the list of many friends she had outlived.

To touch so many lives and still die alone. Among strangers. Her closest kin only allowed to peer in from outside a window. Unaware and unable to comprehend what was happening. She had voted in about twenty elections. And as I looked around the crowded lot of huddled masses freezing our asses off, I would have bet she never saw anything like this.

It takes three hours to even get inside the library. By then we've run out of small talk. Absentee Ballot Lady has had the chance to drop off her ballot and head out to her son. I've decided I can't take much more of Thoughts and Prayers and have had a nice conversation with Tie Dye.

Politics aside, she's excited. Her job as a personal care aid has given so much overtime the past few months that she's finally paid off her trailer.

"What park are you living in?" I ask, hopeful that maybe she's a neighbor I haven't met yet. No such luck. She lives outside of Halfmoon. I congratulate her and think of the Caretaker's words. That for some this is a step up. After paying someone else all of her adult life, Tie Dye now has a place of her own. Except, I think, reflecting on all she's told me about the work she's done. She deserves better.

We all do.

Finally, four hours later, I cast my ballot. Thinking of how the life we all deserve will still elude us, no matter who wins.

Chapter 61

Halloween

Marie

Another Halloween, but this year, no plans to open the door for kids seeking candy. No costume parties. No binge-watching scary movies with friends. No laughing at the ridiculous makeup and special effects of some of the classics.

I think of the older woman. What did she call herself? Crazy Dottie? She'll be standing under the Full Moon tonight, I think, as I set the photos up on a small end table. My grandmother's photo is the newest addition on this altar to the departed. Surrounded by photos of past Ancestors who knew enough to get out while life was still good. I imagine them, heading into the Afterlife with fond memories of their time here on Earth, I wonder if they would recognize what we've become.

And another photo, of Jackie. Tears form in my eyes.

I light candles. A sliver of light appears, and then another and another.

I know Source is still there, but it feels too far away. Maybe the Goddess has better sense than to hang around a place like this. But Dee was right. And so was Crazy Dottie. Death isn't the end.

They're still with us.

But then, why does it feel like I've been left here to rot alone?

You mean, the way your grandmother was left to die by herself? The voice chimes in from the recesses of my mind.

Yeah, like that. I answer out loud.

They're still with me, I tell myself. I just can't feel it because I've gone off grid. From the mundane world, from the Spiritual world, that was the intention, right? To find a place to dwindle into oblivion? Mission accomplished, I guess.

Chapter 62

Dee

I saw Halloween on TV. I didn't get to go to houses to get candy. Because of lock down. I didn't have a costume. Last time I went trick-or-treating, Taylor Bishop's mom took me when we all went with their friends. I asked Mom for a costume. To be a princess. With a dress like Elsa. And a crown. And gloves.

She got me a crown but it wasn't like Elsa.

"What about the princess dress?"

"You have your dress from the Christmas party a few years ago, wear that. I can't afford a new one just for Halloween," Mom said.

She dug in the closet to get it. I didn't say anything. Because you're not supposed to make Mom sad about money. Mom works hard for us, Derrick Torrey says, so don't make her feel bad if we don't have money for something new.

That's the rule.

It's also the rule to wear a costume on Halloween. A new costume, that is just part of the trick-or-treating. What happens if you wear a Christmas dress for a Halloween costume?

The dress was green and velvety, and it fit, but the shoulders were tight. I remember how it itched and squeezed my arms. How Mom had to put the crown on my head because I couldn't lift my arms. How the other kids asked where my costume was. They didn't believe me. Said I was cheating. Just wearing regular clothes for Halloween.

That was bad. But at least there was a fake costume. This year, there is no costume. No friends. No trick-or-treating.

Fiver is in my room now. Mom said he could come in. I give him baby carrots. I wonder if anyone else has a costume this year. Walking through the house, I don't see Derrick. The bathroom door is closed. I open the front door.

I'll only be a minute.

It's crisp and cold out. I don't have my jacket on. No time. I wander from the trailer and look up and down the road. I hear children laughing. Maybe trick-or-treating. Where the new people moved in. They brought their home. It's nice. Better than ours.

They put up a big fence. Like the new lady. But I went into her yard and she was nice.

I walk up to this fence and peek inside. I don't know who all the kids are. They're having a party.

"Who are you?"

A girl inside the fence sees me. Her hair and shirt are yellow. She's skinny and her face looks bossy. Two boys standing with her stop their play and watch as I open the gate. Her hands are on her hips.

"Dani Torrey, but I like to be called Dee."

I look from curious face to curious face. All strangers. Do they live in this house? In the yard? I think of shows on TV with animals in a farm and imagine the kids all in a room like chickens. They're dressed the same. Yellow shirts. Blue pants. Except the girls. They have long blue skirts. Are these costumes?

"Are you having a Halloween party?"

The girl laughs but walks closer to me. I don't know if I want to play with them. The others follow her. There are so many.

"Halloween is for heathens!"

I don't know what that word means. She says it like it's a bad word.

"We're having a meeting. A Golden Appleseed meeting," she says.

"Is it like Girl Scouts?" I ask.

"It's only for people who pass the test." This time, it's a boy near her who answers. He looks bigger than me. I don't like him. I don't like tests. I don't want to come to this party. I changed my mind.

"Hey! What're you doing here?" a familiar voice yells from the back of the group. Don pushes his way through the crowd.

"Why aren't you with your big brother?" he asks. I don't answer. He continues, looking toward the other kids, "this is Dee. She's not one of us. She's white trash."

I've heard that name before. At school. When Becca Cliff found out where I live. I don't understand what she meant. At our house, the white trash is mostly paper, so it goes in the recycling container, not the trash. Maybe Becca Cliff doesn't recycle and was jealous.

"I've got an idea," Don suddenly says. I don't like this. My hands sweat. I can't breathe. I want to go home. I can't move. "Dee the dirty douchebag has a rabbit. Adam," he turns to another boy, "you like rabbits, don't you?"

"Yeah," Adam says.

"I like rabbit too!" Scott joins in.

"I like rabbit with barbecue sauce!" Don sneers. The girl, the one who led them to me, smiles. It doesn't look friendly.

The crowd approaches the gate now and I step back to the road. My eyes fixed on them. I walk backward and try to keep a distance.

"No!" I yell. Louder, and louder and louder. They chant "kill the rabbit!" I shout louder, frozen in place. I don't know when I started screaming.

I only know that suddenly, a lady is there. I've seen her before. She moved in with the trailer. Her blond hair is long and wavy, she's pretty. Her eyes are mean and angry and she reminds me of mean girls at school. Or like the person in a movie that everyone thinks is nice because she's pretty but she's really bad and they don't know until it's too late.

She kneels on the ground and looks at me, blocking my view of the crowd.

"It's okay," she says again and again. I can barely hear her at first. She turns to the crowd.

"Go back in the house. This is not how we conduct ourselves." She didn't yell, but she said it like a teacher. And they listened. Finally, they listened. They went back toward the house. When she turned back to me, Don smiled and put his middle finger up. Like you're not supposed to do. He knew I saw him and turned back around to join the others.

I stand, frozen in place.

"Are you okay?" she asks.

I'm frozen. I can't speak. I've stopped screaming. I can't answer. I want to go home.

"Dee! There you are!" It's Derrick Torrey.

"What happened?" he asks the lady.

"She wandered into one of our gatherings and the kids were joking around. Looks like they may have upset her. But you know, boys will be boys. You should really keep a closer eye on her."

That's not true. It is. But it isn't. They weren't joking. I know they weren't. Derrick takes my hand and pulls me toward the house. I look back once. The lady stands leaning on the gate. Her face no longer soft. Eyes looking mean. A yelling face.

"You can't wander off, Dee." Derrick says, opening the door.

"They were going to eat Fiver." I finally tell him.

"No one is going to eat Fiver," Derrick tells me. "But you need to stay away from that house. That house especially."

He doesn't have to tell me twice.

Chapter 63

November 2, 2020

Cyrus

Almost showtime. The red Ford pickup truck pulls up and I quickly take off my mask. The door opens and as I suspected, none of the guys inside are wearing one. I hope they weren't paying attention. I don't want them to think I was being a pussy.

"Hey! I'm Cy, nice to meet you," I shake hands with the two guys in the back who introduce themselves as Kevin and Steve. Dylan is the guy in the passenger seat. He looks to be about my age whereas the other guys are older, like in their forties or fifties. Old guys, but cool. Mitch is driving. I've been talking to Mitch online for weeks and finally I get to meet him. He's a smart guy. He told me he's been part of Golden Apple for a long time.

The older guys have full, long beards. I instinctively reach and feel the tiny bit of fuzz on my own chin. I've been trying to grow out a beard, but not having the best of luck. I reach for a seat belt but don't find one.

"Hey, don't worry about it, we're in the backseat, and besides, no one's gonna hassle Mitch, ain't that right?"

Mitch grins in agreement and pulls out. The other guys, they have red trump hats. I don't have one. My dad would kill me if I wore one in the house. I suddenly feel left out. Kevin must sense this because he digs around the back and pulls out a bag with at least five and gives me one.

"You can keep it, man."

"Thanks."

We hit the highway and I look up into the rearview mirror. I can see the giant flags flowing in the fall breeze. There are four of them. Two are trump 2020, one is a snake with the slogan Don't Tread on Me, and the other is a Thin Blue Line flag. I still haven't decided if I'm actually voting for trump, but I'm getting closer to deciding. Even if I don't though, we're off on a badass mission to collect liberal tears.

It feels good to be out of Dad's house for once and taking a road trip. I listen to the other guys talk. It feels good to be around people who are willing to tell it like it is, instead of being PC all the time.

Mitch is definitely Golden Apple, but I don't know if the other guys are. I assume they are, but I don't know if I should mention it. Usually, Golden Apple uniforms are pretty specific but Jordan's made it clear he doesn't want his people getting involved in the same antics as the lower rung trump people. So it could just be they aren't wearing their uniforms because we're on a mission.

"So what's our first stop?" Kevin asks.

"We're picking up a few more people and then heading to Jersey. To an official trump train rally through the city and back upstate. Ready to see the libs piss themselves?"

Did he say a few more people? I'm already in a tight squeeze with Kevin and Steve so I venture a question, not wanting to sound rude.

"Um, where are the other guys gonna fit?"

Mitch laughs. "The bed of the truck."

"Is that legal?" I ask.

"Don't matter, you're white, didn't anyone ever tell you that?" Kevin answers. We laugh. I guess he has a point. I've seen people ride in the back of trucks before, but on the highway? Damn, these guys don't mess around. I feel excited and kinda nervous at the same time.

Then things really get interesting.

Mitch suddenly speeds up, and I hit the seat hard, but I don't complain.

"Hey what's that all about?" Dylan asks.

"Look who just passed me," Mitch says, pointing out the front windshield. I regain my balance and lean up, looking far out to the road ahead. There's a tan SUV with a sticker on it that reads Black Lives Matter. The driver is a white dude.

"Fucking race traitor," Dylan says. As Mitch speeds up and changes lanes to close in on the SUV on the left side, Dylan rolls down his window and starts shouting.

I can't believe the words he's saying. I've read the banter online, it's so different actually hearing people say these words. Like out loud. In public. And no one is stopping them. The guys are cracking up now, jeering and taunting, and I laugh along with him, but I honestly don't know if I can say some of these words out loud without choking on them. I listen as the guys go back and forth, one-upping each other.

It's vile. And exciting. I could never be as ballsy as Dylan. Then Mitch slows down to keep pace with the SUV. I have to lean side to side around Kevin, on my right, but I can see the driver. He's shitting bricks. I mean, this guy looks like he's going to freak out and run right off the road.

Mitch has him blocked in now. I can tell the guy's scared because he's starting to drive like shit. Then, Dylan outdoes himself. He takes his giant soda from a fast-food place; I don't get a close enough look to see where, but it's one of the big plastic take-out sizes.

Mitch pulls up alongside the SUV and Dylan rolls the window down further. He leans way out of the truck and dumps the entire fucking thing on the SUV. Soda, ice and the container itself splatter all over the windshield, the roof and the driver's side window.

It's fucking glorious.

We're dying laughing. I swear, Steve looks like he's gonna cry, he's laughing so hard. Then Kevin says, "Run him off the road!"

My heart freezes. Would Mitch really do that? I look out the windows, there's plenty of cars on the road, but no cops around, no one to interfere with a flying soda cup. But a crash? To actually run him off the road in broad daylight and start a crash?

I don't want to seem like a pussy, but instead I suggest, "How about saving that for the way home? When it's dark? I mean, there's all these witnesses now."

"Witnesses to what?" Dylan asks, "If he has a problem driving and hits a ditch, that's his problem, isn't it?"

The guys laugh and I chuckle along with them. But really? I wonder. A crash? Like running the dude's car off the road?

My hands clench into fists and I try to conceal how nervous I suddenly am. Please don't do it, just don't do it, I say in my head, trying to will Mitch to keep driving before things get too crazy. I mean fun and games is one thing.

But.

But what?

What exactly did you sign up for? I hear Jordan's voice in my head.

"This is civil war, people. We're talking about preserving our way of life. Protecting our children and women from corruption. What are you willing to give?"

That's what he says, isn't it?

Now I'm really sweating.

Mitch is still playing cat and mouse with the SUV, letting him get a little bit ahead and then roaring up alongside of him. Then he drops back and roars up on the right side of him, keeping him guessing as he shuffles back and forth between the three lanes on the highway. This is getting dangerous.

But so is a war, right? I mean, when Jordan says civil war, he's not kidding, is he? So what is a minor fender bender in comparison to an all-out war? I mean, this is barely a warm-up, not even a skirmish.

I need to get a grip, and fast. Plans are already set, and I am part of those plans. And if I can't stomach a little fun on an afternoon drive, how the hell do I think I'm going to manage the mission I've signed up for?

Chapter 64

FBI Office

Cliff Rosen/Howard Jeffries

It's taken months but I finally got him. Just in time. Disparate groups are becoming emboldened in their efforts. Planning to target the electoral process, even going so far as to hijack Biden's tour bus.

That wasn't Golden Apple but could have been. I sign out of Howard Jeffries' account after taking screenshots of the most recent conversation.

Me, or I should say, Howard, bragging about the shenanigans from the trump truck rally this past weekend, careful to only observe and get discrete photos and audio recordings, careful not to partake in any of the illegal aspects of the weekend's festivities.

I put all the evidence into a folder and save it to my USB. Then I save it to a second USB, and this one, I slip into a pocket inside my shirt.

The original USB, with all the files needed to incriminate Jordan and his followers, as well as others in their loose network nationwide, are right here. All the proof we need to bring down Golden Apple. And it's a good thing because if we hadn't intercepted their plan, we would be headed for Civil War.

I sigh deeply, relieved. It's almost over.

I grab my phone and tuck it into my back pants pocket and head down the hallway. I knock on the door marked Jim Overton, Director Domestic Terrorist Unit.

"Come in!" Jim calls from his desk across the room. I open the door. He's fiddling with his phone and doesn't look up at first. He always does this. Too busy for everyone and everything, no matter how urgent.

"I got the final nail in the coffin for Jordan. Jordan Tennyson, the head of a loose knit white supremacist group calling themselves Golden Apple. Pictures, direct quotes, conversations, audio, the works. And they're planning something big. It's all here," I tell him, holding up the USB and waving it, trying in vain to get his attention.

"Humph," he grunts, "leave it on my desk here."

"I think we should have a conference about this right away, this is going to be-"

"Leave it, I'll take a look at it. Good job on this one," he says.

I wait a moment to see if he'll so much as look up from whoever he's texting. He doesn't.

I turn to leave and he calls out again to me, "Cliff," I look back over my shoulder. This time he's facing me. The USB is in his hand. He holds it up and repeats, "Good work with this."

I nod and open the door to leave.

Almost walk right into a wall of security personnel standing shoulder to shoulder.

Two on either end step forward, each grabbing one of my arms.

"What the fuck is this?"

NATIONAL SPOTLIGHT

FBI Domestic Terror Expert Found Dead
11/2/2020

The body of FBI Department of Domestic Terror Project Leader Cliff Rosen was found dead of what appeared to be a self-inflicted gunshot wound early yesterday morning. Police were notified after Rosen failed to report to work for several days in a row.

Rosen's supervisor, Jim Overton, reports Rosen's job was in jeopardy when it was brought to light that Rosen was a member of a far-right nationalist hate group. "We just can't afford to have people of questionable character in this department. It's a shame he resorted to these measures, but I think it is a testament to his poor mental health," Overton said, in a statement from the department on Rosen's death.

Chapter 65

Barbara

"I can't tell you how good it feels to finally get to do something for me for a change!" I tell Janice as she rubs the massage oil on my back. It's been forever since I've been allowed to get a good hot stone massage. Thank goodness Janice is a doll and was willing to come to my home and work on my back even during the shutdown.

Now that she's back open, well, it's my civic duty to support local businesses, no?

She's only just started and already I feel like I'm melting. Something's wrong. I lean up and look over my shoulder.

"Janice, would you mind being a dear and letting me take this dreadful thing off?" I ask, pointing to my mask that I've been forced to wear. I swear it's like soviet Russia. What's next? Yellow stars?

She looks perplexed but must see the desperation on my face and nods her head.

"Thank you, and I promise I'll keep my face down here, not breathing in your direction," I say, hoping to reassure her. I take the horrid thing off my face and relax my face back down into the face cradle. Now it feels divine. Everything just as it should be before people lost their minds because the media told them to.

I fall asleep during the massage, it's so relaxing. Even drooled on the face cradle a little. I wipe my mouth before Janice can see. Besides, I'm sure she's used to it. It's what people pay her for, after all.

Golden Apple

When my session is over, I slip back into my outfit, another treat after months of self-sacrifice. I feel like I'm walking on air as I exit Janice's office. She shares a building with several other practitioners. I stop to grab my phone and call Stephanie, whom I'm supposed to meet for lunch. A flyer on the bulletin board catches my eye.

First, the words, "Do you long to get back to simpler times, and connect with people who share your traditional values?"

Sounds good, I think, walking closer to read the details. There's a phone number and a website, and an adorable little logo.

A golden apple.

Chapter 66

The Caretaker

"What the hell did these fools do now?"

There's a chance of course that it was just an animal. Maybe a squirrel got into it. Maybe some mice, God knows there are mice and cats and gophers, raccoons all running wild here.

Somehow I don't think so. It just doesn't seem likely. I can fix it, but it will tie up my morning. If it ain't one thing, it's another.

I reach my gloved hand into the box and push past the telephone and other cables. It's the internet cables. Something doesn't look right. As if someone tried to rig something into the wires.

But why the hell would someone do that?

Chapter 67

Dee

Taylor Bishop hasn't come to class yet. I look around the room again. I don't see her. Maybe she is still on lock down. I look at the board. Mr. Roberts is writing. He writes the date. He writes a message for the day. Someone coughs. I look. It's Matthew Thompsen, across the room. Darren Cleveland pushes him and says he's going to start a pandemic. Gavin Fryer throws a crumpled paper at him. He looks around. No one else talks.

Mr. Roberts saw it. He doesn't say anything. He just stands with his arms folded. He looks mad. Mad looks don't do anything. He's supposed to say something. Eventually, they turn to the board and pretend to be paying attention. They weren't. I saw it. So did Mr. Roberts.

I write the message for the day in my notebook.

"Dee," Mr. Roberts says, "it's your turn to feed Chompers today." I nod and put my pen down, careful so it doesn't fall. I walk to the back of the class. I don't like how the other kids watch me. How my broken sneaker makes fart noises when it scrapes on the floor. How they giggle and whisper when I walk by. I don't look back at Mr. Roberts, but I know he's probably making the mad face. But not saying anything.

Chompers is in the tank in the back of the class. Derrick Torrey says tanks aren't good for rabbits. That's why Fiver has a cage. So he can breathe. Chompers can't breathe like Fiver can. I approach the tank. Mr. Roberts said Chompers, but the rabbit in the tank is Fiver.

Fiver has been in the bad tank. Where he couldn't breathe. I pick him up and rub wood shavings off his twitchy nose.

"Are you hungry?" I ask him with my mind. He says yes.

"Dee…" a voice taunts behind me, "Daaaaani… Dee isn't a name. It's a letter. It means dumbass." I freeze, holding Fiver tight. I know the voice. He's not in my class. Why is he here? I don't want to turn around. I don't want to. I don't. I won't.

"Shhh," I tell Fiver with my mind.

"Dee, I'm hungry." The voice says from behind me. And now footsteps. Walking closer. I pull up the bottom of my t-shirt, wrapping it around Fiver to hold him in place.

"Dee, we're all hungry. You've got to let us eat. We all want to eat."

As I turn to face the direction of the voice, the lights start to flicker. My heart is pounding. It hurts to breathe. Like I'm in a tank. Don Swansen is in my class. He's not supposed to be here. He's supposed to be upstairs, with the big kids.

He's standing in the aisle, walking between desks, coming toward me. The floor screeches as Darren Cleveland pushes his chair back, hovering over his desk. Matthew Thompsen follows his lead. Then Melissa Pompinau.

Now they are all standing, chairs creaking. Lights still flickering. I hold Fiver close.

"We're hungry," Don Swansen says again.

I look to Mr. Roberts again. He's not even making the angry face. He just stares.

"We're hungry," Don Swansen repeats.

He's getting closer now. I back up almost to the wall.

"We're hungry, and we're coming for you."

The lights go out.

I begin screaming. Nowhere to run, I bang the wall with a fist. I hear someone call my name. Again and again and again. Until I open my eyes and see Derrick Torrey.

"Wake up!" he says, "you're having a bad dream."

Part IV Regime Change

Chapter 68

Election Day

Cyrus

I'd been to the park a few times. It's a hangout for jam band followers and people who don't mind living a little rough when they're in town to catch a concert at SPAC. Lined with RVs and the most basic camps you can imagine. But it's right on Saratoga Lake and you can't beat that.

Now it looks nothing like the casual party spot I knew a few summers ago. I don't know how these guys got permission to do this, but right at the entry, beside the electronic sign telling the rest of the world that the park is closed for the season, they've got tables set up, checking guys in.

Not just guys, some families, but mostly guys.

"Name?" A guy in a windbreaker, his gold shirt collar visible beneath, and navy blue pants asks me when it's my turn. He doesn't even look up to see my face. I could be a Black dude for all he knows.

"Cyrus. Cyrus Dixon."

He scrolls down on his tablet screen, looking through some database, then, finding my name, I assume, he touches a button, and proceeds to question me.

"What are your skills?"

"I'm okay with computers. I can build stuff. I know a little bit about fixing cars."

He punches in words I can't see with one index finger.

"Are you trained in armed combat?"

I'm stumped. "No, not really."

"Military service?"

"No."

"First Aid experience?"

"Oh, well, yeah, I was a lifeguard. I can do CPR and stuff."

His finger punches at the screen again.

"Are you the direct descendants of Jews or any mongrel race?"

I wince. I understand the importance of national pride and protecting western civilization, but, do they really need to say it that way?

"No, sir."

"Have you ever been convicted of a crime?"

"No."

"Do you own property, cars or other valuables?"

"Um, no."

"What is your net worth?"

* * *

Right hand stamped with an apple, papers in my other hand, I make my way into the encampment. A man with a lanyard and badge, holding a clipboard, directs traffic. There are hundreds of us. He sees me and checks my papers. Most of it was weird code, stuff I don't understand.

Like net worth.

"What, you mean like my money? I don't know, a few hundred dollars in a savings bank. My dad has some trusts for me, but he manages that. I don't really know the details." I had told him.

It made me uneasy. Why he would even ask.

The unofficial traffic controller shows me to the RV I'll be sharing with a few other guys for the duration of the convention. "And who knows, maybe longer," he joked.

My job, he said, is to join the team of scouts and scope out the area for what he called degenerates.

"What do you mean, degenerates?"

He looks at me blankly, so I try to clarify.

"I've heard that term used a few different ways, so just want to make sure I catch your meaning."

"Derelicts. Homeless people. They sometimes squat here. Now, we don't want to beat 'em up or set 'em on fire or anything like that. If you can, try to see if they're open to helping the cause, if you know what I mean. Offer them some food, tell them we've got plenty of jobs for people willing to work.

I nod. But I'm not sure what the jobs are. As far as I've heard, all of the work we've been doing has been volunteer, or for privileges within the organization. Either way, not my place to question.

* * *

Maybe they keep a low profile or maybe they blend in with the crowds, but I'm beginning to think that if there are homeless people around, they keep to themselves. I'm just about to call it quits, having walked the length of Bob's park, when I see something move quickly in a cluster of trees.

A squirrel? I wonder at first, walking closer just to be sure.

There's a kid there. Face unwashed, clothes too big for his small frame and worn thin. He looks at me like he's going to bolt but there's no place to run. I start to tell him how I can help him get some food, some money.

Kid looks terrified of me. I don't know why. A woman, his mom, I'm guessing, she comes down the path just then and takes him by the shoulder.

"We're all set, thank you," she tells me.

I'm not sure what to do. I was given orders to get them on our side. So I just say "Look, you may as well check out what we're doing. You can get some food and a place to stay and a job and"

"We're good, thanks, we're just passing through."

She puts an arm around the kid and they both walk through the woods, in the direction opposite the camp.

No wonder these people don't go anywhere in life.

Chapter 69

November 3, 2020

The Caretaker

It's something short of a miracle that nothing has gone awry here in the park. What with a good three quarters of my neighbors flagrantly letting their trump flags fly and the other quarter, who knows?

So far, the drama has stayed at bay. Sure, folks were less friendly this summer, but that's fine. Folks stopped inviting me to barbecues, the first time I declined to eat a hot dog. The whole *men eat meat* bullshit.

That's alright by me. I don't give them the satisfaction of knowing where I stand on things. I've found it's far better to watch, listen, let people think what they will. Tensions are high, even if the shit has managed to avoid the fan thus far.

If we can make it through the night, then maybe tomorrow the flags will come down and we can all just go back to being regular old poor rednecks. United in our lack of retirement, credit scores and close proximity to being out on the streets.

Maybe.

I turn on the TV, may as well watch this shit show on a bigger screen, and sink down in the worn sofa. Pundits are boring me with their prattle, so I grab my guitar and start to strum, mindlessly.

"This just in, Vermont goes to Joe Biden," the man on the TV proclaims, perhaps a bit more enthusiastically than he was supposed to.

My fingers find the rhythm and I sing quietly as the projections continue, back and forth.

"I get the news I need on the weather report, yeah..."

The music louder now, it echoes in the trailer in a way that takes me out of reality just enough, just the way I like.

"Yeah, I've got nothing to do today but..."

The voice breaks in

"Kansas goes to donald trump."

No shit, I think, finishing *The Only Living Boy in New York*. In my head I hear the applause. Never much, just a coffee shop full or a crowd on a busy downtown street. Enough that when the crowd disperses, there'll be a few bills in my guitar case. In my mind I see myself pausing so they could take photos or ask questions, do you have a card? can you play Free bird?

To which the answers were always no and no.

I tinker around with the strings again and the rhythm changes a few times. It's been over a decade since I last voted. Since they took away my rights, threw me into a cell and labeled me a felon. Since I decided I would have nothing to do with their corrupt government, and that includes voting. If the whole system implodes on itself, well, so be it.

In all this time I've been waiting. I just never thought the resistance would be so weak when the time finally came.

As I turn to the television again, the anchor, this time a woman, announces West Virginia has gone to trump, and my fingers strum the melody to It's the End of the World as We Know It.

* * *

Shari

I didn't like it at first, to be honest. The meetings, so frequent, seemed demanding. But, it's worked. My boys are suddenly perfect little gentleman. They've become so respectful. And they're actually learning more from the new people than they've probably learned all year from their liberal schoolteachers.

Joni, whose been a mess since she got out of that crazy cult, even she seems to be finding her purpose now. I think she may even have a crush on one of them. But it's changed her, and for the better. She still does her weird woo-woo things, but she's become more practical.

She even helped them build some of the temporary camps down by the lake. For the big convention. I'm sure it would have been bigger if not for Emperor Cuomo's ridiculous fear mongering. But Joni, who never lifted a finger to do anything that may chip a nail or get her hands dirty, she was helping to put this whole community together.

So I said, "what the heck?" Started to give them the benefit of the doubt. Spending more time there, helping with the garden and the kids and the home schooling and the community nights.

So even though I don't usually make a big deal out of election night, I mean I vote, but I don't really follow politics, still, when they invited us to come to their big election night shin dig, I said "Sure!"

I made a few casseroles, Joni actually helped me. The boys got all dressed up in their little uniforms. Suddenly, it's the closest to a party we've had here just about all year.

No alcohol, of course, because that threatens the intellect and dulls the senses. I've learned thanks to Bianca, that this type of mind control is actually a part of the Deep State's agenda. Some of the guys weren't thrilled about that rule, especially Vinny, he loves his homemade wine, but you really can't argue with logic and some things are more important than a glass of wine.

Instead we have punch, lasagna, tacos, and pizzas. I think there's more food here than there are people. Everyone's really put their heads together to make this feel like a community again and that's nice. Even Dave has lightened up a little. Been less grumpy and more excited about the new friendships he's made.

The trailer isn't huge, but it's bigger than most in the park. Still, some are camped out on the lawn and congregating outside in the training areas and meeting areas.

I've been going back and forth, refilling plates, playing the hostess. My favorite thing. Only barely paying attention to the fuss in the living room where the others, mostly the men, are glued to the television.

They erupt in boos just now.

"What happened?" I asked Missy, one of the other wives, who has been paying more attention.

"Biden just won in Virginia. No doubt because their governor is in bed with Antifa and crazy radical terrorists."

I panic. It's early still, I remind myself. Everything I've heard about Biden terrifies me.

"Can you believe our parents fought to end communism and these people want to make it the law of the land?" I ask her.

"It'll be over my dead body," her husband, Joe, interjects, putting an arm around her.

"Well, let's hope it doesn't come to that," I say, smiling. This is the part I don't like. The messiness, the hostility. I turn away to check on the food and supplies.

* * *

Dottie

I don't need the news to tell me what's coming. One wins, the other wins, either way, we're headed for war. It ain't gonna be pretty, either, but who listens to Crazy Dottie?

Fritzie, the oldest of my cats, and the plumpest, has been following me all day. I lift him on to my lap.

"You know it's coming too, don't you?" I ask him.

He doesn't have to answer, I know. He howled me awake last night and there I was in the midst of a dream, fire and destruction. It was too late to run, but there was some hope for the children escaping.

"But then you woke me up, didn't you? With your howling? Because you knew it was a nightmare? Or because you wanted to go out and try to get laid?"

He purrs dismissively as I scratch his ear.

No, tonight is not the time to fawn over the television. There will be no winners, mark my words. Tonight we pray to the Goddess, to guide us out of this mess, whatever the outcome may be. It's all right here. In the *Book of Discordia*. Just as we were warned, but who would listen? Who listens to reason anymore?

I light the candles on my altar and turn on the CD player. I put in an Enya disc for a little mood music and light the incense.

Then, with Fritzie on my lap, I see the doors between the realms open, and She is there.

* * *

Marie

"Ooooooo OAK la homa where the racists run around the plains!" Andre sings in their best imitation of a maudlin Broadway performance.

"Don't tell me, he got Oklahoma too?" I begin, I'd been distracted by the news.

"Well, come on, we know dis," they add, mimicking Kate McKinnon's new character on Saturday Night Live.

"We know dis," I reply, but my heart is racing.

"Have you been able to sleep at all this week?" I ask them.

"No, you?"

"Same here."

"Have you gone door to door converting the people of Dogpatch?" Andre teases.

"You know, for all the trump flags and Gadsden flags in this place, there are actually a few really cool people here. The people next door put up a Biden sign last week and so far, no explosions. I actually am starting to like a few of my neighbors. There's this wild older lady,

Dottie. I think you'd love her. She's full of piss and vinegar. One of the kids here, this girl Jess, is pretty cool, her family is nuts though. The family next door is nice. Another lady, Josephine, she's been friendly. Her son's a creep though. I mean there's still the new people who have a life size target outside on their lawn which is fucked up. But some of them are not so bad."

"That's no surprise. Just don't tell the 'nice white liberals' because the rate this is going, they're gonna need some poor rural folks to blame for dropping the ball again." Andre chuckles.

"Right? Vilify poor people rather than admit that Biden was the weakest possible choice and he's going up against an evil genius."

"Glad you're having a change of heart about the neighbors, fam. But I do just want to call you out on your classism. You need to work on that."

"My classism?" I can't tell if Andre is joking or not. "May I remind you that you were the one calling it Dogpatch."

"True, but I don't move in to take advantage of the low cost of living and then get all condescending thinking I'm smarter than everyone and they're out to get me."

"Okay," I'm getting pissed now, "I didn't accuse them all of being out to get me, I just happen to observe the lack of consideration for pandemic protocols made up for by an abundance of jingoism. Oh, and the park's resident trump supporter killed my dog."

"Alright, but remember, people who are routinely forced to neglect their health in order to make ends meet aren't going to suddenly become health conscious. They've been told to work without concern for their safety. So they internalize that toxic masculinity and aren't going to care about safety measures because no one has cared about their safety in forever. This translates into a denial of vulnerability, not just a denial of science."

I sigh. "You're right. I came in defensive. Maybe I didn't give people a fair chance because of it."

"Glad we had this little talk," they say, "but I'm still not gonna visit you there."

"Yes. We know dis."

We laugh and then I change the subject. "What are you going to do if he wins again?"

"I don't know, but it may taste like almonds."

"Stop!" I yell, louder than I intended. "Don't joke about that!"

"Well, it won't be my first step, but, Marie, if he wins, all hell is really going to break loose. The next four years will make the last four look tame. To be honest, I don't know what I'm going to do. I have family in France, I thought about moving there, but now with COVID that's not an option."

"Well, he got what he wanted, we're walled in for all practical purposes."

There's a moment of silence. My heart is sinking. As awful as another four years will be for me, it will be worse for Andre. And I can't help them.

"Well, I guess we've got to fight then, and this nonviolence bullshit isn't going to do it. I hate to say it, but it's just not."

"I hear you. Are you armed?" I ask.

"No, you?"

"Nope."

"Well, we're fucked."

***

Justin

My favorite thing, if I'm being honest, is the kids. I love getting the chance to teach them the shit no one was around to teach me. No Dad, no big brother, not even so much as a cousin. I mean, it's not that my mom was a libtard or anything. It's just that she doesn't realize how she's stuck in the lies of feminism and multiculturalism.

How could she possible have taught me the truth if she didn't know it?

But these kids… these kids are the future. And they're getting the best possible education. I watch them now, as I'm sitting on Bianca and Tom's porch. The sun has set hours ago, but the citronella torches surrounding the yard give enough glow that they can march around the lawn and play at combat.

"Kill Antifa!" One yells.

That's my man, right there.

Inside, the other guys are watching the election results. I don't have to watch. I know. It's been ordained. He's the chosen one, and one way or the other, we'll make sure we get what's ours.

The time is coming soon. I check my phone for any texts or calls from Jordan. He said he likes the work I've been doing. I haven't heard from him at all this week, and it's so close.

Stay calm, I tell myself, don't be a fangirl. Stay calm. Trust the plan.

* * *

The Caretaker

I watch the colors change and then change again, Florida being contested, and Georgia and Ohio. Fucking Ohio.

He's won in Alabama, Mississippi, West Virginia, Kansas, Oklahoma, Idaho, and fucking Missouri. Not only is he winning, he's winning by larger margins than last time.

Just when you were starting to think people had half an ounce of sense.

My eyelids are heavier now. I put the guitar away and check the clock.

11:56 p.m.

An urgent voice brings my attention back to the screen.

"This just in," the male anchor this time, fills the screen, "A winner has been called. The next President of the United States is…"

And just before he can finish his sentence, the power goes out.

* * *

Marie

"Okay, this needs to end now. Really, I can't take any more." I tell Andre. We've been on the phone for hours now, between video chat and call, each other's support group for the end of the world.

"Well, you need to call out your white friends because apparently they haven't learned their lessons in the last four years, tsk tsk."

They're right.

I watch in horror as one state after another on the screen turns red. It can't be.

Knew it would.

But hoped it wouldn't.

Andre's talking, but I can't hear them, I interrupt, "Andre, they're getting ready to call it!"

Silence.

Andre's still there, I can hear them breathing. The anxiety is palpable. Cold sweat pours down my back.

It's so close.

So close.

Unbearably close.

"This just in, we have a winner."

I try to read the future on the faces of the anchors who are too skilled at professional appearance to betray emotion just yet. They're somber and serious. I wish they would just get down to it already. My heart is racing.

I start to walk closer to the screen as if doing so will somehow speed things up.

"Ladies and gentleman," the anchor begins and I try to search his face for signs of panic or disappointment but he just drags it out so long, looking down at his desk and then back up at the camera.

"Ladies and gentleman we have a winner. The next president of the United States is…"

I hear a something pop and the screen is blank. My phone is dead. The trailer is completely dark.

Chapter 70

Election Day Night

Tom

I turn off the television. I just got the notification on my phone, and though we are the only ones left in the park with power, there is no need to watch the news any longer. "Announcement folks. This just came in from our administrators. A victory has been declared. In our favor."

I let them cheer and hug each other and high five. Very few within the ranks know even Bianca, smiling like the perfect obedient wife, has limited information. That's how it needs to be.

When the excitement dies down I walk to the middle of the living room and pull a stool in front of the big screen, taking a seat. "Honey, call in the folks outside, I have an announcement to make."

She does this. In comes that young man, Justin. Need to keep an eye on him. A bit of a loose cannon, but that could come in handy. And the kids and a few others straggling about, lighting off fireworks and such. Boys will be boys.

I survey those gathered. Only a fraction, I know.

"I have an important announcement to share. From headquarters."

I've got their attention.

"Though we have a victory, we also have work to do. More work now than ever. I've received word that armed thugs are rising up all over the country. They're coming to try to disrupt and take what's ours. They will fight the results of the election. It is now our patriotic duty to make some sacrifices. Each of us has a job to do, young and old. Jordan has asked me to head up the efforts in this area, but rest assured we are in solidarity with people all over the country tonight and in the days ahead."

I pause for effect. Justin looks ecstatic. Some of the younger kids look confused. It's ok. They'll figure it out. Dave sits with his arms folded over his chest like he's indignant. Some of the women look scared.

"Now, I don't want to cause undue fear. The situation is grave. We've had to resort to some emergency measures. For our own safety. For the safety of our women and children."

Throw in the women, that always gets them.

"What kind of measures?" one of the older guys asks. His name is Vinny.

"We have allies nearby in the surrounding area. They are standing guard against Antifa and other terrorists, but that also means road travel is closed for now. We have emergency supplies and food but will need everyone's help with rationing and distribution. We've practiced for this all summer and now the time has come. This is not a drill. We'll dispatch those assigned to guard duty immediately. Others will get their instructions in the next day or so.

"Shit! My phone stopped working!"

This interruption comes from Dave and instantly prompts everyone else in the room to check their phones. I expected this much. They were going to find out one way or another.

"Stay calm. We prepared for this. We expected this much, remember? I was warned by headquarters that Antifa was likely to sabotage our power and internet access interfere with our phone communication. For now it's best to assume all our devices are being hacked. By terrorists. I would strongly advise not using phones or computers until this is sorted out."

Of course, I know damn well they won't have the option anyway but best to not let them know that yet.

The sound of voices outside now causes a panic, I remain calm and walk toward the door. "It's okay folks, like I said, we're well protected here, but only here."

I open the door. A few people from the neighborhood are wandering around, confused, talking about the power being out. One of them I recognize as the Caretaker. "I'm going to check it out, should have the power back on in a bit. This happened the other day as well. Don't worry."

I try not to laugh. Blend in. Act just as surprised as they are.

"Folks," I call out, getting their attention, "I have news that president trump has won the election and the country is now under attack. The power will not be on shortly. It has been hijacked by terrorists. You can check the main service panel, but I assure you, that is not the source of the problem."

They look stunned. Those who were not with us tonight have been on the outskirts, they don't know. They haven't taken the red pill yet.

"I know this may come as a shock, but don't worry. We have guards stationed on the main roadways. But we're going to need to work together. We're going to need everyone to cooperate."

By now more have come out of their homes. There are about a dozen or so, wandering around, gravitating toward me because it's clear mine is the only place with a light working. I repeat the basic message again and again. No need to get fancy. We'll have time for explanations tomorrow.

"We have a backup generator here but will need to conserve our resources. We have enough kerosene heaters for five trailers, so some of you are going to have to spend a few nights together. Tomorrow, meet out here at ten o'clock, we'll talk about plans going forward."

They look confused, dazed, tired, but compliant.

So far.

Chapter 71

Marie

"Grab anything perishable out of your fridge, I've got a nice deep freezer that should hold for a while."

Dottie tells me this as I wander around in a daze. First the power outage. Then hearing trump won. I don't believe it. But why shouldn't I believe it? New guy says the power won't be back on any time soon.

The Caretaker confirmed it. The issue wasn't the service panel. He sounded concerned but acted like he was trying to hide it. All phones are dead. And that new guy suddenly stepping up like King Boy Scout who's going to show everyone how to make a fire. Fuck him. For now I can't think of a better option, so I take my things; a few changes of clothes, toothbrush, my phone, and laptop, and all that was in the fridge. It fits into one canvas bag.

My flashlight battery is almost dead, but the dim light keeps me from stumbling on the ground as I find my way back to Dottie's place. She yells for me to just come on in. The door is unlocked. She's already getting the kerosene heater going.

"They dropped the heater off fast," I comment, trying not to be concerned about the possible implications of using this kind of heater inside a cluttered mobile home.

"This? Oh, hell no, this is mine. I ain't borrowing shit from them. I've been prepared for this for some time."

"You knew this was going to happen?"

"Maybe not down to the letter, but in general, yes. It's all spelled out. In the *Book of Discordia*."

The heater blazes into action. It's too much so she dims the flame.

"Now listen, I know it's cool out, but it ain't that cold yet. So the bottom line is, we're going to have to rely on blankets for us and just enough heat to keep the pipes from freezing so we don't run out of juice, okay? We're in it for the long haul. Okay, hon?"

I nod then realize she probably can't see me and answer with a "Yes."

"Come in outta the doorway."

I hesitate. I haven't been in anyone's home all year. She must see my hesitation because she says "Look, I know the virus is a concern of yours, but right now, we've got bigger fish trying to swallow us up."

I nod, the gravity of the situation still sinking in. "It's all because these people keep voting against their own best interests!" I blurt out, only thinking after it's too late that Dottie may have voted for trump as well.

She lets out a raspy cackle. "Honey, ain't no one in any of our lifetimes had a candidate to vote for who was going to serve our best interests and don't kid yourself by thinking otherwise." She takes a sip from a gigantic bottle of water, then continues. "You're new to this park, and I suspect you're new to the lifestyle folks in this park have spent their whole lives in."

She pauses and lets the meaning of her words sink in. Rich people look down at new money, nouveau riche, the term they use to refer to people who have acquired their financial status but not the nuances that go with being part of the aristocracy. Is there such a thing as nouveau poor? If there is, Dottie apparently can tell I've wandered as clumsily into the class she's used to.

She continues, "No one here has had the luxury of voting in their best interest since Christ was in kindergarten, or at the very least not since you would have been a kid. Reagan sold out the unions, the first Bush started a pissing contest over oil. Clinton signed our job prospects away with NAFTA. Baby Bush sent our kids to war. Obama bailed out Wall Street. trump is bad. He's real bad. But no one in Washington is looking out for people like us. Not Biden. Maybe Bernie, which is why they would never let him stand a chance. But this is all just navel gazing now, darling."

She takes another long gulp of water as if all the talking has dried her throat up. "Bottom line is, we're the ones who will have to clean up the mess, even if they're the ones who made it. I know you don't like it here…"

I try to cut in and explain that I've actually come to like it, to tell her I like her and Jess and a few other neighbors, but she lifts up a hand to keep me from interrupting.

"You don't have to justify anything. They may think I'm just Crazy Old Dottie but I've got eyes and ears all around this place. I know this isn't where you expected to be. Same's true for a lot of folks. We make do, some adapt quietly, some go kicking and screaming. Doesn't matter. Things have been tense but it's about to get a whole lot worse. So you're going to have to take chances now. You're not as prepared as you should be."

I walk in and put my stuff down in a corner of the room. Her home is small but cozy. Posters of animals and Goddess figures line the walls. There are candles everywhere. And books. Lots of books.

In the dim light, I see Dottie eyeing my laptop and laughing.

"What'dya bother with that thing for?" she asks.

I laugh too as the reality slowly sets in.

"Habit."

Her face grows austere now and she walks as close to me as she's gotten. I can see urgency in her eyes. The shadows cast by the candles she's lit add an eerie dramatic air.

"To be prepared, dear, you've got to break every habit. Forget everything you count on. That is the challenge now. The Stellium in Capricorn heading for a Grand Conjunction in Aquarius. Now is the time to break habits, darling, because what we're dealing with is like nothing we've ever done before. Do you understand?"

"Yes, like the virus."

"Like the virus, yes, the virus in our society. It's festered and blistered and now all that infection is coming to the top. It's gonna stink like hell before it gets better. Won't get better in my lifetime."

"Don't say that."

I'm really starting to like this lady, the last thing I want to think about is her dying too.

"Don't say what? It's the truth. Always tell the truth. I've been shown already darling. I know my mortality and I will not see this through. But you might. And you're not prepared. We've got to get you ready."

She sets about lighting some more candles. A grey pudgy cat watches me from the sofa, I hadn't seen him before. He purrs loudly now. I sit and pet him and he climbs into my lap.

"You mentioned a few times, some book…" I begin.

"The *Book of Discordia*. It's some book alright." She laughs and the smoker's cough erupts in her lungs and I cringe out of habit, but she can't see me. She's hovering over a bookshelf. She pulls an old book out from the row of closely-packed tomes and hands it to me.

"I've never heard of it."

"Not many have."

I flip open to the first page and begin reading.

And here She is
The wretched one
Presence void of charm and grace
You'll recognize Her by Her name
In your fellow man, you'll see Her face.

She's made Her mark upon your world
In every Golden Apple spoiled
Your suffering is Her delight
And as you waste the hours in toil
That you may have what others lack
You'll not escape their suffering

For in a mansion or a shack
The gift of strife this Goddess brings
And who would want Her at the feast?
Yet for this rejection, you'll feel Her pain
Destruction of human and beast
To Discordia, it's all the same

I look up at Dottie, holding my place in the book with my thumb.

"Golden Apples, that sounds familiar."

"It should," Dottie answers as she pulls blankets down from a shelf. I help her carry the blankets and bedding to the living room and then she leaves for a moment, returning with a folding bed, I assume for me to sleep on. She continues.

"What have you noticed of the new neighbors?"

"They're creepy. I knew it but I didn't know why. Well after tonight I have some ideas, but even before, I thought there was something creepy about them, but my friends thought I was over- reacting because I hate it here and have been so paranoid."

"Were you? Were you really?"

I can't concentrate on answering her because something else has crossed my mind.

"How far do you think this goes? My friend Andre, they're in the city. We were talking when the power went out. They're a walking target if what that guy said about trump is true."

I'm starting to panic, and it shows in my voice.

"Sit down, and take a breath," Dottie says, lighting a cigarette.

"Now," she continues, "back to the new neighbors, what have you noticed?"

"They're creepy," I begin.

"Yes, we've established that."

"Sorry, they, one day I caught a glimpse of a human sized target, like for target practice, in their yard, after they built the fence around it. They have a lot of people in and out. And they wear those dorky uniforms and march around singing about Jesus and stuff."

"And what else?"

"I've heard them talk about it. Golden Apple, as if it's some kind of symbol or something, the name of a group. Their cult maybe?"

A knock at the door makes me jump. The cat eyes me warily and walks away, convinced he can no longer count on me to be a stable napping surface.

Dottie grabs a meat tenderizer from a drawer in the kitchen and with the cigarette still dangling from her lips, opens the door.

It's Jess.

"Hey, can I stay here with you?" she begins to ask and then sees me on the couch. "Oh, I'm sorry if you've got a full house I can…"

"No, you come on in, you're meant to stay here with us. It's okay," Dottie reassures her.

Jess has a small bag packed. She comes in and sits on the other end of the couch. She looks terrified.

"We were just talking about Golden Apples," Dottie begins.

Jess's eyes widen as if in horror. Dottie turns to her. "Jess, what do you know about Golden Apples?"

"It's the name of the group. The new people. My parents and brother, and even my aunt are all caught up in it. I thought it was another stupid bullshit cult, like the one my aunt was in before. They have all these meetings, and everyone dresses the same. I've never gone to one of their meetings, but I heard my brothers talking about it."

"What did they say about it?" Dottie asks, but by now I've gotten the impression she already knows the answers to the questions she's asking.

"They're like Boy Scouts, but for crazy evangelical Christians who are planning for a white ethno-state. I mean, that's not the words Don and Scott use, but from what they're describing, that's pretty much what it is. I was planning to run away. Was going to go live with my boyfriend after the election. But now, do you think it's true? What they said about armed guards closing down the road?"

"It's true. You better believe it's true. But they're not telling the whole truth," Dottie went on.

"Do you think trump really won again?" Jess asks.

"I think it no longer matters who the president is. One way or another, we've got a fight for survival right outside that door." Dottie points a long finger toward the entry to her trailer.

"Do you know what started the Trojan War?" Dottie asked.

"What?" I ask.

"Um, wasn't it because everyone wanted Helen of Troy, or something?" Jess asked. She's paid more attention to Greek Mythology than I have, clearly.

"The Apple of Discord." Dottie continues. "The Goddess Discordia, also called Eris, all that is wretched and undesirable, cast out by the other Olympians and ignored. Isolated, alienated."

I hadn't heard of the Goddess in this guise and lean in listening intently.

"She's also a representation of raw power. What does the patriarchy fear but the power that exists outside of its clutches? In the stories, She is feared because of Her looks, because She wasn't one of them. Because She reminded them of what they could become."

"Sounds like patriarchy," I agree nodding my head.

"Exactly!" Dottie claps her hands together for emphasis. "So to seek revenge, She created a Golden Apple and presented it at the wedding feast of Thetis and Peleus. With four words, 'To the most fair,' She offered the apple as a prize."

"What's that have to do with us?" I ask.

"She knew how to get to them. Through greed and vanity. The gift created competition. Hera, Athena, Aphrodite, rather than enjoying the wedding feast, became obsessed with proving their beauty, purity, worthiness of the prize. Which led to the misery of the Trojan War."

Dottie stopped to take a drag off her cigarette.

"Eris, Discordia, calls out our weakness. Our greed. Our vanity. She forces us to see when things are fucked up by trapping us in our own misery until we see it for what it is. The shit we fight over, go to war over, it's all a mess of our own making. Our own selfishness. Our ambitions."

"Divide and conquer," I think out loud. "and purity and fairness are like codewords for what whiteness is to America now."

"The pattern sure seems familiar, don't it? Someone miserable about themselves, finding ways to play on the insecurities of everyone else. Distract them with competition. Give them some bullshit standard of perfection. Get them thinking that winning the bullshit prize is the only thing that matters. They'll crawl over their best friend for that Golden Apple."

I think of you, for a moment. Nodding slowly as Dottie speaks.

"It could be whiteness. Thinness. A bigger house. Newer car. Bigger boat. The prize changes. Nothing is every good enough. People with a bitter mind and desperate soul have nothing better to do than to chase. They'll knock out anyone who gets in their way."

"But why would Golden Apple name their group after a Goddess? They're a bunch of misogynistic creeps." Jess asks.

Dottie turns to her and flicks her cigarette in an ashtray. She exhales smoke. "Because, dear, like most of these groups nowadays who like to borrow a little of this and a little of that from older legends, they're only focused on the prize. They don't think about context, the bigger story, the deeper meaning. They're brainwashed not to. They have no idea what their symbol represents. It would be funny if it wasn't serious."

"They've been preparing for a war." Jess adds, her face solemn. She looks as if she's trying her memory for details. "Golden Apple. They blame it on Antifa and Black Lives Matter, but the truth is, it's always the white people instigating violence. They want some crazy white Christian bare-foot-and-pregnant world. Just like that book of yours, *Handmaid's Tale*."

I sigh heavily. Trying to put it all together. I never trusted the new neighbors. But how could they have this much clout?

Dottie added "We don't know how far spread this is, or how much power they have, or who they are connected to. One thing I would say, we can't make any assumptions. Just because it looks like some petty little backyard militia, doesn't mean they don't have a reach beyond what we can see."

"So what do we do?" I ask.

"First thing's first. We've got to find a way to get the children out of here." She looked at Jess, "Do you think your little brothers will cooperate if we try to help them get out?"

"I don't know. They like this thing. They believe it. I don't think they'll volunteer to leave."

"Maybe not yet, but in time, they'll see."

"Dee," I remember just then. "Did her mom even come home from work before all this happened? She and her brother Derrick live next to me."

"Her mom's car was in the driveway, so yes, she was home. But we should try to get Dee and her brother even, and the other kids who aren't directly involved first."

"Is their mom part of the cult?" Jess asked.

"I don't think so. She seems reasonable. Plus, I don't think she gets enough time off of work to get involved with anything like that," I tell her.

"For now, we sleep. Jess, Marie, you ladies can fight over who gets the couch and who gets the folding bed. I'm going to bed to talk to the Goddess in my dreams. Years of complacency got us into this mess, but She may be able to help us get ourselves back out."

Chapter 72

The Caretaker

By the dim glow of a lighter, I look through the drawer to find my good flashlight. I test it and the brightness is nearly blinding in this almost total darkness. I slip out the back door. I know my way through the dark for now, saving the light for emergencies only. I don't want to draw attention to myself.

No one on the road so far. Everyone tucked into their trailers, bundled under blankets no doubt. I check my phone again. Still no signal.

Shit.

Frank probably has no idea what the hell is going on and it's his damn park. If they're just bluffing, I can probably use the phone at Stewart's to make a call.

Approaching 9R now, the coast looks clear. I walk along the edge of the park. Close to the trees that line the road and make it so hard for anyone to know what's really here. As I walk through the trees, closer to the parking lot, I see a figure standing outside of the store. The lights are on. I can see through the storefront windows, but no one is there. At least, not inside. Standing outside is what I expect to be a man. Leaning on the door, smoking a cigarette. A sight I've seen dozens of times.

But never like this.

He's wearing camouflage. And holding an automatic rifle.

My blood runs cold. I scan the parking lot. A few more guys in camo are walking across the lot. One holds a walkie-talkie. They don't see me, I'm pretty sure, but I need to get out of here soon. A voice calls out in the darkness behind them. They turn and gesture back in the direction of the bridge. And then bright lights flash on, facing the bridge, luckily, away from me, not toward me. The bridge is illuminated, and so is part of the lake beneath. Then I see it.

* * *

I slip back to my trailer, unnoticed. Even in the dark, as I write this note, I can see the image on full display, clear as day in my mind. The line of Jeeps on either side of the bridge. The armed men, like a scene from some movie of occupied Afghanistan or Iran. But here, in my neighborhood, it's surreal. Soon it will be morning. The curiosity to check and see if it is true will compel them, tempting them to go near the road. To see for themselves.

Which could be a mistake.

I fold up the papers, there are two. Marie is with Dottie, or so I saw last night. Jess is there too, thankfully. The only one in her family with an ounce of sense. The other note is for the lady with the son and the little girl, the one with the rabbit. I contemplate writing another note, but her son, Justin, is involved, too dangerous.

I slip out for the second time that night and slide the notes under the doors of the respective trailers before anyone is out and about to see.

I know you'll want to check the road. Don't. There are armed guards outside the park. It's too dangerous. Stay here for now. Burn this note.

Chapter 73

Andre

I roll my eyes as her voicemail picks up. Again.

"Come on now, fam. It's Wednesday, November 4th also known as Election Groundhog Day. No, for real. I don't know what's going on with you, hanging up on me like that. But whatever, when you're done with your mood, I'll be here. Watching the news. Waiting to find out who the next president is. Call me. Bye."

Chapter 74

Eric

Maybe this wasn't the best idea. She hasn't been responding to my texts. I stand on the corner in downtown Saratoga. Karentoga. The spot where we were supposed to meet.

"I can't take it anymore. My whole family is in this weird cult. They're like a militia. I need to get out of here," she had pleaded with me. That was a few days ago when we last talked on the phone.

I finally broke down and agreed. Family is fine with it, they like Jess. More than we can say about her family's attitude toward me. Hell, they don't even know about me, obviously.

But she's not here.

And not answering.

"Hey Eric!"

I look up, scared, I won't lie. This town isn't friendly. I recognize Devon.

"I haven't seen you in a minute!" We hug, and I notice he's carrying a sign.

"What's all this?" I ask.

"There's a rally this afternoon. Gonna be big."

"What for?"

"Same old, same old. Doesn't matter who the president is, we're still under attack. You wanna stick around?"

"Possibly. I'm supposed to meet my girlfriend here, but she hasn't shown, so something must have happened."

Saying it feels weird. Like I'm a of fool who doesn't realize when his woman is playing him, but that can't be it. I know Jess, that can't be it.

"She live around here?" Devon asks.

"She's off of 9R, outside the city."

His face changes. "What?" I ask.

"I heard through a source, it wasn't on the news mind you, but I heard something fucked up is going on by the lake. Some kind of militia shit. Crazy ass white people taking over entire neighborhoods, blocking off the road."

"It wasn't on the news?"

"Nope. No surprise right? Me and a few hundred people are about to march peacefully, and it will be all over the news, cops spraying us and all, but let some white people play Bundy Family with an entire neighborhood and it's just another day in paradise, right?"

"True. But she could be trapped with those crazy people."

"Could be. But you'd be better off letting her figure that out unless you've got an army to go with you, you aren't going to make a dent if it's as bad as my friend said. Besides, it ain't our fight anyway. Sorry, I know it's the woman you love, but they're talking about serious shit. Fully armed, they aren't playing."

Chapter 75

Marie

11/4/2020

Day One

I wonder if anyone slept well. Dottie seemed to. I was in and out of dreams, or what I think may have been dreams. Who knows. In the early morning light, I head back to my place for more provisions. Blankets, dry goods. Anything else we may need to consolidate.

No one has been up early in the time I've lived here, but suddenly, with no power, no electronics to distract us, it looks like everyone in the park is scurrying about. No one really looks at anyone else. People look scared, or resolute. Or confused.

I see a commotion in front of the new peoples' trailer. The gate is wide open for once, no longer hiding the lawn. Chairs and tables are set up. There's juice and snacks. It looks like they've set up a fucking carnival. They've even got a barker.

Standing in his gold shirt and blue pants, holding a clipboard, it's the kid, Justin, calling to anyone who walks by. "Hey, you, come on over here. You've got to register. We need everyone to register."

"Fuck off," I tell him and continue walking. I think of the note Jess found by the door this morning. About armed guards. Probably just a scare tactic. But what if it isn't?

Back at Dottie's, I unload the supplies on the living room table. Jess is pacing the floor. "I was supposed to meet Eric today. What if this is going on all over downtown? They might have gotten him! What if he tries to come here? They'll kill him!"

I consider this.

"Yes, this is true. But Jess, do you think he would try to come here? Or do you think he'll just figure plans didn't work out and go home? I mean, if it is just here. And if it isn't, you've just gotta trust him. Trust him to know how to protect himself."

I know this doesn't help.

"Where's Dottie?"

"She's meditating. Said not to disturb her."

"Got it."

Who the hell can meditate in the middle of a... what is this? A coup? An uprising? An occupation? A loud knock at the door breaks my concentration before I can answer my own question.

Jess and I look at each other.

"Everyone I care to talk to is already in here." Jess says.

I'm content with that, but then I think of Dee and Derrick. There are a few other people who aren't nuts in this park. I look out the window. It's the new guy, Tom.

I try to ignore him. He keeps knocking. It's probably interfering with Dottie's meditation, I think to myself.

"I'll go out and talk to him."

"No, don't," Jess starts to say, but I'm already out the door, hooking my mask behind my ears.

"What do you want?"

"Well, that's not very neighborly."

"So?"

"We're in the midst of a crisis here, young lady."

I'm pretty sure I'm actually older than him. His fake patronizing calm tone makes me want to spit in his face. I don't want to take my mask off.

"Are we?" I ask.

"Yes. I was given a report that you were rude to one of our neighbors. Someone who is trying to help maintain law and order."

I laugh out loud at this.

He doesn't flinch.

"We won't tolerate people being rude. We need to cooperate. It's a matter of survival."

"Why are you the only one with power?" I ask.

He feigns offense. "Well, I guess I'm the only one who invested in a backup generator."

"What do you want?"

"We're having a park meeting at eleven. I expect everyone to be there."

"Whatever."

I go back into the house and close the door in his face. There, that wasn't so bad. But then again, he wasn't armed. The others, somewhere, are.

Allegedly.

"What's that all about?" Jess asked.

"I don't know but this asshole who ignored a pandemic all year now imagines we are in the midst of a crisis, so I guess he's calling a meeting."

"Yeah, they seem to really like doing that."

"You going?" I ask Jess.

"I guess we should, I mean if they're going to come around knocking on doors to round people up and shit."

"Maybe we should, just to see what kind of craziness they're gassing people's heads up with."

* * *

Jess was right. Not only did they knock on every door, they actually walked up and down the road ringing a damn bell. Like we're animals being called to the trough to feed. And then to slaughter.

I stand by Jess, not entirely sure if she's safe, but also assuming maybe she is because her whole family is part of the cult. Or militia, or whatever they are. She doesn't seem as worried as I feel. Dottie was still back at the trailer meditating.

We stand around in a cluster. I'm the only one wearing a mask. I see Dee and Derrick and their mom on the other side of the crowd and nod to her in solidarity. Why are they dragging kids out here? I remember Dottie's words about helping to get the kids out. How, I have no idea.

Scanning the park, I see no sign of anyone being armed. I know each and every one of these rednecks has a gun in their home, so the thought of armed guards doesn't surprise me. It's hard not to laugh. The right to form a well-organized militia to defend the citizens against a corrupt government has become the organization of militias of the deluded in favor of the very tyrannical government it was supposed to defend against.

"Can I have your attention please!" Tom calls out. He's actually standing on his deck, like a wannabe dictator in his balcony.

Yeah, you've got our attention, asshole, you dragged us out here, didn't you?

The crowd quiets down. Some have grabbed snacks from the table. I wonder what's in the cups. Kool Aid?

"That's more like it," Tom continued. "We are in the midst of a serious crisis. We've got to work together. I know that's a hard message to hear when we all love our freedom. But those of you who know me, you know nobody cares about your freedom and safety more than I do."

"That's right!" a few remarks of admiration arise from the crowd.

"I believe we have a fair stockpile. We need to be careful about our supplies. So, we have assigned designees to manage the garden and to keep an eye on the store down the road here. We have been granted access to these supplies."

"Granted access by who?" I turn to follow the sound of the voice. It's the Caretaker, leaning up against a tree, arms folded over his chest.

"We've worked out the logistics, that's all you need to know." No one else asks questions. How can they just go along with this? But then, I'm not asking questions either.

"Now, for safety purposes, since we have to look out for each other now, I've enlisted the help of several of our designees to take a record of everyone who lives here, in case of emergency. Let's all make this go as smoothly as possible and get these forms filled out over at the table." He points to a table set up at the far end of the yard. Sitting behind it, three women, like the grown-up version of kids selling lemonade on the side of the road. Smiling.

I turn to look at Jess. Her expression nervous now, for the first time. She looks to me and I give her arm a squeeze. "It's okay, we'll figure something out."

"Now, we are also going to have to put all our resources together. We're asking everyone to pitch in. We've got to share and be willing to help our neighbors out, right? So we're looking for volunteers to help with various tasks. We are also sending volunteers around to gather up some critical supplies that we may need in case of an emergency."

I want to speak up then, start to even, but a commotion from my left distracts me, all of us. It's Dottie.

"We found a straggler," one of the two men who have her by the arms and are practically dragging her to the group calls out to Tom.

"Don't fucking touch me, you assholes! I said not to bother me when I'm fucking meditating!"

I find my voice then.

"Is this what you mean by volunteering?" I ask. A few others start to speak up as well. The men shove Dottie, and she stumbles forward. I catch her before she hits the ground.

She brushes her arms off and walks right through the crowd, until she's standing face to face with Tom.

"Now you listen to me. I know who you are, and I know what you're doing," she turns to the crowd. "First, he's going to demand all your belongings, then he's going to enlist you in his little fascist army. He's full of shit. There is no terrorist uprising coming to steal your white women. The only coup going on right now is the one he's responsible for."

The men start to advance toward Dottie now.

"Dottie! Dottie! Look out!" I yell. It makes no difference.

"Fucking traitor!" people begin to shout.

"Commie!"

"Damn Socialist!"

"Satan Worshipper!"

I stand in front of Jess to block her from the crowd. They're losing control. This time, a group of four men, men I don't recognize from the park, dressed in camouflage, grab her and drag her back through the crowd. Dave spits on her face.

"Dad! Cut it the fuck out!" Jess screams.

"No," I try to keep Jess from running forward into the mix.

"No! Stop! Knock it off!" my screams are easily drowned out by those who see her as the enemy.

She starts to laugh. Turning toward the crowd, pointing a finger. "This is your mess now. You think he's telling you the truth? Call me whatever names you want. I'm not afraid of you. I'm not afraid of you weak minded easily led men and Stepford women."

One of the men kicks her in the stomach and she doubles over. When she lifts herself from the ground, her bloodied lips form a grimace that sends chills down my spine. I think the others are freaked out too because they stand down just for a moment. Long enough for her to raise a finger to the crowd like a scolding teacher.

"Eris has risen. She's dwarfed mighty Pluto. December of this year, She will square off with Him. In the years to come, the wealthy, the greedy, the heartless, She'll bring them to their knees." She turns to Dave, stares him down and he actually flinches, then tries to hide it, folding his arms over his chest. She looks Tom in the eyes and then spits on the ground, turning again to the crowd.

"The age of Men is ending. The era of patriarchy is ending. Everything your leaders have killed and lied for will burn. It is written in the *Book of Discordia!*"

Her words hang in the air a moment. I swear time has frozen. Until one of the guards punches her in the face, hard. I hear a crack as she falls to the ground. This time, they grab her by both arms and begin to drag her.

"No! Knock it off!" I yell. I start to run toward them, but I'm restrained by an arm around my waist. I can't see who it is, and I try to jab with my elbows and kick behind me.

"Stop! Calm down! You're not helping."

I hear the familiar voice.

"She knows what she's doing. Let it go for now," The Caretaker whispers again. A jeep pulls up and the men lift Dottie and throw her in the back seat. They drive away.

The commotion has stopped. In place of the cheers and name calling and the few shouts of protest, there is only silence now.

"Now, as I was saying," Tom resumes his speech as if nothing just happened. "Sign up and register at the tables. Be sure to enjoy some snacks contributed by our women's Auxiliary."

I look to Jess. She's pale. The confidence natural to teens who fashion themselves immortal is gone. "Ladies, I trust you received my note?" The Caretaker asks, his face blank.

"Yeah, what you're with them? I knew it. You're one of them." I start to jab him in the chest with my finger after every word. He grabs my hand midair before I can get in a final jab.

"I've told you before," he says this as if there is more he wants to say but can't, and part of me knows he's telling the truth.

"Then why? Why won't you do anything?"

"Who says I'm not?" As he asks this, he leans in for just a moment. Just long enough to say, "play along for now, I'm working on it."

He looks into my eyes again to make sure his words register.

"Come on, Jess, let's just do their stupid paperwork. For now."

* * *

"Hiya Sweetie, thanks for volunteering to fill out a form!" The bubbly blonde next to Bianca greets me as she leans over the table and hands me a pen. I reach for my hand sanitizer on instinct, but then remember I don't have it with me. I take the pen reluctantly.

"I don't know what reality you're living in, but based on what I saw this morning, it doesn't appear that 'volunteer' is the word you should be using."

She stares at me with vacant eyes and the same big, fake smile. I wonder if she was able to comprehend what I just said.

I look at the form. Name. Age. Emergency Contact. Ethnicity.

"Why do you need my ethnicity?" I ask.

"Just fill out the form sweetie, okay? It's for emergencies. For safety protocols."

Fucking kept woman, I think to myself. I don't think this phrase is feminist, but under the circumstances, I don't care.

Please list all medical conditions

I list every STD I can think of. Not because I have them, but because it suddenly occurs to me that these fools may get rapey at some point.

Are you able to breed?

Bingo.

"What is this?" I ask again.

"It's your registration. Just fill out the paperwork." This time she doesn't pretend to be friendly or patient.

List any assets you currently own.

Well that's easy. Not even the trailer is mine. I start to write 'Nothing' when Fascist Takeover Barbie leans over and asks about my car. Fuck. The one thing that's paid off.

"Nope," I lie.

"Cash on hand?"

"Nothing." I stare at her coolly. How the fuck would she know the difference.

"Alright then," she points toward a tent in the back of the yard and says, "now proceed over to the swabbing station for your DNA test."

Chapter 76

Dee

11/4/2020

Day One

Mom was home last night to watch the Election. She calls it the Shit Show. Mom is allowed to say that. I'm not. She let me stay up late to watch. It was a boring show. She was also home this morning when I woke up.

And that's not normal. Neither is the cold.

I heard Mom talking to Derrick Torrey. She sounded upset. She's probably upset because it's cold in here. I stayed in my room, playing with Fiver. He's cold so I wrap him in blankets and snuggle him. Thinking of going into the living room to join them. It's like Christmas, sometimes, when I go out of my room and sometimes she's got the day off and sometimes there's surprises under the tree. Sometimes she's excited. Sometimes she's upset. Usually, when she's upset, there are no presents.

I put Fiver back in his cage and wash up in the bathroom. Light comes in the window, but the real lights don't work. Still hearing Mom and Derrick Torrey but not really listening. I get washed up. The water is cold. I join them in the living room. Mom has bags under her eyes, like when she works a lot, even though she just had a night off. Derrick Torrey tells me to go in my room. He follows me. He tells me to sit on the bed with Fiver.

It's weird, Derrick Torrey never wants to play with Fiver unless I ask him. I pick up my bunny and snuggle him in my arms. Derrick Torrey sits on my bed and looks at me. I know this look. It's the look he had when the cat died. When school was locked down. When everything changed.

It's a bad look.

"Dee," Derrick Torrey begins, "You know how we went to Uncle Bert's house that one summer, and we saw people in costumes playing war?"

I do. I nod.

"Well," he continues, "remember how I explained that they were re-enacting history, as a game?"

"Yeah."

This is boring. I start to kiss Fiver's head and blow my warm breath onto his back. He puts his paws on my shoulders and gives me soft rabbit kisses. I giggle.

"Dee, you need to pay attention."

"Ok." I look at Derrick Torrey, but I stay petting Fiver's back and stroking his ears.

"Our neighbors are playing a re-enactment game too."

Why is he telling me this? I don't care. I want breakfast. My stomach grumbles.

"Can I have pancakes, syrup, butter and…" I begin.

"Dee," Derrick Torrey sounds mad now. I shut up and he continues. "The neighbors are playing this game. Ok? They're playing re-enactment. But you know what the rule is with re-enactment?" he asks me.

I shrug.

"The most important rule of the game is that everyone has to pretend it's real. Okay?"

"I guess, but re-enactment is a boring game. Can we play hide and seek?"

"We may have to at some point. For now, this is why Mom is home. Everyone is playing. And we have to play along. Follow me and Mom. And don't try to break the rules of the game."

Golden Apple

"Why couldn't Mom take days off of work to play with us?" I ask him.

"Never mind that for now. This is…" he pauses, scratches his chin and looks at the ceiling, "it's like an emergency drill. Like a fire drill, but a game. Okay? And part of the game means no electricity for now. So, we have to keep the fridge door closed. We have to dress warm and play along with the game. It's not real. But we have to pretend it is."

"Ok. Can I have breakfast now?"

Chapter 77

Jordan

11/4/2020

Day One

The call comes in through my stereo.

"Hey, it's T-Boss, checking in to let you know we've secured Lakeside."

"Great, thanks, let me know if there's anything you need."

I round the corner and slow down. Driving down Broadway in downtown Saratoga Springs, it looks like everything is working out according to plan.

Up ahead, a caravan of trucks slows traffic even more. It's all good. I'm in no hurry today. Their trucks decked out with flags, signs, even hood ornaments all with the same message: trump 2020.

Another call comes in.

"Hello, It's Thor, from team Saginaw, we have conquest. I repeat, Golden Apple Operation Saginaw is a success."

"Great, thanks Thor."

So that's Saratoga, New Paltz, Queens, Staten Island, Saginaw, western Vermont and of course, Ohio.

Not bad, not bad at all.

Traffic has come to a halt. I lean out my window. An entire section of the road is blocked. Police in riot gear and a lot of liberal clowns, of course. It was to be expected. This can work to my advantage. I pull over and park the car, grabbing a flash bang and my cell phone.

I don't usually wear a mask, but for occasions like this, I can make an exception. A crowd has gathered now, people on the sidewalks for the most part jeering at the crowd assembled in the street. Protesting. Peacefully. For now.

I take out my phone and start recording. They chant Black Lives Matter and Who's Streets?

Who's streets, really? Look around you. These are my streets.

I make my way through the crowd and past the shops. Women eye the crowd with disgust and some cling to their children, pulling them away from the commotion. Good idea, because it's about to get interesting. No one seems to notice me. They're focused on the shouting, drumming, marching anarchists in the street. Just as well. I toss the flashbang and quickly turn around the corner and lean against the wall.

The sound and light behind me, I cue up the video on my phone again. Re-emerging in time to take footage of people running about. A young Black woman with a bandana over her face is crying and screaming. A Black man with a bullhorn, is shouting, and a different woman with a Black Lives Matter shirt grabs the bullhorn from him.

"Calm down, remain calm! Anyone who needs medical attention, medics are over there!" She motions in the direction of a car with several people standing around with masks and rubber gloves on. I doubt anyone can hear her. The noise and commotion escalate. "They're shooting us!" another screams. "Fuck the police!" yells another.

A few white guys on the sidelines stand by their motorcycles, taunting the crowd. Now they're coming in, using their bike helmets to knock people out of their way. I cut away for that part but bring my camera back in time to show the retaliation. Three protesters get in the biker's face. They're screaming and one even tries to grab at him. Now it's just a free for all.

I stick around long enough to catch footage of the police coming in, batons swinging, tear gas at the ready, and to see protesters now throwing empty water bottles at the cops.

Mission accomplished.

I cut through an ally and take the long way back to my car.

Mask down now, no longer needing anonymity, I can't help grinning at how easily people are played. My phone chimes. I grab it from my back pocket.

It's a text.

Olympia is secure.

Sweet, I think to myself. West Coast, represent.

By the time I reach my car, I've gotten confirmation of Northampton, Ogunquit, Western Pennsylvania and parts of Virginia and Alabama. Well, we knew they wouldn't be too hard.

By the time I get home, we've got Decatur, We've got Hoosiers, and we've even got Northern California. And most people have no idea.

Chapter 78

Marie

11/5/2020

Day Two

"Did you sleep at all?" I ask Jess.

"No, you?"

"Not much."

"What do you think they've done with Dottie?"

I pause for a moment, not sure how much I should say. I hear Dottie's voice. *Always tell the truth.* "Well," I begin, "I don't know if you'll believe this, but I had a dream about Dottie. She was walking by the lake. Said she is ready to cross the bridge. I think she meant she's dead. Or going to be dead soon. She wasn't worried about it. I know she sees death differently. I know she's not afraid to die. She also said to get the children out."

I turn to Jess. She seems to be taking it better than I expected.

"I just don't know how we're going to manage that. It's not like we can really go anywhere."

"I don't know. The Caretaker, I think he's on our side. I think he's trying to figure something out."

"I don't know how long we have, until things get worse."

As if on cue, a rapping on the door interrupts us. Jess looks to me.

"I'll get it, you go in the back room, don't come out unless I call you to, okay?"

She retreats back to Dottie's bedroom.

I remember Dottie grabbing the meat tenderizer and I find it on the kitchen counter. Holding it slightly behind my back, I open the door, just slightly. It's the blonde woman, from "registration."

"Yeah?" I ask.

"We're starting another meeting now. Everyone's attendance is requested."

"Requested?" I ask.

"Requested." She says again, her lips pulled tight in more of a sneer than a smile. She nods her head in the direction of the path and I look over her shoulder.

Pacing up and down the road, men in camouflage, carrying guns.

"Requested," I say again.

***

It's unusually warm, I left my jacket back at Dottie's. I try not to think of her. I know she was ready for whatever is happening. But I'm not ready to deal with this. *You're not prepared.* I hear her say again.

Today, it's the same crowd, but this time, people are more subdued. Less exuberant than yesterday, even the followers. Disciples, whatever they're called. "Stick with me," I told Jess, "and for now I think we need to do what the Caretaker said, as much as I hate to admit it. Play along, until we can get the kids out of here.

A handful of the guys in the park, the same ones who have been kissing Tom's ass since he moved in, are parading around with their chests puffed out. Like they think they're hot shit. That kid, Justin, is the worst.

Tom once again takes his place on his front deck, gesturing for everyone to crowd in on his lawn.

"I've got some disturbing news, and I know some of you won't believe me unless I show you. So, here it is. He gestures to one of his minions who brings out a portable projector screen. They set it up and Tom uses a remote control to start a video. It could be anywhere, any time since the summer. It's not just anywhere. I recognize Broadway in Saratoga Springs.

Jess grabs my arm, and I can tell she's straining to see. Then a look of recognition crosses her face. I know she's trying to hide it and I don't want to draw more attention to her. I turn back to the screen. Protesters being corralled by police. The video cuts to another scene, a few of the protesters are pushing back.

"This," Tom begins, was yesterday. Only a few miles from here," he stops the film before proceeding. "Didn't I tell you they were here? Coming here? To our neighborhoods? Bringing terrorism to our streets? And here you have it. They looted and rioted in downtown and then they headed here. Our guards subdued the mob, and they were dealt with. This is how close we are to danger, ladies and gentleman. We're not playing around. We're trying to keep you safe."

The few murmurs that spread through the crowd died down.

"We can't take any chances. Now, in a few more days, I'm sure we'll have the power back on, and this is all going to be resolved, but for now we are vulnerable to attack. And it's not just here, there have been riots all around the country. Liberals and terrorists who don't want to accept that the people chose trump, again. We've got to be vigilant against these forces of radical socialism."

God, he actually believes what he's saying. I look around. Looks like the majority of people here also believe the bullshit. I spot Derrick in the crowd. He looks confused. Dee is on the far perimeter of the group.

You've got to get the children out.

I hear Dottie's voice.

"What about Dottie?" I ask.

Tom looks annoyed, but he stifles this with a professional poker face. "The instigator," he begins, "left us with no choice but to defend ourselves. She tried to attack one of the guards overnight. She had been in communication with Antifa, and they were planning to raid our supplies."

Bullshit.

But everyone else is buying it.

"What about Frank?" the Caretaker asks.

"Who is that?" Tom asks.

"The guy who owns the fucking park."

The guards don't seem to like his tone of voice, a few of the armed men in camo reach for their guns. Tom motions for them to relax.

"Oh, Frank, yeah. I'm in touch with Frank. It's all under control."

"But you just said you didn't know who he was." The Caretaker persists. God, what the fuck is he doing? Didn't he say to play along?

Tom is obviously annoyed now.

"Yeah, well, it's a common name, so, I needed to be clear about who we were talking about."

The Caretaker smirks.

"Hey, what's the matter? You can't stand the thought that someone else is running things now?" The shout comes from the front of the group. Vinny. He's got his arms folded over his chest and is staring down the Caretaker.

"I just think it's mighty unusual that you don't know who the guy is one minute, but you've also talked to him. I don't know, I guess if no one else finds that unusual. Or finds it unusual that a hoard of terrorists came down 9R last night and were subdued by guards and no one heard anything, right?" He looks side to side, but no one backs him up.

"I heard shots," Justin volunteers. Then a few others concur that they too heard a raucous.

"One of them tried to get into my bedroom last night," someone volunteers. I recognize her as Jess's aunt, Joni. Jess grunts and rolls her eyes.

"Really?" the Caretaker asks. "One of who?"

"Antifa," she said, nodding her head for emphasis.

"How do you know? Were they wearing a nametag that read, Antifa? Did they try to offer the secret Antifa handshake?"

"Hey!" Dave yells now, stepping forward from the crowd, pointing a finger in the other man's face.

"When a woman says she was the victim of an attempted assault, it is our duty to believe her!" he practically spits in the Caretaker's face.

"Oh? So you were upset when Brett Kavanaugh was appointed then?"

The crowd devolves into rumblings and a few insults shouted at the Caretaker. Race traitor is one, another calls him a Commie. It's beginning to sound like a repeat of yesterday.

From either side, armed men in camo approach. Again, I don't recognize them from the park. They can't be older than thirty.

"Hold it!" Tom calls out, calming the crowd. He motions for the armed men to step back. "It's okay. We don't need to do this. It's okay to let people have their own opinions, right? This is America. You're allowed to have your own opinions, you just can't have your own facts, right?"

He shoots a plastic smile at the Caretaker.

"We have important work to do today, folks. But before we get started on that, I am requesting that everyone drop their cellphones, laptops and tablets off at this table. We have some trained volunteers who are checking for infiltration and bugs."

No one speaks up. By now I don't see the point.

Jess looks horrified and that's when I remember her boyfriend. If they are able to hack into her phone, they'll see her conversations with her boyfriend.

"It's okay," I mouth the words, rather than speaking them. I notice the Caretaker watching over her shoulder. He approaches.

"What's up?"

"Jess's phone," I try to find some reasonable excuse. "She can't find it," is all I can think.

"Oh, well, that reminds me," he reaches into his back pocket and pulls out a phone.

"Little lady, I found this on the ground outside of Dottie's house. Be more careful next time, okay?"

She puts two and two together and nods in agreement.

"Hey, Marie?" she begins.

"Yeah?"

"Remember that time you told me about how your mom used to read your diary, and how you did that thing as a result? And you told me about the thing you did?"

"Yes."

"I think you should tell him that story sometime," she says, and it looks like she's trying to be discrete and casual at the same time.

I look at the Caretaker who raises one eyebrow.

"That's not a bad idea."

* * *

We got our assignments. My job for the day is to take stock of medical supplies and then food. The park is overrun with men in camo, carrying guns of all shapes and sizes. Every so often, a golf cart with a crew of them rolls through. Others pace back and forth on foot. They guard the garden, the food supplies and even the shed in Tom's yard which is now the medical supplies unit.

We work until we're told we can stop.

Tom uses that obnoxious bell to summon us again in the evening.

By now, no one thinks to not show up. It's amazing how quickly crazy becomes normal. "I've been told that there is a spy in our midst. We found an explosive earlier today in one of the mailboxes. Luckily, we were able to de-activate it. This begs the question, who among us is our enemy?"

Everyone is silent.

"So for the sake of security, we will collect all shoes as well. You may wear your shoes while you are working if your task for the day requires you to remain outside. You will turn in your shoes before retiring home. Also, your jackets. And one more thing," he paused for effect here, his face fixed in false sincerity. "These are unprecedented times. Many of you have reconnected with your faith, which is marvelous to see. We will begin offering prayer services every evening. All are expected to attend. To make the most of our food, meals will be twice daily, and communal. After dinner, at 7, we'll gather for prayer. Men will be expected to wear a Golden Apple uniform. If you don't have one, it will be provided."

By this, it's understood he means those horrible golden shirts and navy-blue pants.

"And women and girls, we have dresses for you. You will be expected to wear these at all times."

Bianca comes out on cue with a plastic bin. She lifts off the lid and holds up what I can only describe as a smock. They look like third graders sewed them together, and perhaps they did.

"Now, shall we have some music before dinner?" Tom asks, grinning.

Someone in the crowd starts to sing and the hymn spreads until almost everyone is singing. Almost.

I may never march in the infantry
Ride in the cavalry
Fire the artillery
I may never shoot for the enemy
But I'm in the Lord's Army!

"Don't forget to turn in your shoes!" Tom's voice calls over the singing.

Chapter 79

Barbara

Carol looks stunning as always. I adjust my top, the last purchase (I promised myself!) from the boutique on Broadway. I only bought it last month but since I haven't been back to the gym since they reopened, it's already feeling a little snug.

There's a nip in the November air. No sitting out on the patio today. I walk Carol into the house where guests have already gathered in the great room. "How nice of you to come over for my birthday!"

"I wouldn't miss it for the world! I mean, now that police cleared the riffraff from BLM out of the streets," Carol replies.

"Oh God, did you see the mess they left? Windows broken everywhere, the whole of downtown trashed. I mean, for once I'm glad there was no track season, could you imagine if people came from all over the world to see downtown looking a mess like that?"

"I heard they tried to take over entire neighborhoods, but some patriotic citizens have squashed the riot, thank God!" And truly, a mess like that could have destroyed the turn out for my sixtieth birthday party, and I've been planning all summer long.

"But enough of this negativity," Carol waves a hand as if waving away the discussion. Her eyes sparkle as she smiles widely. "It's your birthday! Time to party, is that psychic here again today?"

Chapter 80

Jordan

"It's a good day, Odin."

The cat looks up at me from his favorite spot on my desk. I give his chin a scratch. A map of the country hangs on the wall. More pins today. We've got Gloversville, Westchester, Lodi, Tulsa.

Before they know it, we'll be in charge. Not the Supreme Court, not even the White House. And they'll never see it coming, because they think we work for them.

Chapter 81

Marie

11/6/2020

Day Three

Today it's colder. They still don't give us our jackets. I wonder how cold it will have to be for that small concession.

"We can't risk you running off now, can we?" Tom had said. So, his minions had handed out shoes but kept the coats. I lift a hand to my hair, now growing shaggy around my head. I can see my breath.

The trees are shedding leaves now. As if on cue, the takeover of the park coincided with the dwindling of any last blaze of color and beauty from the trees. A cyclical harbinger of the cold winter to come that all Northeasterners recognize. Of course, it's usually accompanied by higher heating bills, snow and shorter days. This year, the live performance of the *Turner Diaries* is just an added bonus.

I try to remember when exactly they collected our coats and shoes. Maybe it was after they passed around a waiver? This one acknowledging that all property and worldly goods of the undersigned were now property of Golden Apple. Relieved, for the first time in my life, to not have shit. Well, except the trailer. I told them I'm renting. If they find out otherwise, so be it.

Today, my task is to pick vegetables from the garden first, then to help with canning. The final canned sauces and preserves are stored in a shed "adapted" meaning confiscated, from Kate, Derrick and Dee's mom.

"I'm sorry," I mouth the words to her, as I trespass on her property to bring handfuls of canned food to the shed that others cleared out the day before.

She shrugs, acknowledging, what can you do?

I hear men's voices nearby and freeze. Taking a chance, I step past the shed and train my eyes on two figures, just a few feet away, in the wooded area behind the park. I can make out the form of the Caretaker, and he's talking to a kid.

A kid I've seen before. First, when he tried to steal Dee's rabbit. Then, when the Caretaker brought him food, down by the lake.

I try to listen, but they're beyond my earshot now. If I found them, it won't be hard for the goons wandering around this place to spot them as well.

I look over my shoulders. The guards are around, but they're not focused on this side of the park now. I linger, taking longer than necessary to stock the shed, planning to create a distraction if any of them come nearby.

My hands are getting colder. The smock I've been given is the color of a canvas shopping bag and about as warm as being wrapped in a paper towel. I try to move from side to side to stay warm. Moments later, I see the Caretaker walking out of the woods. He sees me, and I turn away, pretending to be busier than I am with the canned food. I glance again from the corner of my eye and watch as he, too, appears to pretend to be busy with some inane task he's been assigned.

Later that evening, as we gather for supper, I intentionally walk past him. Close enough to slip a paper in his hand. A paper with a message that no one but Jess, and myself and now he, can decipher.

I saw you in the woods today with that kid. Be more careful next time.

Chapter 82

Dee

11/6/2020

Day Three

I can't wait for this game to be over. It's so boring. I don't know why all the grown-ups decided to play a game together. Maybe it was lockdown and the pandemic. People are doing weird things. They say it on TV all the time.

The new people must be "It" because they get to keep their shoes and coats, but they took everyone else's. If we get to play hide and seek like Derrick Torrey said, we will all probably hide, and they will probably have to find us. They need to learn about how to make games fun though.

You would think they would have had practice, since they always have all those kids around.

We lined up to get new clothes. I thought it would be like when Mom brings home the big bags and boxes of clothes that don't fit her friends' kids anymore, or clothes from my cousins. She would sit on the couch with piles of fancy clothes all around. One by one, I would try them on and we would play fashion show. I would walk up and down the hallway and Mom would look to see if the new clothes fit me.

Sometimes the pants were too long or the shirts too tight in places. I didn't care because these were the clothes the popular girls wore last year, and I finally had some of my own. I was excited when we stood in line for the clothes in the game. I thought maybe it would be the same.

It wasn't.

These weren't the fancy jeans and nice blouses that came in the garbage bags, that other girls had outgrown. These were more like the worn smocks at school that we wore over our clothes during art class so we wouldn't get paint on our outfits.

I found this out when it was my turn in the line. There were no big bags of fancy clothes. Just a box filled with plain looking dresses. We're playing re-enactment and people are supposed to dress bad because that's part of the game.

"These are not clothes for winter. They're for summer. You have to put your sweaters over them." I tried to tell the new lady at the table, who was handing these out in exchange for our shoes.

"Shh! Dee, enough!" Mom had snapped at me and pulled me out of the way.

"But it's what you always say!"

"Remember what I said, Dee." Derrick Torrey said then.

In order to play this game, you have to be cold and do work all day. I really don't like this game.

Chapter 83

Cyrus

11/7/2020

Day Four

I gotta be honest, I wasn't sure about all this at first. This far in, I can tell you. It's pretty bad ass. My dad still doesn't know where I am, and he wouldn't get it. Until it's all over. When we've secured the streets from Antifa, like we did the other day, and restored law and order. Then he'll look at me and say "Well, you were right, how could I have ever doubted you?"

I mean, it's not that I personally was part of the battle against Antifa, but I heard the other guys talking about it. How they came as close as the bridge before being shut down. Feldman and some of the other guys, they said the mob came all the way down Route 9R to the Lake and were beaten back from the bridge. Close. So we've got to be ready.

I don't even mind the camp. Sharing a place with some other guys. No alcohol, no problem. We've got plenty of food, and music, and every night it's like a party. We work our asses of in the daytime. Training starts at six in the morning.

It's all good, like a work-out every day. I'm helping with the training patrols now. We do drills, workout, strategy, target practice. I told the guys, like Feldman, that my thing is computers, and I can help with their IT needs, and he says he'll keep it in mind, but that what they really need most is help with training.

I'm good at shooting a gun, it turns out. I'm learning about all the different kinds of guns these guys have. It's pretty cool. Feels powerful. When Antifa comes, I'm ready.

The sun is rising over the lake now. It's beautiful. Can't beat the view. This is definitely the life. I walk up and down the road, warming up my body for drills today. It's gonna be intense. Other guys, Chuck and Dylan and Aiden, I see them coming out of their RVs now too. We start by jogging around the park, then around the lake, over the bridge, into the rich neighborhoods. They're happy to see us. They know we're keeping them safe from rioters and looters.

I can see my breath this morning as we start to jog. Some of the guys sing while we're running.

That song they like. I hated it at first. But it grew on me. Some of the guys changed the words.

By the time Antifa got here
We were half a million strong
And everywhere, we're takin' back our nation
And civility and freedom, are rock of our foundation
Now our flag waves in the skies
No more being poisoned by liberal lies
We've saved our civilization.
We are Aryan
We are golden
*   We are patriotic guardians*
And we've got to get ourselves
Back to the garden

* * *

I'll tell you what's more. The higher ups, they're noticing me. I know it. Feldman, the guys don't take him seriously. They rag on him and call him a Jew. I know they want to try to shit can him. I think I could take his place if I play my cards right.

"Cyrus," A voice calls me as I'm finishing up my last round of pushups.

"Yes, sir," I'm out of breath but try to hide it. The guy approaching me, his name is Tom. He's in charge of the operation nearby and pretty much in charge of our unit too. He drives a golf cart down here a few times a day to keep an eye on things.

"New assignment for you," he tells me.

This could be it.

"Sure, what can I do for you?"

I try to not seem too excited.

"There is some riffraff hanging around. Reports have come in. I need you to round them up. Go into the woods if you have to, inro the nearby neighborhoods. Homeless people, scum, check near dumpsters and all. Feldman and some other guys will go with you on one of the golf carts. When you find them, bring them back."

"Yes, sir."

* * *

It's funny to think of it, but on the other side of the bridge, they really have no idea what is going on here. Or if they do, they don't act like it. It's alright. They'll figure it out eventually. And then they'll all know who to thank for keeping their neighborhoods safe.

In about four hours, we were able to round up about a handful of people. I wasn't sure how many to expect. We used zip ties to secure their hands behind their backs. Some were drunk. They're scared shitless of us, though. I gotta admit, it feels good.

We bring them back to the training zone, right in the center of the RV park. Feldman radios over to Tom who is next door at the trailer park, and in a few minutes, he's down to survey the situation.

Then, like he usually does, Feldman says something stupid. Handing me a rifle, he tells me to execute them. Luckily, I'm not a bone head who only follows orders. I look to Tom. He puts his hand up.

"No, no we're not going to do that."

I lower the gun to my side.

"These guys will come in handy, won't you?" They don't respond.

Tom looks at me and says "Train them. If they won't cooperate, keep them in John's RV, he has it set up as a holding station. If they don't prove useful, we'll have to go to Plan B," and as he says this, he looks right at them to make sure they understand clearly what he means.

"Yes, sir."

Tom turns to leave and I catch sight of Feldman. He looks pissed, but I wasn't the one who told him to play Rambo.

Chapter 84

Jess

11/8/2020

Day Five

"Today's the day," Marie tells me. She didn't need to remind me. I couldn't sleep last night after I learned the plan. The Caretaker's been talking to some kid, a homeless kid nearby. He's coming tonight after dark to smuggle the kids out. First Dee and Derrick.

"They're planning to do a purge, a eugenics purge. They've mentioned it like a culling, and I know they're thinking about the little girl," the Caretaker had said, after overhearing two guards discussing their plans. He's got eyes and ears everywhere. I guess it makes sense, if you're a crazy delusional nazi, to start sorting people out this way.

Then, later in the night, Scott and Don. They don't know yet. Couldn't trust them to know in advance.

My heart's been racing since.

"And you," Marie says now.

"What do you mean?"

"You're going too. Last one out."

"I can't leave you here."

"Sure you can. You have to. Do it. Not another word."

The truth is, I've become more afraid of what happens when we try to escape than by what is actually happening here.

"Have you talked to your family since this all happened?" Marie asks me.

"Only once, briefly. To my brother Don, he's the older of the two boys. Funny thing is, he's the biggest bully. Thinks he's badass, but now that he's in the midst of all this, he's shitting himself. I could tell. I think he'll be ready to go."

"What about the little one?"

"He's usually not a problem, if I tell him it's okay, make it sound like something Mom and Dad want, he'll do it."

I hope.

***

The Caretaker

I've watched each night. The heaviest patrols seem to be between nine and midnight. In the early morning, even fascists get tired. So that's when it has to be.

Why do you even bother? Comes the familiar voice. *These people did nothing to help when you were in prison. Did nothing to help when you were homeless. Do nothing to help anyone but themselves now. Let them get what's coming to them.*

Because, I tell myself. Because those kids weren't involved. Because if I don't do something, I'm no better than they are...

I argue with myself for a few more moments. The thought of abandoning the plan is tempting.

But I know what these zealots have in store. Even if the rest of the park doesn't. I spent years on the inside, with their kind. Eugenics, rape, forced breeding, culling of the old, the weak, those who are not useful.

I force the anger and resentment back down. My decision is made.

I slip out the back of my trailer and walk through the trees on my lot, to the very edge of the road. The gravel underfoot is rough but bare feet are quieter than shoes.

This may be their last chance. I hope they don't fuck it up.

Winding through yards, I finally make it to the far corner of the park, to the carport.

Under the tarp, I told them, behind the woodpile. And you can't make a sound.

Walking slowly behind travel trailers, piles of old tires and other crap strewn about, using my hands to feel in the dark, an outline catches my eye.

It's the girl, emerging from under the tarp, open for anyone to see. In her arms, a large lump of fur. That damn rabbit. I look quickly over each shoulder. No one is behind me. For now.

"Derrick," I whisper.

He comes out as well.

"Why is she out like this?"

He stands and brushes his legs off. "She wouldn't stay in one place. Better to let her go than have her yell or talk or make a fuss," he answers.

I roll my eyes.

"Okay, come on,"

He guides her by the shoulders. Under that ridiculous frock they've been given, she must be freezing. At one point, she lifts the skirt of the frock and covers her rabbit, keeping him warm, completely unconcerned with modesty. I didn't think to bring blankets, too risky.

It's only a few feet now to the edge of the yard and the entry to the woods. I hear a click and pull the two kids behind a shed. Derrick claps a hand over Dee's mouth, but she didn't utter a sound.

She's lived out here long enough to know the sound of a gun being pumped.

We wait in silence. I hold my breath. From the path on the other side of the shed, I can hear two of the tin soldiers talking.

"When do we get to start the fun?" one asks.

"What, this isn't fun for you?" the other answers and pumps his gun again. "Bam!" he says, "bam, bam, bam, dead liberals!"

I look down at Dee as the rabbit struggles to run at the sound of the loud voices. She holds him tight and he settles back down. I can tell by the look on her face she understands the stakes. She won't make a sound. In the distance, the men laugh and the other continues, "no, you heard what they were talking about? The breeding program!"

"Once the DNA tests come back, be patient."

Fucking assholes. Next we'll have to find a way to get all the women out. Those who aren't Golden Apples or whatever they call themselves. Which brings the tally to about three.

In the distance, through the trees, I see Ben approaching. I put my finger to my lips in the universal gesture of silence and pray he sees me. Whether or not he does, he stops and backs up against a tree.

The sound of the guards dissipates. But that doesn't mean they're gone. I look to Derrick, who also looks to me, questioning. I shake my head "no," and wait several more minutes. Then, I slide down the back of the shed, pick up a stone, and throw it out to the side.

Nothing.

Standing back up, I turn to peer around the corner of the shed.

They're gone.

I motion to Derrick and he lifts Dee, and we cross the small yard into the woods.

Ben sees us. We walk side by side several feet, deeper into the darkness. Farther from the park. Then, I whisper to him, "Ben, this is Derrick and Dee, take them to where you're staying."

"They rounded up some other guys, but they didn't get us, I'm going to change the path we take this time," he replies.

I reach in my pocket. "Here's all the cash I have to hold you over for now if you need it. Don't trust anyone. Not the cops, not anyone."

He nods.

Come back before dawn for the next three. Two little boys and a teenage girl, okay, she will be able to help you. Thanks and good luck,"

They move on a few feet and I stand by to see them off. Dee stops, turns to me.

Don't ruin it. Don't do it, just keep walking, I think to myself.

She waves silently, then turns back and follows her brother and Ben into the night.

To avoid commotion, I wait by the back of the shed for Jess to come with her brothers. If we can get through this without incident, it will be a miracle, but I didn't tell them that. Sneaking this many people at once is a sure fail. It's better than nothing.

And nothing is exactly what happens.

* * *

It's almost sunrise. Jess hasn't shown up.

I make my way back hoping for the best. Maybe they just got cold feet.

Maybe.

Chapter 85

Jess

11/9/2020

Day Six

It's time.

Dottie's home only has a front door, so I climb out the back window, onto the deck and drop to the ground. I pause, listening. All is still. Don and Scott were supposed to meet me behind a pile of wood near Marie's neighbor's carport in the back of the park. They know the spot. They repeated it back to me.

My nerves are on edge as I approach

I pause, look over my shoulder, no sign of anyone else on this side of the park. I let my breath out slowly as I walk along the tree line, through the last lot. Almost to the carport.

Out of anxiety, I expect to hear footsteps, or a gun shot. In my mind I hear these things. Again, and again. I stop just to steady my breath.

Almost there.

I slide along the side of the carport. My foot hits something sharp. Damn!

I clutch my foot, now cut from where I stepped on the rake, which is on its way to falling to the ground when a hand reaches out and grabs it, midair.

My breath catches.
I trace the hand to an arm, then follow along to the face.
It's Don.
I let my breath out in a heavy sigh.
"Where's Scott?" I mouth, afraid to even whisper.
Don just shakes his head from side to side.
I take his hand, assuming all I need to know. Scott chickened out.
Taking a step outside of the carport, a sudden light blinds me.

The beam of the flashlight so big, I can't see who is behind it. I hear one voice, then another. "What do you think you're up to?" It's one of the guards. I pull Don closer to me, trying to stand in front of him.

"I'm kidnapping my brother, before you can fuck with his head anymore!"

"Liar!"

The second voice is Scott.

Chapter 86

Dee

11/9/2020

Night Six

It's cold. The dress they gave me to wear isn't warm. It's probably a summer dress. But when it gets cold, you're supposed to wear sweaters over your summer clothes. Maybe no one told these people. Or maybe they don't have sweaters yet. Sometimes we have winter clothes. Sometimes I get new winter clothes in big bags from my cousins, and it's like Christmas and my birthday all at once. Maybe these people are waiting to get their bags so they can give us winter clothes to wear. I don't know. Derrick Torrey said we have to wait here. And be quiet. No matter what, he said. No talking and no getting upset.

He said we're going to go get food. We have to go at night. Mom can't come.

That must be because we're going to get some good food for a change. I don't like the new people. I don't like the meetings. I don't like the food. I don't like the dress I have to wear.

Derrick said it's a play. It's not real. It's a play like the re-enactors we saw at the park one summer. I don't know. It looks real.

"They're playing a game," he said. "But it's serious. So you can't make a mistake, OK?"

I just nodded. It's not okay. I don't understand.

I start to grab Fiver's wagon.

"No," Derrick Torrey says in a whisper. "Carry him. It's warmer." So I hold him, and we wait.

A long time.

I have to pee but I'm too scared to say anything. I hold it. I pretend I'm a statue. I have a contest with Fiver, who can be quiet longest. I wait. It's dark. Why does it take so long?

This must be really good food. The kind you have to sneak to the refrigerator for when everyone else is sleeping. Cake. Brownies. Cookies. I imagine the treats we're going to get for the game. Or maybe we'll just eat the food ourselves. Not bring it back. That's good. I don't want to share my treats with these mean people. Even if they are just playing.

I see the man who fixes things.

Max Atrillion. He smiles. It's time to go.

Chapter 87

Marie

11/10/2020

Day Seven

Like clockwork, I make my way to the morning meeting. Relieved, slightly, because by now Jess and her brothers are well on their way to someplace far from here. Dee and Derrick too.

"Ladies and Gentleman, I have disturbing news," Tom begins as we assemble in the cold, shoeless, coatless, huddling. A cough breaks out somewhere in the crowd and I cringe.

Great, just what we need.

"We've been infiltrated by spies. Last night. While good patriots were sleeping, terrorists walked about in our camp."

He turns to his right, and motions for Justin, standing there, grinning like a sycophant. "Let's bring them out now."

Justin disappears into the trailer and returns a few moments later.

My worst fear is confirmed.

He's got Jess. Her wrists are bound behind her back and he's dragging her by her upper arm. A gag is in her mouth. He kicks her to the ground. Then he goes through the door one more time, this time, he's got his hand around the back of Don's neck.

"These two were attempting to escape, and they arranged for the murder and kidnap of two of our brave patriots. Two children."

Shocked cries and murmurs circulate through the crowd. Tom waits and then adds, "We suspect this was an Antifa plot to infiltrate the camp and cleanse it of those the radical left deemed unworthy of joining their ranks. I know that's an ugly idea, but we think this because one of those captured and killed is a little girl."

Bullshit.

I want to search the crowd for Dee's mom, Kate. For the Caretaker, but I don't want to draw attention to them.

"We've got to protect the purity and sanctity of our land, and our community." Tom goes on.

"Can I take care of this for you?" Justin asks, with a psychopathic eagerness.

"No, that honor," Tom pauses for a moment, "goes to our youngest hero. A boy who alerted us to this plan and proved himself a true patriot."

My stomach lurches. I feel the bile rise to my throat. I look to Jess; her eyes are wide in horror.

"Scott, come on up, son." The boy walks to the deck. He holds his head high as he ascends the steps, looking proud of himself. "Do you know what happened last night?" Tom asks.

"Yes," Scott begins, "Antifa spies were trying to kill the young and the weak."

"Why?" Tom asks.

"Because they are communists, and that's what communists do," he recites.

No, they can't do this. They can't. They can't.

I spot his parents in the crowd. Dave's eyes are cast down. He looks embarrassed for himself, not afraid for his kids. Shari's fingers are in her mouth. She's chewing her nails.

"And what do we do with Antifa? How do we protect our families and neighborhoods?"

"Shoot Antifa!" he replies, pumping a fist in the air. The crowd cheers.

"No!" A voice breaks through the crowd. It's Shari, their mom. *What took you so long?* I think.

She's broken from her husband's side and rushes to the front of the crowd. Climbing the steps, her arms flailing in desperation. But before she can get too far, Justin jumps down from the deck and grabs both of her arms.

Shari screams. On the floor of the deck, both Jess and Scott kneel, bound, and gagged. Jess has stopped struggling. Don whimpers as tears and drool run down the gag in his mouth and wrapped around his head.

"Now Scott, we need your sister to remain alive. Understand?" Tom asks.

"Uh-huh," Scott answers, mindlessly.

"Good, now, you showed us you are a hero last night, now you get your reward."

Tom picks up a rifle that had been leaning against his house, and hands it to the boy. "Just like target practice, okay?"

This can't be happening.

The crowd is cheering him on, calling slurs and insults.

"Wait!" a voice booms from the front of the crowd. Dave walks forward now, trying to maintain composure but looking as if he's about to piss himself.

"Maybe he can be rehabilitated, okay? I mean, he's a kid. He had to have learned this from somewhere, right? Maybe he can be given another chance, right?"

"Where would he have heard it from?" Tom asks now.

Don't do it, I think. Don't play into his hand, he's fucking with you. Don't do it.

Tom is playing cat and mouse, a game of wits, and Dave isn't well armed.

"His aunt," Dave blurts out. Of course. Anything to try to bail out his kid.

"That's ridiculous!" Joni shot back. Tom seemed unmoved by the allegation. He went on with his Socratic method.

"Joni? What makes you think Joni put these ideas in his head?"

"She's always hanging around with the kids putting this New Age crap into their heads. And she's already been a known member of a dangerous cult. A sex cult. She's just the kind of person groups like Antifa recruit.

A few guys raise their eyebrows and make catcalls at the reference to a sex cult.

"I'm sorry, Dave, you need to have solid proof if you're going to accuse someone of something like that. Doesn't sound like solid proof to me. Still," he thinks for a moment then calls for one of his armed guards.

"Steve, be Joni's shadow for the rest of the week. She doesn't so much as use the bathroom without you standing right there watching."

Steve pumps his gun for effect and takes a stand right behind Joni, awkwardly close. She's not happy, I can tell by the look on her face. But the last thing she's going to do now is complain.

My heart pounds in my chest. I look back to Jess. She's eyeing the crowd but won't find sympathy here.

"But I do find your case compelling," Tom continues. "Maybe he is just young and impressionable, like we all were once. Shall we put it to a vote? Like true patriots?"

The crowd cheers. It's not just the neighbors, I notice then. Armed men in camouflage have surrounded the lot. I have no idea where they all came from or who they are.

Tom puts his hands up to silence the crowd. "Okay, fine, a vote. Raise your hand, if you're in favor of our youngest hero getting the chance to prove he's a man by eliminating a dangerous enemy."

Dave looks stunned. As if it's just starting to dawn on him that the group he put his trust in has no interest in preserving the democratic process. His mouth is agape, eyes wide, he turns from side to side and realizes in horror that the majority, the overwhelming majority, of hands instantly rise into the air.

"Well, the people have spoken."

Tom steps back and picks up a mug from the table. He sips from it, licks his lips, and then gestures to Scott.

Don't do it, I say inside my head. Don't do it.

I should stop him. I should yell out. I should do something. I look to the Caretaker now, his face grim, but still unwavering. Why won't he do something? I look from side to side, why won't anyone else do something?

Why won't I do something?

Do something.

Do something.

Dave's face is cast down now. Shari is crying hysterically. Scott notices. He looks to his mother. I see something pass over his eyes. Compassion. Hesitation. He's not going to do it. He starts to lower the gun. Then looks past his mother. To a different woman.

Bianca. She's smiling her fake television smile. She nods her head slightly and says "It's okay, baby, you go on ahead. Just like in practice."

He turns back to his brother, now screaming through the gag, eyes shut tight, face turned red, a pulse throbbing through his forehead.

And fires.

Chapter 88

The Caretaker

11/11/2020

Day Eight

If there is one thing that is sure, it is that things will get worse. The breeding program. The assassinations. The time to act is now. I pace the floor inside my trailer, bare feet scraping on the linoleum.

If there is another thing I know, it is that I won't be able to save everyone here. But maybe a few more. Just a few more. Jess, Marie, Josephine, Justin's mother. And Kate, who can then be reunited with her kids Derrick and Dee.

It has to be all at once.

I try to play the guitar, to stimulate my thoughts, but no deal. Not tonight. I rip a paper off the pad on the fridge and grab a pen, writing out in code. If I can get the note to Marie, I can count on her to pass along the plans to the other two women, she comes into contact with them easily enough during the day.

But Jess. I don't know where they're keeping her.

Last I heard from Ben, before the botched escape, the group had some kind of encampment down at Bob's Park and were using one of the RVs as a makeshift jail. There perhaps?

It may take a few days to organize, but we don't have much more time.

Chapter 89

Vinny

11/12/2020

Day Nine

"Tom, sir, can I speak with you for a minute?"

I approach him after breakfast, when he doesn't seem too busy. I mean, he's always busy, but the morning meeting is over with and all.

"My name's Vinny, sir," I begin.

He smiles. "Yeah, sure, I know who you are."

"Aw, thank you, well, sir, you see, I have a, um, my mother is in a home. Usually I check on her every day and bring her here on weekends, because she's all alone. It's been a few days sir, and I was wondering, since you have the power generator here and all, could I use your phone to call and check in on her? So she knows I'm okay?"

A few of the other guys are gathering around. I start to get nervous. I don't like the way they're looking at me.

One of them starts to laugh and whispers something to the other guy. Now they're all laughing. Except Tom. He turns to them with a hand up, to signal them to shush. Then he turns back to me.

"I can't let you do that, Vinny."

He starts to turn away. "Sir, um, sir," I try again.

Now he looks annoyed.

"Yes?"

"I just don't understand what the big deal is. I mean, I've been helping out. Doing my part, it's just one phone call."

His face darkens. I clench my hands in to fists and then let go.

"You expect me to trust you with a phone call? Well, the problem is, we're having a real issue with people being disloyal, aren't we fellas?"

The guys circle around nodding in agreement.

"And, we have to be very careful about who we grant privileges to."

"Well, I'm loyal to the mission, I've done everything you ask."

He pauses to consider, then says, "Vinny, you're Italian, right?"

"Yes, sir. My grandmother came here from Sicily."

"So, you're basically Black." Tom says casually.

"What?"

"Italians aren't Aryans. You may say you're with us, but you're not really with us. It's in your blood. Like Cuomo. And Fauci."

"What are you saying? I'm as white as you are."

"Watch your tone. And don't insult me again." Tom's voice is stern. A few of the guys reach for their guns. He gestures again for them to back down.

I feel sick, now. I can't make sense of what he's saying. Cuomo? Fauci? I'm nothing like those guys. Haven't I proven it? Then I remember the first day. The registration. The DNA tests.

Italian.

Not really white.

If I'm not one of them, then who the hell are they, and who the hell do they think I am?

What the hell is gonna happen now?

Chapter 90

Marie

11/13/ 2020

Day Ten

You did this. And I want you to know.

With nothing left to do, I sit, alone now, by candlelight in Dottie's trailer. Writing in a notebook I found.

You did this. I scribble again and again.

You voted for this. You threw all your faith behind this. You did this.

I see you, in my mind, smiling, joking, dancing. On vacation. On Christmas morning. On our anniversary. And then, years later, on election day.

"I voted for... not Hillary."

You did this. Every person dead. Every child in a cage, everyone in line for food, everyone in this park, and wherever else this is happening. You did this. And I want you to know.

I write down every detail. With no reason to believe you'll ever see it. Motivated only by the hope that maybe you will.

By then, I'll most likely be dead as well.

* * *

I wake to the sound of scratching and jump up in the couch, breathing heavily. A note under the door.

I read it.

Tomorrow night, Josephine, Kate, You.

Chapter 91

Marie

11/14/2020

Day Eleven

Josephine may be older, but she's not shabby. It's probably two in the morning by now and right on schedule, here she is. Kate had less ground to cover. She got here early, and we huddled together behind an old chicken coup that hasn't been used in who knows how long. We decided against using the carport since that location has already been exposed. We aren't meeting Ben, since we can find our own way through the woods.

Josephine reaches our meeting spot, and without stopping to take a full breath, I motion toward the trees a few feet away. She nods. I turn to Kate. She nods as well. Shoeless, without jackets, in nothing but these ridiculous smocks, we make our way into the woods.

It's dark and dizzying with only the light of the Moon to go by. Sticks stab at my feet. I hold Josephine by the elbow to keep her steady as our feet softly crunch through the fallen leaves.

My eyes are so fixated on the darkness, I don't notice a hand grabbing my arm and pulling me to the side. My heart stops. But it's Kate. She leans to me and whispers "There's swamps back here. Be careful. You were headed right for one. Follow me."

We make our way like this in a train of sorts, Kate, then me, and Josephine. To the other side. I don't know where we are when we reach a clearing, but the road is empty. We walk along the edge of a road in the dark. I don't know where we're going or what we're going to find.

It suddenly occurs to me that the occupation may extend to the entire county. The whole state. The entire country.

trump won, didn't he? We don't know what state the world is in at this point.

Chapter 92

Vinny

11/15/2020

Day Twelve

"I'm terribly sorry about your boy."

I am, it's true. But I'm also testing the waters. Maybe, if there's anyone here who may be feeling like enough is enough, like things are getting out of hand, maybe it is her. Shari looks like my words stung her, and I feel guilty for bringing it up. Our tasks for the day, yardwork, winterizing the lots one by one, brought us into contact. I didn't go looking for her. Just figured while I'm here, I could make some small talk. Gauge her attitude on things around here.

"Are you?" she asks, with an edge in her voice.

I don't blame her.

"Yes. Maybe more than you know."

"You didn't do anything to stop them."

"Do you think the time has come?" I try to sound casual. Not too forward.

"For what?"

"For things that have," I choose my words carefully, "gone too far. To be stopped."

"We're past that point." And that's the last she'll say to me. As I do my work, it occurs to me that much fuss has been made about the road going into Saratoga, 9R over the bridge and whatnot. But the other direction, headed to the other side of the lake, no one seems to be talking about. What's more, I know the road.

There's the storage facility, the firehouse, I can go through the woods alongside them places, and then it's all residential. Lotta yards, not many fences.

An idea starts to take shape in my head.

***

"Sir, I owe you an apology," I begin, hoping he won't think I'm pushing too far. Tom sets down the stack of boxes he had been carrying and looks at me, as if he's reading into my expression.

"Oh?"

"I shouldn't have questioned your judgment, sir. I've been thinking about it. I want to up my involvement. I'd like to train with the guards, sir. I think I would be useful, being that I know so many of the neighbors and all. I may be able to spot any future, what d'ya call 'em, infiltrations."

He seems to consider this for a time before responding.

"Report to Bob's Park tomorrow. Ask for a man named Cyrus, tell him I sent you for training. Whatever the young guys are doing, tell him I expect you to do double. Got it?"

I nod my head, "Yes, sir, I will do that."

***

It's my last day here, one way or another, and that I know for certain now. After spending the day training, and I thought it would kill me, I felt my heart nearly give out twice. I've learned my way around the park. The RV where the prisoners are kept. I found it.

Heading back to the park, I seen the young guy standing outside that same RV, he was shifting his weight side to side, like he had to use the bathroom. I know the look, working long hours at the warehouse back in the day, believe me.

"Hey, you look like you need a break. I got this, go ahead, take five."

He nodded his head and handed me his gun. Then he run off in the distance. The other guys, they were home washing up. Most of them. Bob's Park is full of guards and guards in training. No one guards the guards. I saw that real quick. Most of them seem to like to slack off when they aren't training hard. A hard day's training was over now.

I know I don't stand a snowball's chance in hell, but there's one last thing I need to do. To try to make up for my mistakes. One small thing. I step inside. There are about five guys tied up, looking sick. The inside of the RV stinks. Then I see her, Jess, the dykey haired one. No other girls in there. I reach into my pocket and bring out my knife. Working quick to cut her loose, I tell her, "You let these other guys go, it's up to you, but I ain't supposed to be here. So lay low for now and make your move late. After midnight. Do it quiet, they're armed to the teeth. And head through the woods and then south, got it?"

She nods. I think that she looks confused but relieved. I cut the rope but remind her again to stay put until it's safe to cut the other guys loose and make a run for it. I leave the knife by her side. Then I'm out again.

I pace back and forth in front of the RV, looking around. Smoke from fire pits down the path rise up through the sky and guys start to congregate, eating their dinner as they sit or stand around in little circles.

If anyone saw me go in, they don't let on. I doubt anyone saw. I pace around some more.

"Hey, thanks, I needed that break," the young guy says, coming back to retrieve his gun and take his place outside the RV.

"Don't mention it."

* * *

I wait up late. Then I wait 'til it's even later. The most direct route would put me in the line of sight, as they got patrols up and down the road all night. If I take my time, go the long way, I can sneak through the lots and toward the back of the park. Then head away from the boat launch, go south, I can get to civilization again. Maybe into the Stewart's on the far end. Call the cops.

Chapter 93

Andre

11/16/2020

Day Thirteen

I called you three times again. Now your voicemail is full.

Girl, where the fuck are you? Now I know you're not gonna make me call those racist ass cops to come after you. I call around. No one's been able to reach you.

I call Krissy as a last resort. She answers on the third ring. Unlike some people.

"Marie isn't answering her phone. I think something may be going on."

"She's probably just in one of her moods. She got all pissy with me when I tried to talk sense into her."

"It's not like that. We were having a regular conversation, then she hung up. Or her phone died. Or something. And that was back on Election Day."

"Maybe she's moping again."

"This isn't like her. Can you just drive by? Maybe swing by the park, knock on her door?" I ask Krissy, again. Now I'm seriously losing patience.

"I'm not her keeper, Andre. She's probably just being a Drama Queen."

"I don't know about that. I'm telling you it was weird, she just dropped the call, and then nothing. For days now. Something's up."

Chapter 94

Vinny

11/17/2020

Day Fourteen

I should be at the Stewart's already, the one at the far end of 9R. Maybe it's too late to wonder, but it only now occurs to me that they may have that one blocked off too. In which case, I'm dead.

It's still dark, but the stillness, the quiet, it's the early hours of the morning I'm sure of it. No sign of the convenience store. I may have gotten turned around in the woods. This ain't where I usually go hunting. I'm surrounded by trees and a road with no damn markings I recognize.

Yep, Vinny, you screwed the pooch this time. Didn't even bring a damn flashlight. My lungs burn. Didn't bring an inhaler either. No meds. See if you don't drop dead right here in the road now.

Way out here, it ain't like you can just walk up to someone's house, knock on their door at two, three in the morning, whatever this is. Couldn't even do it if there was a house in sight.

I stumble further along the road. Movement off to my right catches my eye. I damn near piss myself.

Lights shining from the distance.

I freeze.

I don't even breathe.

The lights come closer, and a shadow behind 'em and it ain't nothing but two beady little raccoon eyes. I'll be damned if that bastard didn't give me a heart attack.

He ambles into the road, his big hairy ass acting like nothing's wrong. Like all hell hasn't broke loose. Like he's got all night to wander this road, and no one is gonna bother him.

Must be nice.

I watch him walk across the road and disappear into trees on the other side.

Quit stalling, move your ass, I tell myself. The road curves ahead and this time the lights coming around the bend ain't no damn raccoon. They're headlights. I step back into the trees and watch, hoping I moved fast enough. They're coming toward me.

Chapter 95

Derrick

What did the Caretaker say this guy's name was? Sam? Ben? Whoever he is, I haven't seen him around. I don't ask questions. We walk for what seems like days, but I know it can't be. I don't know where we are. No place I've been. I can tell he knows. He just keeps focused, like he does this all the time.

And it's a miracle Dee doesn't complain or drive us crazy with a million questions about everything. I think by now she knows we're not going to get food. She's asked about Mom a few times. I tell her we're going get help and get Mom, but we have to get farther away first. That seems to appease her for now.

Our destination is the underside of a bridge. It's near a highway. Eighty-seven maybe? None of this looks familiar. Sam, Ben, whoever, he knows this route and he knows how to stay hidden.

And so do the people who live here. A handful of them. In tents. Some with sleeping bags.

"These the kids from the park?" a woman asks. She looks like Sam-Ben but older. Like his mom or maybe grandmother.

"Yeah. I figure they can stay just for the day, rest up. Then we'll figure something out."

"Geez, Ben, that's fine. We don't have anything to feed them."

"I got it covered." Ben replies.

A lady sitting by the fire notices Fiver and smiles. "Cute rabbit."

Dee doesn't smile, doesn't talk. Doesn't even ask the woman's full name.

"Thank you, don't mind her. She's had a rough few days." I tell her.

* * *

"What on earth are you wearing? And where are your shoes?" Aunt Jenn asks, as we file into her SUV. Dee holds Fiver on her lap in the backseat. I slide into the passenger seat. The air blasting from the heater a reminder of a luxury I forgot I was missing.

"You're not going to believe it. It's crazy. A bunch of people, they took over the park and basically cut us off after trump won."

"trump didn't win, honey."

As she pulls away from the Price Chopper parking lot where I had used the phone to call her a half hour ago, I fill her in as best I can on the details.

The new people. With their classes and weird uniforms. Justin, the creep, and how he went all Rambo as soon as they gave him a gun. The patrols. How they beat Dottie and took her away, killed her for all I know. The registration forms. The breeding program.

Even as I tell her, it doesn't seem real. I wonder to myself if I'm exaggerating. If I'm making it up. One look down at my scraped feet, frozen raw, convinces me. No, it's true. It did really happen.

"And Mom's still there. We have to call the police."

"That man said no." Dee suddenly pipes up. It's the first time I heard her speak in so long it takes me by surprise.

"What?"

"Max Atrillion said trust no one. Not even the cops."

"That was while we were there," I tell her. She doesn't understand these things. "we're out of danger now, Dee. We're away from those people."

"Dee, you watch too many movies," Aunt Jenn tells her, using her soothing voice to try to calm Dee down. The discussion is over. Aunt Jenn hands me her cell phone. I make the call, repeat the same insane story. Hang up. Aunt Jenn is silent. I don't know if she even believes me. I stare straight ahead and as we pull to a red light I see a truck pull in front of us. Tinted windows. All stickers on the back. trump 2020. The yellow sticker, with the snake. And another sticker.

The same as the logo on the registration forms. On the golf carts that rolled through the park. Manned by armed patrols.

A golden apple.

"Aunt Jenn," I begin.

She takes her eyes off the road to look at me. For just a second. That's all it took. For the truck in front of us to cut sharply to the left lane and slow down. Side by side with the SUV.

"What the fuck?" Aunt Jenn screams.

Fiver jumps loose from Dee's arms and leaps into the front of the car. I grab him. He's frantic. I hold him tight. Dee is screaming. The truck slams into the side of our car. Lightly the first two times, then holding back, letting Aunt Jenn gain some ground.

The final shove, the one that launched us off the side of the road, that sent us barreling to the bottom of a ditch. Right before the explosion.

Family Found Dead, Authorities Suspect Kidnapping Attempt

Southern Adirondack Tribune
11/18/2020

Two minors were the victims of an attempted kidnapping that resulted in a fatal police chase. According to Officer Matt Sheffield, of the Saratoga Police Department. A Call came in alerting authorities that Derrick and Dani Torrey had gone missing from their home outside Saratoga Springs around November 16th. An anonymous tip led authorities to pursue a kidnapping suspect who then drove off the road, resulting in a crash that killed the driver and two children. The name and identity of the kidnapping suspect are not being released at this time. Reports are the suspect also died in the crash.

Chapter 96

Vinny

The car is closer now and as it passes, I see the words Saratoga Sherriff on the side. Not bad for my luck, huh?

I run out from behind the tree, waving my arms like a maniac. I even take a chance on calling out "Hey! Hey! Stop! Here!"

The car slows to the side of the road.

"Officer, officer, thank God it's you." I run to catch up with him. Out of breath, I try to force the words out as fast as possible. Hands on my knees, the cold catching up with me.

"Officer, I need help. My whole neighborhood. It's been taken over by these whackjobs. They've taken everyone hostage. I think they've even killed people. I know they killed at least one person. A kid. Officer…."

My panting slows now, and I lift my head up.

"Officer? What, what are you doing with that?"

He snaps a glove on hand. Then another. He doesn't speak.

"Officer, let's go, we gotta go, it's down that way," I point down 9R, or what I hope is 9R. I start to stammer the address.

He fingers something on his shirt front. I think he's calling it in. But he still doesn't speak. I realize now. I know what he did. That thing he just turned off.

He reaches for his gun, now in both gloved hands. I look to his cruiser. No one else. It's only him and me. Pretty soon, it'll only be him.

Chapter 97

Marie

11/17/2020

Day Fourteen

My feet are now numb. Which is a good thing because if I could feel anything, it would be pain from cuts and scrapes along the ground. Josephine is limping. Kate also seems to be slowing down.

"We're far enough now, I think, maybe we can rest if you need to?" I suggest, still whispering by habit.

"No, let's keep going 'til we get to someplace secure," Josephine offers.

"Yeah, I agree, I don't want to slow down now."

So, we trudge forward, along the road.

"There's a light up there, I think?" I point to a glowing orb about a mile down the road.

"That's probably Gill's," Kate comments.

"What's that?"

"One of those twenty-four-hour convenience stores. What do you think, should we try to go in?"

"Maybe just one of us," I offer, "that way, if it's crazy everywhere, we don't all get caught."

"I'll go," Josephine offers.

"No, I'll go," I interrupt her. "Look, they want women who are breeding age, for their crazy populate the world with white babies plan, right? So that means, no offense, but if either of you two get caught in a trap, you're not likely to be spared. But I will, for what it's worth."

"Wait, take this with you," Kate stops me. She rummages in her bag and then hands me a small plastic box."

"What is it?"

"A lethal dose of barbiturates, don't ask. Only use it if you truly have no other way out. There won't be anyone to resuscitate you."

I understand her meaning and grip it tight.

* * *

When I get to the store, there's a clerk inside and one other customer, though it seems like she's hanging out flirting with the guy behind the counter.

"Hello," I interrupt them. Both turn to look at me, their faces twist into disgust and confusion, not sympathy.

I realize that I am a shoeless, jacketless, disheveled woman with a crazy DIY haircut and a smock who is about to tell them a story about a militia takeover of a mobile home park.

I take a breath and continue. "There's been an emergency. I need to call the cops. I don't have my phone."

* * *

"Now let me make sure I have this straight," The officer, Matt I think he said his name was, leans toward me as Josephine, recounting the story as Kate, Josephine and I file into the back of his car. "There was a hostile takeover of your trailer park, and there's been a murder?"

"At least two murders, possibly more."

He drives along in the dark, on the way to the emergency shelter.

"Where exactly is the shelter?" Kate asks.

"Well, the address is undisclosed. For safety reasons. But it's in downtown Saratoga. We'll be there soon."

Finally. Finally, we're almost there. And the park will be raided before they can do too much more damage. Maybe in time for Jess. I close my eyes and can finally rest.

The car brakes squeak as it rolls to a stop, and the noise wakes me. Kate has fallen asleep as well and Josephine may be, her head is down and she's motionless. I look out the window to get a glimpse of the shelter.

And see only trees. A row of mailboxes. I shake them awake. The officer steps out of the car.

"He brought us back! He brought us back!"

"Take the pill," Josephine tells me. As she says this, the door to the car opens.

"What have you done?" I shriek at him.

"Now, now, I'm sure we can figure this all out."

As he talks, another cop car arrives. The driver pulls up alongside us and rolls down the windows.

"We just got a call of some militia activity here. People being held against their will?" the second officer says.

Who would have called them?

"I just arrived myself. Seems pretty quiet, but that is what these ladies allege as well."

Daylight breaks through the crowd. The flashing lights and commotion has begun to draw a crowd. I see the Caretaker approaching. Tom, Justin, and the armed minions. A few of the women in the park are also emerging from their homes, squinting in the morning light, to see what the fuss is about.

"Look!" I tell the officers, gesturing down the road to the armed men blocking the bridge. They talk amongst themselves, ignoring me. I try to catch the one, Matt's eyes, "Look, there they are, right there, that guy with the slicked back hair is their leader."

Matt only regards me with a look of annoyance, the way you'd look at a mosquito.

"Officers!" Tom says, "thank you for coming by."

"Any time," the officer answers.

I watch, in slow motion as they approach the Caretaker.

Okay, I think, he's a guy. Maybe they'll listen to him. Not to hysterical women. My anger is replaced by terror when I see what happens next.

The first officer, Matt, calls out to the Caretaker.

"So, not surprised at all to see you again, Bishop. Not surprised at all." Before the Caretaker can respond, both officers grab him and pull his arms behind his back.

"No!" I scream. "It's not him, it's them, it's all of them!"

Now my arms are being pinned behind my back as well. I drop the pill on the ground. This can't be happening.

But why? Why can't it?

The cops hold the Caretaker as one of the armed guards punches him in the face.

"Looks like he's resisting arrest, officers," Tom says.

"That's right," Matt agrees. He removes his gun from his holster. And shoots.

Chapter 98

Jess

11/22/2020

Day Nineteen

I don't fully understand why Vinny came to get me, why he let me out of that crappy prison. Maybe it's because he wasn't really with them? That couldn't be it, though. Maybe it was seeing them kill a kid. Whatever his reason, I'm grateful.

It was a miracle I found my way through the dark rural street when I did. A miracle none of them saw me. A miracle that after walking for hours, I found someone who didn't ask questions when I asked if I could use their phone because it was an emergency. They must've been high. Why else wouldn't they have questioned my crazy looking outfit, and why I didn't have a phone of my own. Eric and Callie showed up right away. They were worried sick about me but had no idea what was going on. Of course. Not like it would've been on the news.

I was able to take a hot shower and Callie let me borrow some of her real clothes. I must really be sleep deprived to let them talk me into being here now. I squeeze Eric's hand in mine, even though I'm sweating like crazy.

"I'm not so sure about this." I tell him, again.

"Going to the police isn't my prerogative either, but if the situation is as crazy as you say, and you know I believe you, then it may be the only way to get the others out," Callie encourages me.

"Your choice," is all Eric says.

Callie's right. But I don't want to go. Callie pulls up outside the Saratoga Police Station. Eric leans over, kisses me, and offers one more time to go inside with me.

"No," I tell him. I can't make you do that. I'll deal with it."

"We'll wait here for you," Callie says.

"Thanks for letting us stay at your mom's place, and for the ride," I tell her.

I knew this was a mistake. From the minute I walked through the door. A guy named Todd stares across the desk at me. He takes an occasional note, but mostly smirks, looks me up and down, and makes that skeptical grunt you make when you're humoring someone.

"I'll have to run this by my boss," he says, "wait here."

He leaves me alone in the office.

Officer Todd

I wait while the phone rings. He picks up. Took him long enough.

"FBI department of Domestic Terrorism, Jim Overton speaking."

"Officer Todd Parsons, Saratoga PD. You put out a notice in case anyone showed up related to Golden Apple?"

"Yes."

"I got one."

"What's the story?"

"Pretty wild. Actually. Militia takeover, some kind of bizarre claims about a neo-nazi cult or something. Allegedly off of 9R outside Saratoga Springs."

"I'll send someone right over to take care of this."

* * *

Jess

By the time he comes back, I've already bitten my nails down as far as I can. Two fingers are bleeding. This was a mistake.

Always trust your dreams Marie had said. Christ, where was she? More than anything, I did this for her. Maybe that Caretaker guy who wasn't so bad after all. And maybe for Don. Fuck the rest of them.

The door opens. Three guys in uniform, not police, not that I recognize, step in. I can't see their badges. Officer Fuckoff behind the desk seems to be expecting them.

This was a mistake.

"Overton sent us," one of them says.

This was a mistake, a voice repeats in my head.

Officer Fuckoff looks at me and says, "You're going with these two."

I try to make a run for it, too late. They slam me against the wall, face first. Then to the floor. These fucking pigs, they're putting my hands in cuffs.

Chapter 99

Marie

12/3/2020

Day Thirty

No one has heard from the kids. They could be dead. We were told Dee and Derrick were kidnapped and killed. No way to prove it happened. No way to prove it didn't. Those of us who remained, well, we didn't remain. We were taken to Bob's park. Phase Two, they're calling it.

Do you know what is happening here? An hour away from where you are? Do they tell you on the news? Do they even know?

I want you to know.

I stole a pen. I have no shoes. I have no coat. I'm losing any shred of sanity I had. But I have a pen, and an old notebook I found in the Women's RV. Oh, it's nice. The best of accommodations. Overflowing toilets. Stinking blankets. The only good part, forgive me, I'm bound for hell anyway, the only good part is that Joni and Shari are stuck here with us.

Funny, isn't it? All their bowing and placating and bullshit. Where did it get them? Starving, freezing and stinking in an RV in some shit park. Waiting for their number to be called for the breeding program.

I live for two things now. The day their numbers are called. Joni is number sixteen. Shari, number twenty-seven. I'm number twelve.

And to write this to you. I hope you find it someday. This, and the *Book of Discordia*, and all the other journals I've left. If Golden Apple or whatever they call their lame little gang; if they don't torch the place to the ground.

I want you to read it.

Every word.

You voted for this.

These are your people.

You did this.

I'll be long dead. And I hope you live with the truth for a long. Fucking. Time.

Chapter 100

Cyrus

12/16/2020

Day Forty-Six

I moved up quick, through the ranks. It's not hard to do if you just follow orders and don't act like a douche. Some people get half the formula right, on a good day. Like Justin. I know he's pissed. I can see it. He thought he would be the next deputy. He's actually in with Jordan, who is higher up than Tom. But I got promoted. Not him.

Not too hard to figure. For one, he's not that smart. Secondly, he's nuts. Everyone knows it. He can't hide it if he wanted to.

He's pissed because Deputies get first dibs in the breeding program. He'll be lucky if he even gets sloppy seconds. I tried to tell Tom, without sounding like a pussy, that I don't trust Justin. I wouldn't put it past him to do something stupid. Really stupid.

***

Tom

There's one in every crowd. It's true. And it's not so easy putting the genie back in the bottle. I tried to explain this to Jordan. That once you give a guy a gun, some status, some authority, you can't just take it away. But he wants that. Wants me to strip Justin of his rank. Leaves me to do the dirty work when he could do it just as easily. Knowing I'll be stuck babysitting.

Someone, one of the other Deputies no doubt, sent word back up the pipeline about the stunt he pulled. When those bitches escaped. Tried to. One of him, Josephine, his mom. Maybe that's why he took things into his own hands. While we were all dealing with the cops, he got his hands on her. Dragged down to Bob's Park. I heard about it afterward from the other guys on Patrol. How he dragged her by her hair. Beat the crap out of her. Tied her hands behind her back, cut her clothes off with a knife, and hung her, by the wrists, from the bridge.

Of course, I told the guys to cut her down. We can't have that kind of publicity stunt. And they did. Well, they tried to. They pulled her up onto the bridge and were about to cut her loose. Crazy bitch heaved herself over the rail. Into the water. Freezes my balls just to think about how cold it must have been.

That wasn't the first time he'd needed redirecting. By far the worst, but not the first time. He's become a liability. He's a liability I don't want to deal with. Which is part- not all- but part of why I promoted Cyrus. Dealing with Justin will be his first assignment. Tomorrow.

* * *

Justin

He's got plans for Cyrus, does he? Deputy. Let me guess, he applies himself. Doesn't he, Ma? I'll show them.

The smell of ammonium nitrate burns my eyes. I loosen the valve on the oxygen tank that I grabbed from the medic unit. The fireworks are coming early this year.

Explosion Rocks Local Landmark; Antifa Suspected

Southern Adirondack Tribune
12/17/2020

Residents of Saratoga Lake area are in shock this morning as Bob's Park, a well-known campsite, was destroyed by a series of explosions authorities believe were set intentionally. Authorities have no solid leads just yet but believe the act of terrorism was related to violent riots and Antifa activity that has been on the rise in several nearby cities.

A number of casualties are involved, and police suspect the residents, who were illegally inhabiting a number of RVs in the park, were part of a radical left-wing cult.

Afterward

August 2030

Jordan

Stopped at the light, I check the rearview mirror. My hair has grown out from the close cut 2020 pandemic-do-it-yourself haircut. I feel my smoothly shaved chin. No one does the whole beard thing anymore. A man needs a new look. Rebranding, what we call it in the business world. And that's all it ever was. A brand.

Did I ever believe all that white power shit?

No way. The fools, it's what they wanted to hear. Rile up a bunch of mouth breathers, give 'em exactly what they think they're missing. That's all Golden Apple ever was. Just business.

It worked for me. Like it worked for Mike Cernovich, worked for Alex Jones. Build an audience and then sell supplements. Colloidal Silver. Pillows. Why not?

Of course, I don't use that business name anymore. Too much baggage after a while, when things got really exciting. They called it a Civil War, but it was no more of than a string of small skirmishes.

Sleight of hand, really. The turmoil, the pomp and circumstances. The most lunatic of the fringes who branched off and decided to do their own thing, parading a few mayors and governors to execution on what would later be called Insurrection Day. Oh, I had nothing to do with that. At least, I never pulled the trigger and when the dust settled my hands were clean.

I didn't tell people to go nuts, I just gave a few motivational speeches on Zoom during a time of need. The first pandemic, remember that? COVID 19, before the pandemic of 2022, which some people ended up calling the "Rebound COVID."

The light turns green, and I drive down the hill, crossing the bridge than spans over Saratoga Lake. Now tranquil. No remnants of the occupation, a minor disruption really. I was never really into all of that.

I pull into Stewart's and gas up my company car with the newly branded Eden Real Estate logo printed on the side.

Am I even into the whole Bible thing? No more than I care about purification of the white race and that bullshit. But it's all about perception. I jiggle the handle to shake out the last of the gas, fulfilling my ration for the week in a system that any of those Golden Apple morons would have called "communist" without having the first inclination it was put into place by their hero.

Or a succession of them.

Like the old man said, nothing fundamentally changed. And it didn't. The crackpots pounded their chests and pissed on the capitol. There were a few massacres. But no dramatic revision to the system of government. The militias, they eventually cooled off and went back into hiding, waiting for their next opportunity. My favorite scene in the reality show was seeing the Proud Boys round up the former president and half his family. Romanov style.

And they were reckless enough to livestream it. But I had nothing to do with that.

I slide back into the car and pull out on to 9R only to hang a left just a tad farther down the road.

God what a dump.

I wasn't here during the siege. Like I said, kept my hands clear of that end of the business. But the deeds and assets and bank accounts signed over, some voluntarily and others, with some.... encouragement. Even got the park owner involved. Wasn't hard once he became one of us. Give people a sense of community, they'll sell their families and give you the money. Amazing. Well, it's all part of the Eden Real Estate Empire. And not just here. Prime real estate from coast to coast in these little throw away zones. While the people of Dog Patch fought against each other, I sat back and cashed in.

Cha-ching.

If you look deep enough, you can see how those events lead to where we are now. The widespread crackdown. The Integrity Protection Act which is just as bullshit as the Patriot Act and about fifty times more restrictive. Wish I could take credit for it. Kinda brilliant, actually. Gave the Biden Administration a legacy of fully enforcing the militarized police state the trump administration dabbled with, all in the name of preventing another Insurrection.

How's that song go? Meet the new boss… same as the old boss…

I get out of the car and check my phone. No message from Rob yet. I decide to give him a few minutes before assuming he missed this little piece of shithole country and needs better directions.

It's been years since the park was condemned. The siege, I guess you could say it didn't end well. Do they ever?

I walk down the path. A trailer to my right is overrun with squirrels. The roof has caved in. Junk on the lawn, well that may have been there even when it was occupied. Little ceramic moons and stars and cutesy gnome statues strewn in the overgrown weeds.

A few stray cats hover in the distance, eyeing me suspiciously.

Can it really be?

I walk a bit further down the path, past the singed frame of a burned-out trailer to another, just barely intact, a damp, moldy cloth clumped on the ground. I grab a stick and use it to pull at the edges of what used to be a flag.

trump 2020, it reads in faded red and blue. Would have been quite a collector's item, at least in the way that some idiots collect nazi memorabilia and civil war shit.

Some of the trash is newer, broken bottles, used condoms. No one has legally resided here since it was condemned, and the town decided to let weeds take it over and forget about everything that went down. But someone has been here. Looks like they had a good time, too.

I start to turn back, when a trailer catches my eye. On the sides, the words painted in an amateur's tag, "Golden Apple- Getting Back to the Garden."

I chuckle. Dumb shits. Ate it all up, hook, line and

"Jordan," a voice interrupts my thoughts.

I turn back toward the road and see Rob standing outside his car. Must be one of the newer models, fuel efficient to get around the gas rations. Liberal fucker.

"Hello," I call back, walking in his direction. We shake hands again, though it's not our first meeting.

He looks around the place and I swear his face is wary. Like a kid who walked into a haunted house on a dare.

"So, this is it?"

"Yes, and it's gonna be golden." I tell him.

"You want everything razed?"

"All ancient history. Destroy it. Every last bit."

"What's going here?"

"Boat Storage. Way of the future. Almost no overhead. And what these people wouldn't do for their boats." I tell him.

"Sounds like a perfect business plan," he says.

"That's why it's Eden," I tell him, winking. Like everyone else, he eats it up alive.

***

Frank P., Northern Lights Construction Contractor

The heat has been so unbearable, but if anyone is going to make any money in demolition these days, you gotta break up your schedule or else only work in January, and that won't bring in enough.

So, I was there, pausing for a break, in that place where everyone went batshit crazy what with the militia and the battle of 9R oh about ten years ago. I wasn't in the area then and didn't pay it much mind. But it's become legendary. Like Waco and Jonestown.

That was a crazy year. First Portland, then Michigan, and it was all Antifas and crazies everywhere. And then right in NY. And that virus. Nothing good came out of that year. Like it was cursed. Then again, the following few years weren't much better.

I take a break to lean on what's left of a shed wall and drink my water. Then I pour some on my face. I squint it out of my eyes and as I turn to put it down, I see something.

Well, I see a lot of things. I mean, there's shit everywhere in this place. It's fascinating. Like how people go to Deeley Plaza to stare at the book depository where that guy shot JFK.

I look down and see a book, red with gold lettering. It's one of them fancy books, bound all nice and whatnot.

The *Book of Discordia* says the title.

So, I pick it up, flip it open and start to read.

"Hey, Frankie, what you got there?" Bill asks.

"It's some book, The *Book of Discordia* or some shit."

"What is it?"

"Some poetry, Shakespeare. It's all this bleak destructive, take a look here," I say.

I read it to him as he looks over my shoulder

"The cruel work of Discordia
  I can hear them saying now
  But it was not I who had the power
  It never was within my control
  To place the darkness come to life
  Into your mortal soul
  So ask yourself, what was the draw
  To a Golden Apple as a prize?"

He pops it closed with his hand.

"Lose that faggy shit, will ya?"

"Hey, I was gonna keep that, give it to my daughter, she's all into history and shit."

"No way, you heard what the boss said, nothing comes out of this place.

Nothing."

Epilogue: Book of Discordia

Chorus: And here She is
   The wretched one
   Her presence void of charm and grace
   You'll recognize Her by Her name
   In your fellow man, you'll see Her face.

She's made her mark upon your world
   In every Golden Apple spoiled
   Your suffering is Her delight
   And as you waste the hours in toil,
   That you may have what others lack
   You'll not escape their suffering
   For in a mansion or a shack ,
   The gift of strife this Goddess brings
   And who would want Her at the feast?
   Yet for this rejection, you'll feel Her pain
   Destruction of human and beast
   To Discordia, it's all the same

Her shrieking brings the freezing wind
   As each dream rots upon the vine
   Her laughter at your suffering
   As you continue chasing lies

You'll never see the puppet strings
That lead you to the trap She's set
Lured by bright and shining things
A fetid harvest you will get
Any treasure within reach
You'll destroy in due time
Never knowing the poison She unleashed
Convinced that you have won the prize

Until friend becomes foe
    Left with nothing but regret
    And when it's too late, you'll finally know
    What it is to be
    Alone.
    o
    Chorus:
May we have but one reprieve?
Have we not suffered now enough?
Can our Heroine succeed?
Will love or hope finally triumph?
Or will you strip us bare, Lady of Strife?
To satisfy your vengeful lust
Will you let some silver lining show?
You must know now, we've had enough.

Discordia: As long as you place blame on me
    You'll never allow yourselves to see
    What you've reaped you now must sow
    Blame the other, that's your way
    But never toward the mirror go
    Not once have I forced your hand
    Nor have I the power to take
    What you would not eagerly throw away
    To satisfy your own greed.
    And if it be your secret will

Angela Kaufman

To suffer when you could have joy
Is that my doing after all?
Am I to blame for your ills?

You say my wretched ways are known
That I whisper in the ears of those
Who would be happy, planting seeds
Of jealousy, fear and woe
That I deny the innocent
A life of happiness deserved
Just for my own amusement
You ask why suffering must befall those you claim did nothing wrong?

I see then, you presume to know
Whose soul is pure and whose is not
But if there exists one righteous hero
Among those in this sorry lot
My reach would not extend so far.
The darkness lies within the hearts
of those Who follow my call.
And who are you to pity one
Trapped in her own misery?
If a heroine she is
where then is her empathy?
While she sulks the day away
and suffers as the death toll grows
She'll let the world around her burn
As long as she is out of reach
I ask again, why is it me
You blame for mankind's darkest night?

For as you make your demands
What eludes you even now
The truth: there are no innocents here

All have blood upon their hands.
Those who neglected their fellow man
Exploited the Earth for their own gain
Whose eyes remained closed to suffering
Believing it was all a game

Until what you call misfortune came
   Knocking on the padlocked door
   And is it too late to turn things 'round?
   They've no one but themselves to blame.
   Before you jump, so quick to judge
   Who is deserving of mercy
   And who is not.

Ask yourself, is your plea
   A desperate hope that you'll be spared
   A similar fate
   for all you've done
   To disregard your fellow man?
   Thinking first of what you want.
   And when nothing is ever good enough
   Is that a divine punishment?
   Or is it a failing on your part
   To see the truth for what it is.

Chorus: How can it be near four years in
   That hatred still has so strong a hold
   Surely we're better than this result
   Surely now the truth we know?

Discordia: Have you now?
   It doesn't look that way to me.
   The cast wretched have made their presence known
   And now you see
   They've walked among you from the start

Angela Kaufman

    Did you really believe your pithy pleas
    Your data, facts and righteous memes
    Could ever possibly compete
    With what all men and women desire
    More than your approval
    More than gold
    The blessing they seek comes
    Only from the hands of their foolish King
    Why wouldn't they back him once again?
    And why would not their numbers grow?
    If you'd been watching all this time,
    All of this you would have known.
    Did you not believe the persecuted?
    Who told you of deep seeds of hate
    Written into your constitution
    Cemented in your institutions?
    Or did you dismiss them
    As paranoid

Not wanting your comfort to be destroyed
    Do you not want to know the truth?
    You've slept right through the siren's song.
    Do you have any but yourselves to blame?
    For tolerating injustice just as long
    As you were winning at the game
    And now you feel that you've been wronged
    To see the seeds you've planted grow
    You'll blame the poor, you'll blame the old
    But do you really want to know?
    How your silence all these years
    Allowed the harvest to be sown

And what will you do now
    That the fire is burning beyond control?
    Will you pray and hope the numbers swing

GOLDEN APPLE

In your favor so
You won't have to worry anymore
Leaving those around you again to drown
Just because you've found sanctuary
Will you bar the door again, leaving those
Who tried to warn you all these years
To fend for themselves out in the cold?
Keeping the downtrodden at arm's length
A convenient step upon to stand
Leaving breadcrumbs of charity
While keeping power in your hands
Not wanting to sacrifice too much
The bare minimum has been enough
To assuage your guilt
But maintain your place
Preserving the privilege of your race

And what is more,
   You'll gladly take
The liberation they've not yet won
Denying with your every breath
That you are doing any wrong.
But it's easier to pretend
You're not the villain on this set
That your symbolic gestures equal blood sacrifice
Made by those you too oppress
Tell me, who is it really
Who has not learned their lessons yet?
o
"The cruel work of Discordia!"
I can hear you lament, laying blame now
But it was not I who had the power
It never was within my control
To place the darkness come to life
Into your mortal soul

Angela Kaufman

So ask yourself, what was the draw?
What was beauty in your eyes?
What treasure did you turn to God?
What made you allow evil to rise?
Why did you trod upon your neighbors
To chase a Golden Apple as a prize?

o

An apple that cannot sustain you,
A fruit that you can never eat
And why were you so easily led
To sacrifice your very soul
To listen to the words of hate
And chase an apple made of gold?

And when the dark chaos of strife
   Has descended upon all the land
   You act as if I wrote the book
   When it was penned in your own hand.

Fact from Fiction

This book was written in 2020, during a time when the question of what is real, what is propaganda and what can be believed came to have both urgent necessity and epic consequences. Long before *Golden Apple* was even a thought in my mind, I began reading critiques of media, information distribution and the changing nature of how people consume and are shaped by information.

Some of the intriguing works that influenced me to question content sources and discern the agendas inherent in each were books like Neil Postman's brilliant work *Amusing Ourselves to Death* and more recent books like Ryan Holiday's *Trust Me, I'm Lying; Confessions of a Media Manipulator*. The warnings and examples outlined in each of these works came to a horrifying crescendo embodied by the rise of trump and trumpism.

As a writer of fiction influenced by fact, and in the service of encouraging others to dissect truth from imagination even when digesting a work of fiction, I am compelled to break down what of this work is true. At least at the time of this writing.

The nameless park our protagonist calls Park Reaganomics is based on an actual location that I know well. None of the characters in this book are representations of the residents of that park, nor is this work intended to mischaracterize or vilify the residents of that park or any mobile home park, for that matter.

Writing about class and class warfare, it is my intention to challenge the tropes that exist- intentionally- to discredit or demean those of us who are low income. Though this work references class-based assumptions and stereotypes, it is for the purpose of exposing and challenging such stereotypes. After all, it was not the low-income people of Park Reaganomics who were the true source of conflict, but who were incited by more affluent characters such as Tom and ultimately, Jordan.

After writing the first draft of this work, I heard familiar convenient mischaracterizations about low income people repeated by centrist and even center-left news sources as many of us watched horrified as the Capitol was raided. Yet careful examination of the Capitol Riot/Insurrection-an actual historic event- revealed that many of those directly involved were financially comfortable and did not actually fit the characterization of the "financially insecure angry people" that served to suppress low income people and fuel class tension.

How perfectly Discordian.

This familiar narrative of blaming the poor and assuming that low income is synonymous with uneducated, and further assuming that lack of formal academic education means ill equipped to make sound decisions has been perpetuated for decades but became a tool of class suppression (not to mention elitism and ableism) in particular since 2016.

When I set out to write Golden Apple, this was one of the narratives I wished to challenge.

Joni, for example, is of a more affluent economic standing and presents as having a formal academic education and yet she succumbs to the propaganda and influence of not just the cult of Golden Apple- a fictional hate group, but also NXIVM, an actual cult that preyed on people interested in healthy living, spirituality and self-improvement.

NXIVM had a broad reach beyond the U.S. but had a stronghold in a suburb between Albany and Saratoga Springs, NY.

Though Golden Apple is a fictitious group, it was based on a combination of ideologies that are, unfortunately, all too real and growing in popularity. These bigoted ideologies are on the rise even among young people, "academically educated" people and other groups of people that moderate liberals like to believe are "immune" to such ideas.

It was very difficult to write dialog and description based on the ideologies espoused by such groups as these words are not only incredibly offensive but also potentially dangerous when acted upon. Yet in the service of accurately portraying a threat in our midst, I tried to make the dialog authentic. Jordan Tennyson is a fictional character, but his role in using social media to spread hateful ideology for ultimately dubious and self-serving purposes is loosely inspired by actual leaders in the modern white supremacy movement. Rather than listing their names, I would instead prefer to offer a resource to learn more about them in context of comprehensive research. Accounts of their personalities and tactics are outlined painstakingly in the book Antisocial: *Online Extremism, Techno-Utopians, and the Hijacking of the American Conversation* by Andrew Marantz and also *Culture Warlords: My Journey into the Dark Web of White Supremacy* by Talia Lavin.

Locations such as Stewart's Shops and Saratoga Lake are real. The events described in this work did not actually happen at any of these locations as of this writing.

Cyrus's road trip with his fascist buddies was a fictionalized account of actual reports of aggressive drivers forming "trump trains" with their trucks and cars and stopping traffic while also intimidating others. These events took place throughout the U.S. and locally to the Saratoga area, in the weeks prior to the 2020 election.

Likewise, the scene in which Jess witnesses white supremacists intimidating a family with their boats on Saratoga Lake is fiction. Although the fact is, in the summer of 2020, there were plenty of boats sporting trump 2020 flags. In lakes nationwide, boaters sporting trump flags swarmed other boaters, intimidating them, which partially inspired this scene.

Scenes involving harassment and violence toward unhoused people conveyed in this book are fictional but are based on actual accounts from people who have experienced such treatment directly.

Characters make references to various songs which are not in any way tied to the political views presented in this work. The disturbing song "*I'm in the Lord's Army*" is real. The anthem Golden Apple adopts as their own is a reference to Joni Mitchell's 1970 song Woodstock, though to be clear, Joni Mitchell and her music are in no way connected to the ideology presented by this fictionalized or any actual hate group. One of the recruiting strategies used by modern hate groups is to align themselves with "holistic" lifestyles touting the benefits of organic food and getting "back to nature" while infusing online interactions with eugenics and white supremacist ideology.

Finally, to my knowledge there is no *Book of Discordia*. However, there are stories of the Goddess Discordia, also known as Eris. Eris is also the name given to a recently discovered asteroid so references to this discovery are accurate.

The poem attributed to the *Book of Discordia* was written for this story. As an archetype, Discordia symbolizes alienation and social rejection but also could represent the absence of various forms of social privilege. Discordia is often synonymous with strife, but on a larger scale and when applied to institutions of white supremacy, sexism, ableism and classism, becomes the symbol of chaos and discord created in order to maintain competition and infighting and distract from solidarity and revolution.

Discordia can be seen as the catalyst for revolution as well, as this archetype compels us to examine our inner motivations and how we do, or don't, feed into such divisions and oppressions or competitions.

While the book Principia Discordia does exist, it was not the basis for this work and the referenced Book of Discordia described in this story is imagined, though it would be a tribute to the spirit of Discordia to discover this is not the case.

About the Author

Angela Kaufman is a freelance writer, activist, Astrologer and Intuitive Reader, and is author of several books. Past nonfiction work includes *Queen Up! Reclaim Your Crown When Life Knocks You Down-Unleash the Power of Your Inner Tarot Queen*(Conari, 2018). She is also author of *Quiet Man* published in 2020 by Trash Panda Press. Angela is a proud member of the IWW and resident of a mobile home park that is currently under threat by a real estate developer in Saratoga County. For news about upcoming fiction and nonfiction work, visit angelakaufmanauthor.com

Barbara Bouchey

Nancy Salzman